CATCH ME IF YOU CAN

⟨～⟩⟨○⟩⟨⟩

"What brings every young woman from the country to London?" she said. "Adventure."

"Adventure?" His lips curled. "Most women come during the season to find a husband."

"That is an adventure to most women, Your Grace."

"But you seem much more interesting than most women," he said.

A tingle passed through her. "I am sorry to say you will likely be disappointed in me, Your Grace."

"I'm sure that will not be the case." A sinful glint lit his eyes. She bowed her head.

"I'm sure you will find some other lady to attend."

"But there is no other lady's interest I wish to *catch* so much as yours." He pulled her slightly closer than was proper and his leg brushed hers.

The inflection made her heart skip. *He was suspicious, but he didn't know. He couldn't or else she would already be in prison.* But a devil inside caused her to say: "You long to *chase* endlessly after something you can never hope to catch, Your Grace."

He threw his head back and laughed, and his laughter vibrated through her body as she saw the mischief shining in his eyes.

Other **AVON ROMANCES**

Anne Mallory

Daring the Duke

AVON BOOKS
An Imprint of HarperCollinsPublishers

This is a work of fiction. Names, characters, places, and incidents are products of the author's imagination or are used fictitiously and are not to be construed as real. Any resemblance to actual events, locales, organizations, or persons, living or dead, is entirely coincidental.

AVON BOOKS
An Imprint of HarperCollins*Publishers*
10 East 53rd Street
New York, New York 10022-5299

Copyright © 2005 by Anne Hearn
ISBN: 0-06-076223-3
www.avonromance.com

First Avon Books paperback printing: August 2005

Avon Trademark Reg. U.S. Pat. Off. and in Other Countries, Marca Registrada, Hecho en U.S.A.
HarperCollins® is a registered trademark of HarperCollins Publishers Inc.

Printed in the U.S.A.

10 9 8 7 6 5 4 3 2 1

To Mom, Dad,
Matt, and Selina

Chapter 1

London, 1824

A sliver of moonlight broke through the dense clouds, and the cold fingers of the night encompassed Stephen Chalmers, the new Duke of Marston, as he watched the figure in the window.

But heat spread through his body when the silhouette arched upward and grasped an object in a graceful steady motion.

With energy and anticipation thrumming in his veins, the passing minutes felt like an eternity. From his position in the shadows, the figure's act of reaching upward was a lover's hand skimming a thigh, grazing a side, gliding across a chest. And the motion of pulling an object off a shelf became a hand running down a neck, down a breast, skimming a hip.

He shifted uncomfortably, trying to ignore the way his body was responding. It wouldn't be much longer before the papers in the house across the street were secured; the thief's reputation had been well earned.

The silhouette lifted its shirt and tied what appeared to be a sheaf of papers around its waist. The body lines unintentionally revealed more than an added padding of paper.

The figure slid from view, and the light in the room was extinguished. A long leg stretched from the open window, and the intruder landed a smoothly executed jump.

Stephen admired the graceful landing and held his position. The figure scanned the empty street, lowered the window, then sprinted to the east. Stephen motioned eastward to the man at his side, who nodded and silently followed the retreating form.

It had been a stroke of genius and good luck to find the notorious thief Hermes' destination. With it came confirmation of the thief's identity.

A satisfied smile eased across Stephen's face. Patience wasn't his strong suit, but some tasks were definitely worth the wait. He had tracked the thief's movements for too many years to carelessly spoil the hunt.

Years of tracking Hermes had finally come to a close. Stephen had thought he was out of luck when the thief had abruptly retired and disappeared from London the previous year. But something had lured Hermes back to the game with renewed vigor. The thief was single-handedly responsible for six robberies in the last week alone. Seven, counting tonight's work.

Having stolen the papers, Hermes' next stop would be the modest brick house near Mayfair. The thief's temporary home.

Stephen stepped into the street and walked the few blocks to his carriage, whistling. He would visit the unpretentious brick house soon. An introduction to Hermes was well past due.

His blood heated. It was time to toss a kink into her plans.

Chapter 2

Stephen casually twirled a pen, splattering ink on the papers covering his desk. "What did the informant say?"

Marcus Stewart, Baron Roth, leaned casually against the leather chair on the opposite side of Stephen's desk. "The same as the longshoreman. He only noticed that the papers had been switched because he had been informed earlier in the day that the spice ship was coming in late. Otherwise, the ship would have been rerouted in the same manner as the others."

"Any new information on the villains' identities?"

"A few of the men on the docks recall a short man with a nervous twitch and a floppy hat. Seems to corroborate the earlier descriptions of one of the men we are searching for. Still no recognizable facial characteristics."

"What about information on any of the others?"

"The thefts all point to Hermes. At least one other person besides Mr. Floppy Hat has to be involved. Probably the coordinator between the thief and the man in charge."

"Hermes will be taken care of."

"You know who the thief is?"

"I do indeed." Stephen dabbed at the splattered droplets with the ink blotter.

"Well? Who is he?" Roth, usually a patient man, sat forward in his chair.

Stephen smiled at his friend's expression. He was in no hurry to satisfy Roth's curiosity. He examined the shape of his inkpot, the curves vaguely reminiscent of the ones he had seen the night before. "You'll know tonight. I need to put some plans into action."

"Get Hermes, and you have the others. Without the thief there is no way for them to get the papers or to sneak in and use the necessary seals to create the new documents. No one else is as good."

"True. But we need to make sure that we get the others."

"What's wrong with the usual methods? Hell, Angelford will be back tonight. He'd probably love to help with the interrogation." Roth smirked. "Provided his wife lets him."

Stephen smiled briefly. "Yes, but I've decided to try something new with this one."

Roth gave him an unreadable expression. "Why?"

"I have my reasons." *Not that those reasons are necessarily good ones*, Stephen thought darkly.

Roth leaned back and studied him. "Why the secrecy?"

"Why the impatience?"

As planned, Roth took exception to his flippancy. "You know damn well why, Stephen."

"Someone is wreaking havoc with the dock and shipping records. Flanagan is marshaling forces in St. Giles and stirring action in the stews. Someone's trying to kill me, et cetera, et cetera." Stephen twirled the pen again. A small flow of liquid jetted toward his friend, landing just short of the papers on the edge of the desk.

Roth grimaced at having taken the bait, but persisted. "That's a rather blasé way to state the situation, even for you."

"We don't know if Flanagan has direct involvement with the shipping trouble. Shipping ventures aren't his style."

"How much does it take for a criminal to develop an interest in another aspect of the criminal underworld? This is your area of expertise. I shouldn't be the one quoting it."

Stephen sighed and set the pen down, the exhilaration from identifying one of Flanagan's top thieves receding along with his enjoyment from nettling Roth. "I know. But Flanagan is a thief at heart, not a murderer, and with the dead longshoreman last week and the merchant the week before, it just doesn't fit. And his minions are cut from the same cloth. They all belong in prison for their crimes, but I don't believe they are treasonous. It's just not their style, Roth."

"Hermes was one of Flanagan's best and we *know* he is involved in this. Besides, illegal shipments and rerouting cargoes fit into the category of theft."

Stephen acknowledged Roth's point. "Yes, and maybe Flanagan has some involvement. But my gut says there are new players involved. Besides, I believe we are searching for someone with greater prestige and position than flunkies in the St. Giles gangs. Someone who has access to specific, confidential information."

Stephen began ticking off points on his fingers. "We know there are at least three major players: Hermes, who is stealing the papers and authenticating the fake ones with the appropriate seals, the person who is serving as the intermediary, and the man behind it all. I need to confirm a few details this afternoon, then I will meet you at the Taylors' party. That way I can tell you and James everything at the same time."

Stephen pulled one of his fern hybrids over and plucked a dead leaf. "We'll uncover the plot in time to save the day and rout the villains, just like we did with the Cato Conspiracy, don't worry."

"Sometimes I worry about *you*, old friend."

"No worries, Roth." Stephen flashed a grin. "The next few weeks should be quite exciting. Wait and see."

Roth threw a balled-up piece of paper at his head. Stephen grinned as he caught it, but promptly grimaced as the action aggravated his sore shoulder. The shoulder hadn't fully healed in the year since he had "fallen" into the Thames. He rotated his arm and felt the slight pop.

Roth watched him, concern etched in his eyes. "Still paining you?"

"Feeling better every day."

"Discover anything new about your savior?"

"I have the men following a few leads, but no, nothing new."

His friend tapped a finger. "That is odd."

"And frustrating. You don't have to remind me."

It had been a year, but Stephen could still feel the dark grip of the Thames before he had blacked out. Jumping off the bridge while barely conscious had not been his smartest move, but in the end it had saved his life. As a result of his involvement and investigation, justice had been served. The treasonous members of England's Foreign Office had been apprehended.

Everything had worked out satisfactorily, with the exception of the shoulder injury and not finding the faceless savior who had fished him from the river. Both loose ends still bothered him.

He rotated his shoulder again. "Only one more thug to corral from the Foreign Office investigation. Leonard Peters. The dullard has been absent from London since the incident, which is fortunate for him. A stone would give him a good beating in a test of intelligence."

"He works for Flanagan," Roth pointed out.

Roth was relentless. He wasn't going to dismiss the Flanagan connection until he was satisfied.

"So did some of the other conspirators, but they all maintained they were hired for an outside job. No connection to Flanagan." Stephen cracked his knuckles, an annoying habit taken from his father. "And there was plenty of incentive for them to implicate Flanagan."

Roth nodded but looked unconvinced. "But most of his folks are loyal. I still think you should investigate Flanagan's bunch."

Stephen stroked his fingers down the curves of the inkpot. "I have. As a matter of fact, investigating his gang is exactly how I determined Hermes' identity. Icarus's too. Two of his favorite thieves."

Roth leaned forward, careful to avoid the ink-stained papers. "Excellent. Tell me who Icarus is then."

"Tonight, old man, tonight," he teased the man only two years his senior.

"I do believe I dislike you these days, Chalmers."

Stephen grinned. "I promise the Taylors' party will be interesting."

Roth raised both brows in disbelief and rose. "I find that hard to believe, but I'll see you this evening."

Stephen released the curved inkpot and leaned back in his chair. Tonight *would* be interesting. The carefully structured impromptu meeting this afternoon would guarantee it.

A lighthearted feeling of anticipation and excitement thrummed through him. The chase was going to be even sweeter this time. He felt it in his skin. He would finish the game started years before when Hermes had pilfered important government documents. While not a treasonous affair, and therefore not in Stephen's usual line of work, the papers contained secrets that had caused consternation among his superiors and a lot of official sweating. Stephen had retrieved the papers, but the thief had been long gone—an indescribable shadow by witness account.

Since he had been needed on the Continent, Stephen had assigned numerous men to catch the thief. Hermes had slipped through the fingers of every runner and hired guard. Slipped through every time without a trace.

But this time the thief was making mistakes, just as every criminal eventually did. Rather than confining activities to the general populace, the thefts had once more crossed into government affairs. This time Stephen was going to catch the thief himself and not delegate the work.

And it was a task he expected to enjoy thoroughly. The thrill of the chase pulsed through him again, forcing him to temper the feeling with cold realism. The ending to these cases was always the same. Prison and often a death sentence. Justice was the cornerstone of English society and civilization. Societies that had laws without justice crumbled—justice always needed to be served.

Stephen fiddled with the tangled fronds of the

fern on his desk. Tangled just like he had planned, but maybe a little too twisted to unravel.

He lifted the plant and walked to his conservatory, whistling. He needed the right amount of twist to get the desired effect. Too little was boring; too much created a mess. He needed the perfect combination.

He loved a challenge.

"Good afternoon, Miss Kendrick. The cabbages are particularly plump this day. My son hauled 'em in from the country early this morning."

Audrey Kendrick smiled at the stout grocer and examined the healthy vegetables in his stall. A hearty cabbage soup would complement the roast duck she planned for supper. "In that case, I believe I'll take two."

"How is Mr. Maddox? Is he feeling better?"

Audrey gritted her teeth but assumed a hopeful expression. "Yes. He is no longer bedridden. The doctor said he has made an inspired recovery. He's well enough that we shall even be attending a gathering this evening."

The grocer leaned forward. "Pardon my saying, miss, but I've never seen that doctor around these parts afore. Now, the good doctor around the corner, that's who you should have looking in on your father."

Audrey loosened her knit fingers from her skirt. Father indeed. "Oh, Dr. Smith has been very kind to us. Father took right to him. I don't think he would be doing as well without the dear doctor."

The grocer smiled and bundled her purchases. "Well, then that's what matters. Here you go, miss. Have a good day. And give your father our regards."

Audrey forced herself to smile back. She wouldn't be surprised to find her skin stretched permanently across her face from the strained smiles and fake cheer. If she had to refer to that vicious old goat as her father one more time, she was going to scream. The lies were growing more difficult to utter. Especially in the face of such people. Round, jolly vendors hailed her, and motherly, cheerful women called out greetings. They were too damn nice here.

This pleasant little slice of London, on the outskirts of Mayfair, was almost comical in its contrast to her old territory. Mayfair was nothing like the dregs of London, where one foul word could find you with a knife embedded in your ribs.

Absently, she rubbed her right side. She was

never going back. A voice in her head mocked her. *You're already back*.

No. No, she was temporarily "assigned" to a few tasks. As long as she and Faye survived this mess, there was enough money saved to ensure they'd have a new life. A new life far from London. If there was one lesson the entire experience had taught her, it was that she and her sister couldn't remain in England. The past would always haunt them.

Moving away from the vegetable stall and her dark thoughts, Audrey stepped into the center of the market. The smell of warm bread and delicious meat pies filled the air. The atmosphere was festive. It was another way that life in Mayfair was better. In the dregs, women hawked their wares to visiting merchants. Here, merchants hawked their wares to women and servants eager to return with the best of the day's meat and produce.

"Fresh vegetables!"

"Tasty cutlets!"

"The finest potatoes in England!"

A street urchin breezed past and she felt a slight brush. In a trice she had shifted her packages and seized the boy's arm with her free hand. The boy looked at her in surprise, then panic.

"Not today, boyo." She pulled him forcefully toward her to keep him off-balance, reached into his pocket, and retrieved her money pouch. He regained his footing and scampered into the crowd.

She absently memorized his features. He was new. The boy had promise; he just needed a little practice. It was the same for all new recruits.

Audrey continued down the lane of colorful stalls, letting the cheerful atmosphere temporarily soothe her. These rosy bursts of humanity were the only things that kept harsh reality away, and unfortunately such moments were becoming fewer and harder to come by.

A bright reflection drew her attention. The summer day was cloudless, and the rays easily caught the gleaming steel in the stall on the right.

The new smith was flipping knives. She sighed wistfully. He might be an apprentice, but the quality of his craft was evident. Balanced, tempered, and sharp. His was the stall she most wanted to visit. But if Miss Audrey Kendrick, fainthearted gentlewoman from the country, strolled in to toss the blades, the grocer and half the other vendors she frequented would become suspicious.

No, she couldn't afford to indulge in her hobby. But maybe she could sneak into the smith's house.

Of course, she'd pay for the merchandise. Her honor demanded it in this instance. But she'd relieve him of a few of those crafted beauties and—

A fresh forest scent assailed her, momentarily breaking her concentration. An odd smell to find in London. "Oof." Audrey felt as if she'd hit a pine tree.

"The Fates are kind today."

The tree had a smooth, deep voice. Audrey looked up at the handsome blond-haired man she had just crashed into, and the expression in his devilish green eyes caused her breath to lodge in her throat. One second. Two seconds.

"I've been waiting all day for a beautiful woman to fall into my arms. But I am a reasonable man and will accept a collision instead."

Dear Lord, he was here to arrest her. *Move*, she shouted to her traitorous limbs. But she was rooted in place, rendered speechless and incapable of flight.

"You look a little shocked, miss. Are you hurt? I didn't mean to startle you, but you were so intent on watching the smith that you didn't see me." A mischievous glint lit the familiar stranger's face, belying his words.

Air whooshed from her lungs, and she stammered, "No, I'm fine, thank you. And you?" She nearly winced as the words spewed forth.

The lazy smile reached Stephen Chalmers's eyes. "I'm interested."

Audrey swallowed and again murmured something less than intelligent. But her mind was screaming danger. Did he know who she was?

She watched in a trancelike state as he released her and twirled his walking stick with casual grace. It had been a long time since she had been this close to him, but his sheer presence still overwhelmed her. Still caused that breathless feeling, like she was being sucked into her own stomach.

"Good. Great. Good-bye." She shuffled backward in a dazed manner, her purchases swaying precariously in her arms.

"Here, let me help you with those packages."

Audrey snapped to attention, but he took advantage of her momentary brainlessness and smoothly relieved her of her day's purchases. His fingers grazed her side, and she had to force herself to breathe again.

He watched her frozen state in amusement. Undoubtedly, he was accustomed to causing a flustered reaction in women. Audrey's wits returned at the thought, and, feigning gratitude, she reached out for the packages. "Very kind of you, sir, but not necessary. It's late, and I must be on my way."

He waved a dismissive hand, having no trouble

balancing all of the parcels in one arm and his walking stick in the other. "In my own self-interest, I can't leave you to wander into someone else. Then our encounter would be nothing special. I insist. Where to, miss?"

His green eyes were twinkling. Damn. She cast a quick glance around. A few of the vendors were smiling at her apparent "fortune" in attracting the attentions of such a handsome, well-dressed man. There was no way to extricate herself from this sham without causing a scene.

And what difference did it make if he accompanied her home? If he knew her identity, he already knew where she lived. And if he didn't know who she was, denying him might cause his suspicions to rise. The shock of seeing and touching him faded, and she felt the familiar rush of the chase slither through her.

"I'm on my way home." She looked away from him and pointed to the small house at the end of the street.

She peeked at her escort from beneath her bonnet. Did he never stop grinning? He looked exceptionally pleased with the situation and matched her pace as they walked.

"Did you find everything you needed?" he asked.

She nodded and slipped into character. "It was

an eventful day at the market." Well, it had started out normally enough . . .

He peeked into the top bag. "Onions and cabbages? Fixing something tasty, are you?"

"Actually, they make perfect replacements if a head falls off a doll. Especially if you imagine it to be someone in particular and jab it with sharp sticks."

"Not good news for you," Stephen said to the unresponsive vegetables in the bag. He looked back to her. "The smith has a wonderful stall for sharp implements."

"All of those shiny objects. I couldn't help but be dazzled."

He waved a hand, imitating a romantic young buck. "Shiny and dazzling. A woman of your beauty should be swathed in glittering gowns and priceless jewels."

Audrey nearly snorted.

A wicked look entered his eyes. "Yes, your legs would look lovely draped in dark silk. And if you were scandalous enough, you could don breeches and strike a man dumb with longing."

Audrey couldn't restrain the blush that shot to her cheeks. She tipped her chin up and walked faster, tilting her head to the side to prevent him from seeing the effects of his words.

The comments seemed pointed, but his face was that of a seducer. He was a rogue, and rogues made comments like that. It didn't mean anything else. Dear Lord, she hoped it didn't mean anything else.

They reached the door, and he allowed her to take the packages inside.

He smiled broadly, swung his walking stick, and tipped his hat. "What a pleasant afternoon it has become. Good day, miss. It would be my greatest fortune to see you again soon. Perhaps the Fates will be kind twice."

Not waiting for a reply, he tipped his hat and ambled down the steps, whistling.

Audrey's heart raced at his parting shot. She stared at his retreating back and the tapping of his walking stick. There was a wicked blade in that stick. She knew the type. And a wicked man wielded it. She knew that type too.

She didn't know whether to follow and hit him in the alley or just thank her lucky stars she was still free and standing in her doorway. She decided on the latter as she watched Henry Travers stalking toward the house in his "Dr. Smith" disguise. Later she would figure out what to do about Stephen Chalmers and his merry little whistling.

"Inside. Now." Travers gritted through his straight

white teeth, grabbed her elbow, and propelled her forward.

Audrey cocked a brow. If Travers thought he could intimidate her after she had just come face-to-face with her number one adversary, he had another thought coming. Travers stormed past her and slammed the door.

"What the hell were you doing with Stephen bloody Chalmers?"

She shook herself free and called for her maid. The sullen woman appeared and took the packages.

"Well?" Travers demanded.

"I was bringing groceries home for supper." Audrey walked into the overwhelmingly purple drawing room, Travers hot on her heels.

"What?"

She sat in one of the violet straight-backed chairs, casually resting her elbows on the arms. Her nerves were frayed from bumping into the blond Adonis on the street, but she didn't want Travers to see her consternation. "He offered to assist me with my packages."

"Why? Where did you meet? What did you tell him?"

"I told him about all of the papers I have stolen and changed recently and that you are planning to assassinate the Exchequer."

Travers looked on the verge of exploding; he hadn't even bothered to remove his wig and fake spectacles. His normally unblemished skin mottled in anger. "So help me, girl, I will have you whipped if you don't tell me right now what passed between you."

Audrey experienced a moment's unease. Travers was a thorn in her side, most definitely, but this unnatural anger was unsettling. He was usually a calm devil, measured and precise. Not a screeching demon.

"I bumped into him, literally, and being a gentleman, he took my packages and insisted on accompanying me home. That is all."

"What did he say to you?"

"He just chattered."

"He said nothing? Didn't say a word to you other than small talk?"

She crossed her arms. "No. I have no explanation of what streak of bad luck put me first in your path and now in his."

Travers swore. "We're going to have to adjust the plans and schedule."

"Perfect. Release my sister and good luck with your new plan."

He laughed unpleasantly and twenty years vanished as he removed the wig and glasses of his disguise. He trailed a finger down her arm, and she jerked it away.

"I don't think so, my dear."

"Where is Faye?"

"She's safe, for now."

Audrey hated herself for the weakness, but she walked to the window, putting the table between herself and the angelic-looking devil. "She's out of Newgate?"

Travers absently played with his pocket watch. His eyes were dark and brooding, and she wondered how much longer she'd be able to play his game.

"I'm making arrangements for her release."

As soon as her sister stepped foot from prison, Audrey could relax. Faye would easily be able to escape from a dozen of Travers's guards.

His eyes mocked her. "She's in no danger . . . of harming others. She'll make a delightful . . . guest."

Audrey's heart quickened. "What do you mean?"

Travers shrugged. "The last report said her condition was poor. All the more reason for you to successfully complete your tasks and speed her release."

She couldn't keep the anguish from her voice. "What have you done to her?"

He laughed and dropped his lean aristocratic frame into the chair she had abandoned. "Nothing, my dear. The damage has already been done. Why, you remember what it's like."

Cramped spaces, rats, moldy bread, and the smell of rotting flesh? Yes, she remembered what it was like. She also remembered who had incarcerated them without a whisper of proof or semblance of a trial. All under the table, all too effective.

"If anything happens to my sister, I'll kill you. I don't care about your connections or threats to do me harm."

Travers looked unconcerned, his patrician features unmarred. "We'll see, my dear. So far I've managed to stay remarkably healthy in your presence. Now, do you have them?"

"Yes."

Audrey strode from the room, head held high, and climbed the stairs to her bedroom. Once there she quickly retrieved the bundle from one of her hiding places. She was afraid to linger too long, Travers might follow her. Lately he had been making more overt gestures. She gagged at the thought of him touching her and wiped a hand across her clammy forehead. He hadn't tried anything other than light touches designed to torment and unnerve her, perhaps not yet ready to test her boundaries. For all of his vices and sins, she would never call him stupid, but one couldn't be too careful.

She returned to the study and dumped the bundle into his lap. "All the papers are inside, along with another parchment with a copy of each seal."

His eyes devoured the worn cloth as he carefully unwrapped the bundle with a gentleness that surprised her. "So they are. You have done well, Audrey. With the proper incentive, I knew you would succeed, or I'd never have acquired you for these tasks. Your sister will live another day."

She sat across from him, using the low center table as a barrier. "When will I see my sister?"

"Tut, tut. Patience and trust, my sweet. I have another task for you."

Her fists clutched the arms of the carved chair and darkness seeped into her soul. She had known this was how it would turn out, had known Travers was the last person to keep his word, but she couldn't resist fighting. "Our deal was the papers for my sister."

"But now there's something else I want from you." Travers surveyed her. "Besides your begging, of course. But that pleasure will come in its own due time. Until then I shall only dream of the moment."

Audrey fought the anger and fear, instead keeping her features flat as she always did when he insinuated something sexual between them. If only Faye were free. If only Audrey could scoff at Travers's increasingly suggestive innuendos and ridicule his demands. If only they had left England last year. If only . . .

Travers crossed his ankles. "And then there is the Chalmers situation. How very strange that you sit here before me instead of locked in Newgate with your sister. Why do you suppose that is? Chalmers would put you there in a heartbeat."

"I have no idea, but it is dangerous to continue as we are."

A flash of something, perhaps fear, passed through his eyes. "For Audrey the adventurer? The notorious thief? I think not. I know you won't let the Duke of Marston interfere in my plans or in your desire to have Faye safely home."

He practically spat Stephen's title, and a splinter of wood broke from the chair beneath one of his short nails. The brief flitter of fear she had seen in his eyes was gone. His expression was hard and angry—something more than his usual bitterness. What was Chalmers to him?

Travers looked at his pocket watch once more, as if it had somehow betrayed him, before violently shoving it back into his pocket and withdrawing a paper. He shoved the paper across the table. "This is your next task. And I have a little plan for Stephen Chalmers as well."

Chapter 3

Stephen accepted a glass of champagne and circled the Taylors' ballroom floor. A few women tried to catch his eye, but he smiled and worked his way through the crush, nodding to acquaintances but not pausing to converse. As long as he smiled, the ladies would think they could snare him later in the evening. He had been using the tactic for the past two weeks, ever since gaining the title, and so far it had worked. He kept moving.

There was only one woman he wanted to speak with this evening. One woman with long legs that made breeches look sinful.

Roth was announced, and Stephen nodded to him over the crowd but continued purposefully through the throng, searching for his prey. The information he had received said he would not be disappointed.

Never had he looked so forward to interrogating a suspect and extracting information more than he did with this woman.

Two more guests were announced.

Music drifted through the room, but Stephen was no longer listening. The vision that had just entered the ballroom blotted the noise. Wearing a white-trimmed lavender gown she stood elegantly next to a well-dressed gentleman who looked slightly out of place. Long white gloves covered her hands and lower arms. Raven hair was pinned to her crown, loose strands escaping down her shoulders. He couldn't see her eyes clearly from the distance, but he knew they were silver-blue. She appeared to be simpering, but her eyes were too quick, too assessing to be submissive.

Those icy blue eyes took in the gilt coverings, the heirloom candlesticks, the expensive paintings, and the bounty of silver. And then her gaze assessed each person she was introduced to in the same manner. Stephen would bet she could estimate the earnings and holdings of each person within a few hundred pounds of his or her actual worth.

Anticipation surged through him.

The pair moved into the room and chatted with various guests who approached them. The lady's eyes kept moving, constantly assessing, weighing, and judging.

He wanted to push through the crowd, but instead he made a slow circuit and watched her work. She knew how to handle herself in a ballroom. Her behavior was correct, her manner changing between a blushing young woman and a lofty maiden depending on the person introduced.

Stephen switched his gaze to her companion, who seemed ill at ease in the formal setting. His clothes were well tailored, but he fidgeted as if he were desperate to remove his cravat. The woman soaked all of the attention, effectively deflecting any from the man, her supposed stepfather. Clever girl.

Stephen's anticipation surged again as he walked toward the couple. As opponents, they were well matched. The board was set. He had moved his pawn earlier in the day, and now it was time to implement his next strategy.

"Stephen!"

Turning, he amended his earlier statement. There were two women with whom he wanted to talk. He winked at the lovely blonde woman as he made his bow. "Calliope. James. Good to see you back for the season."

"Your Grace," Calliope's voice held amusement, and a devilish smile appeared as she curtsied, then gave him a warm embrace.

"This imp of yours grows more beautiful each day," Stephen remarked, grasping James's outstretched hand. "And sassier too."

"I wouldn't have it any other way." He laughed, bestowing a loving glance on his wife. "May I add my condolences on your newly acquired title?"

"You know me only too well, James."

Stephen continued to exchange pleasantries with the Marquess and Marchioness of Angelford at the edge of the crowded dance floor, his eyes tracking his opponent as she made her way through the swarm.

"Roth said you would be here tonight. Have you seen him?" James said.

"Yes, he is lurking about."

Calliope put her hand on Stephen's arm. "We will have to speak later in the evening. There are so many things we wish to tell you."

She looked at her husband, and a light blush stained her cheeks. Stephen fought amusement and a slight twinge of envy at the shared glance.

That they loved each other was evident. That they were happy was even more so.

His parents had enjoyed such a relationship, and if he could have gifted a lucky star to any couple, it would be the one in front of him.

"I'm sure you will both nauseate me with your blushes and caresses, but please don't make it too early in the night."

James tried to cover a laugh, and Calliope rapped Stephen lightly with her fan. "Rogue."

Stephen smiled and turned to locate the icy-eyed woman. After a quick search he spotted her near the refreshment table. A few admirers had taken up court. He grimaced as he saw Henry Travers make a dashing bow.

A fan tapped him on the arm. "Stephen? You just ignored two questions. Which lovely lady holds your attention?"

Calliope was smiling, and James's brows were raised in inquiry.

"Just thinking about fetching you some punch, my dearest butterfly."

Calliope laughed. Roth sauntered over to their group, greeting all of them.

Audrey tried not to stare at the foursome across the crowd. Her new admirers were beaming and asking for permission to dance, permission to recite a poem, permission to fetch lemonade. She accepted the last offer and wished she could give the rest permission to cross a busy street. She felt suffocated in the mansion, surrounded by glittering popinjays. Of those people she had no fear. The well-tailored and handsome folk in the tight group, however, were a different story.

"Hmmmm . . . I see you have located your next target."

Audrey blanched as Travers whispered in her ear, pretending to recite poetry.

"Please, sir, your declarations are outrageous," she twittered aloud. A number of the men protested his intrusion, but Travers held up a helpless hand and turned on his charm.

"I do apologize, Miss Kendrick, but your beauty is intoxicating."

The men readily agreed, and Travers took the opportunity to whisper, "I want the butterfly pin Chalmers gave to his old flame, the Marchioness of Angelford. Prove you are the best, Audrey, and I will give you news of your sister."

Audrey's heart leaped, and she gratefully accepted the glass of lemonade an eager suitor offered. Travers smiled and walked away, taking her inept stepfather with him.

The musicians launched into a lively reel. "Would you do me the honor of this dance, Miss Kendrick?" a young man with curly brown hair asked.

She nodded and handed her half-finished lemonade to another suitor. They joined the dancers on the floor. Maintaining a proper distance, they traversed the floor with the others in tempo to the music. Audrey scanned the group on the edge of the dance floor. Her eyes met Stephen Chalmers's, and heat and cold rushed through her. So dangerous. What was she doing here?

She stepped away, then met her partner, performing the appropriate steps, every step taking her closer to her adversaries. Every step one closer to a four-walled cell.

One of the men in the group was speaking to Chalmers, but the duke's attention was focused on her. She felt herself pulled toward him and sensed her partner's shock as she led him in that direction.

She looked at her partner for the first time. "Oh, I beg your pardon, sir. It's a bit stuffy in here."

The man nodded enthusiastically. "Indeed. Would you like to take some air, Miss Kendrick?"

The dance ended. "No, thank you. I think I will return to my stepfather."

A brandy-smooth voice caressed her ear. "Miss Kendrick, how wonderful to see you again."

He addressed her dance partner. "I'll return Miss Kendrick to her stepfather."

Her partner looked crestfallen, bowed awkwardly, and deferred to the duke before moving into the crowd.

Audrey faced Stephen Chalmers. "Good evening, Your Grace. I don't believe we have been properly introduced."

"I thought our introduction today quite proper." He drawled lazily, examining her from head to toe. "And if you wish to do other than speak, I have no objections."

Heat uncurled within her. "You are a scoundrel."

He smiled slowly. "And you are the perfect foil for a scoundrel." Another set was forming on the floor. A waltz. "Would you care to dance with one?"

Lord help her, she put her hand on his arm and walked with him onto the floor.

"You are from Cheshire, I hear?"

Audrey pulled herself into her role. "Yes, we are only in London for the season."

"How are things in Cheshire these days?"

"Quiet. Normal. Peaceful."

"Sounds pleasant. Why did you decide to venture to the city? London is noisy and full of strange happenings and . . . crime." The pause was nearly infinitesimal, and Audrey forced herself to pretend it was absent. She had to keep her wits together tonight.

"What brings every young woman from the country to London? Adventure. Excitement." She tipped her head back and felt burned. His green eyes were smoldering, but she couldn't read the emotion.

"Adventure? Most women come during the season to find a husband." His lips curled suggestively.

"I suppose that is an adventure to most women, Your Grace."

"Too true. But you seem much more interesting than most women."

A tingle passed through her. "I am sorry to say you will likely be disappointed in me, Your Grace."

"I'm sure that will not be the case, Miss Kendrick. I have a feeling London will be particularly exciting this season."

A sinful glint lit his eyes, and she bowed her head. "I'm sure it will be when you find some other lady to attend."

"But there is no other lady's interest that I wish to

catch so much as yours, Audrey." He pulled her slightly closer than was proper, and his leg brushed hers.

The inflection made her heart skip. He was suspicious, but he didn't know. He couldn't, or she would already be in prison. But a devil inside caused her to say, "And too long to *chase* endlessly after something you can never hope to catch, Your Grace."

He threw his head back and laughed. The reverberations vibrated through her. Other couples turned at the sound. He tugged her closer still, and she pinched his arm. He laughed again, returning them to proper positions. The music ended, and she saw the mischief shining in his eyes.

"Come, I will introduce you to my friends."

Panic caught her. In no way did she want to meet the two other men who would love to have her head on a platter.

"No, thank you, Your Grace. I must return to my stepfather. Good evening to you."

She curtsied and tried to keep her pace calm as she walked toward her stepfather, before changing directions and climbing the stairs to the ladies' retiring room.

She opened the door and was relieved to find the

room empty. Walking around two chaises and multiple cushions to get to the mirror, Audrey pressed a hand to her cheek and looked at her reflection. At least she appeared composed.

Was Travers going to make her attend more of these engagements? She didn't know how many more she could handle. She was a back-alley worker. Being so exposed was a new and frightening feeling. And damn if she didn't hate being frightened of anything or anyone.

The door opened, and a lovely lady with honey-colored hair entered. Audrey assessed the newcomer with a mixture of dismay and interest. A gem-studded butterfly brooch was pinned to the dress of the Marchioness of Angelford—Stephen's ex-mistress, although society at large had not seemed to grasp that fact yet.

"Good evening," the woman said, with a cheerful smile.

Audrey returned the greeting and praised the good fortune that had prompted the lady to enter the room. If she could lift her brooch, she could leave the damn ball. She pretended to arrange her hair in the mirror as she surreptitiously studied the pin. It seemed to be securely attached.

Why would her husband allow her to wear a gift from another man? It went beyond all of Audrey's reasoning abilities and her knowledge of the marquess.

"We haven't been introduced, but I'm Calliope."

Audrey looked at her in surprise, then at the rest of the retiring room. They were still the only ones present.

Covering her lapse, she said pleasantly, "My lady, it's a pleasure to meet you. My name is Audrey Kendrick."

The woman waved her hands. "Please call me Calliope. After all, I saw the way you and Stephen were dancing."

What? What was the lady prattling on about?

"If that was any indication of the future, we will probably be seeing each other frequently."

What was this *lady* implying? If she thought she was going to join them in any tawdry activities, well she could take her pretty little fan and stick . . .

"You look flushed. Are you feeling well?" Calliope peered at her and held out a towel.

"The house is a bit warm, is all." *Thank goodness for tired excuses.*

Calliope nodded. "I know, but one becomes accustomed to it. This is your first season?"

"Yes, although I have attended a few balls." Mostly masked balls, which made it relatively easy to relieve the owners of their possessions. Since she had been raised in a genteel home, she had always been assigned to the upper-class functions but until recently had never attended as herself. That she did now only underscored her danger.

"Would you like me to fetch you something to drink?"

She seemed genuinely nice, and Audrey had to stop a frown. What was happening here? It was difficult not to like this woman, even though Audrey didn't want to. She was married to one enemy, good friend to another, and the ex-mistress of the most deadly one, no matter that Calliope and Stephen had always acted a bit too fraternally toward each other whenever she had seen them together.

"No, thank you. My father will worry if I'm gone too long." She couldn't snatch the pin while Calliope was looking at her.

"I'll return with you." Calliope walked with her to the door. "We shall have to meet for tea sometime."

Three ladies entered the room and collided with them. During the confusion Audrey took the opportunity to smoothly relieve Calliope of her beautiful pin. Guilt kicked in, but she needed the pin. The marchioness probably had thousands of brooches and other pretty trinkets.

They walked down the stairs while Calliope

chattered good-naturedly. Audrey felt worse with every step. They reached the bottom step, and Audrey saw Stephen walking toward them.

"Wonderful to meet you, Lady Angelford," she said, and quickly slipped into the crowd, heading in the opposite direction. For once she was relieved to see Travers standing near. She surreptitiously motioned to him and wended through the crowd toward the door.

Stephen saw her rushing toward the exit and decided to let her go. He wasn't pleased with his decision, but he needed to consider his next move. The game pieces were ready.

Calliope whispered to Stephen, "I like her," as she passed by to rejoin her husband. Something was different about Calliope, but he couldn't pinpoint it. Perhaps it was the secretive smile. He ignored it, as there was nothing to be gained from getting irritated with friends.

That Calliope liked Audrey made sense. They were both unconventional.

He frowned. No, Audrey was different. She was a criminal. All criminals were cut from the same cloth. Damn. This assignment might prove maddening.

Roth came to stand next to Stephen. He too was

observing her retreating form. "Lost your touch, Marston?"

Stephen scowled. "Don't call me that."

"Why? That's your name now. Can't go around calling you Chalmers anymore."

"Bloody title."

Roth's smile turned slightly wicked. "Looks like the girl wasn't impressed."

"Oh, I think I just turned her head a bit too much."

"Must be why she ran to the retiring room after dancing with you and is now making to leave the ball entirely."

Stephen told Roth what he could do with his suppositions in unflattering terms.

Roth laughed. "You were right. Tonight is proving to be vastly entertaining." He took a sip of his drink. "You should have seen the two of you on the floor. Set the tongues wagging, you did. Beautiful girl. Who is she?"

"Her name is Audrey Kendrick."

"And?"

"And what?"

Roth shook his head but continued to smile. "You are in a foul mood. And because of a girl running from you, no less."

Stephen didn't answer so Roth continued, "Since

you don't want to talk about the girl, how about finally telling me the identity of Hermes?"

"I'm debating whether I want to tell you anything now, old man."

"Sour grapes, *Marston*, sour grapes."

Stephen held back a smile, suddenly in a much happier mood. Oh, he'd get his revenge all right.

"Hermes is here tonight."

Roth looked around suddenly serious. "You're teasing. Here? You know, I always thought he might be someone connected to society." He studied the crowd, and Stephen debated whether to let him suffer all night. Roth would assuredly make a very thorough search of the entire ballroom. Probably interrogate the populace while he was at it.

"Yes, here."

Roth continued his study of the crowd. "Dammit, Chalmers, are you going to tell me or not?"

Stephen smiled. Victory was so sweet. "Actually, the thief *was* here."

Roth frowned.

"Regrettably, Hermes fled from the ball, immediately after I danced with her."

Chapter 4

~~~~~~~~~~∽◦◦∽~~~~~~~~~~

Audrey slid through the open window and landed in a crouched position on the floor, listening. No creaks, no stirrings; all were abed. She straightened and peered into the darkness. A rare wave of nerves swept through her. Something was odd tonight, but she couldn't pinpoint exactly what.

Thin beads of moonlight streamed through the window, allowing just enough light to outline a bulky desk and portion of the floor. She pushed her nerves aside and crept toward the desk.

The papers were supposed to be inside a secret compartment at the bottom of the desk. Audrey crouched and skimmed her fingers along the underside of the wood. Her fingers grazed a clasp.

Disgustingly easy. It must have been the multiple brushes with Chalmers today that had set her on edge.

This was a job for a green lad. If she was going to risk her neck while being pressed into service, the least Travers could do was come up with something more challenging. She activated the mechanism. A concealed drawer popped open. She removed the stack of papers, closed the door, and reset the lever.

Audrey tucked the papers under her shirt and into her breeches. She would read them later, before giving them to Travers. She needed all the ammunition she could accumulate to save Faye. And if blackmailing her blackmailer was the only way to free her sister, she'd do it.

Audrey moved toward the window. There was no use dawdling. Only striplings made the mistake of lingering at a scene. She was halfway to freedom when she stopped.

The air had changed. Her scalp prickled, and she whirled around to face the other person in the room. So silent. How had she missed him? Why had he waited to show himself? And why hadn't he sounded the alarm?

She lashed out with her right foot, but her blow was deflected. A shaft of moonlight settled in front of her, cut in twain by her body. She was silhouetted in the light, easy to see. Cursing inwardly, she dove and somersaulted away from the desk. She grabbed one of the knives from her left sleeve and hurled it at the figure.

The knife was somehow blocked, and the steel clattered harmlessly across the floor. The sound was deafening in the otherwise silent house. Audrey could hear the walls waking from their heavy sleep. The inhabitants would be next.

She needed to incapacitate her assailant as silently as possible and get the hell out of the house. She could discern a faint outline, and though the man was tall and broad-shouldered, he wasn't a beefy thug. She might be able to sustain his weight before he hit the floor. She grabbed a bust perched on the edge of a side table and launched herself at the figure.

Her aim was perfect, but at the last instant the man stepped to the side and pulled her tightly against him. The bust dropped soundlessly on a padded settee. The man's ironclad grip sent alarm bells ringing in her head. He was so quick, so steady. She jerked uselessly for a few seconds but was unable to free herself. He was too strong.

If she were caught, all was lost. She couldn't be caught, wouldn't be caught. A dark cell and malicious smiles swirled in her mind. Panic gave her strength.

She was off-balance and made a final effort to swipe his legs. It worked. The poorly executed maneuver sent the man to the floor, but he never loosened his grip, and she landed on top of him.

The thud echoed through the house. The stirrings began. Audrey tried to break free, but the man's grip was firm; he wouldn't release her.

A door opened downstairs. Footsteps sounded in the foyer.

Audrey squirmed and tried to kick her captor. His legs coiled around hers, locking her in place. No mere toady, but a seasoned professional. Her panic neared hysteria. She was headed straight to jail, or worse, straight to the hangman's noose.

Footsteps sounded on the bottom of the stairs.

She tried to free one of the knives at her waist. His hold tightened. Confusion joined the panicked emotions flitting through her brain. The man wasn't trying to hurt her; he was restraining her. Toying with her. If she didn't know better, she'd say he was testing her.

She pulled her head back to slam into his nose, but he anticipated the move and rolled them over, pinning her beneath him. The action rolled them into the patch of moonlight streaming through the window. Audrey got a first look at her captor and froze.

Eyes that would be bright green in the daytime speared her with their darkness. She caught a brief whiff of pine as the footsteps continued their ascent.

She would have known his identity earlier had her mind not gone into a panic like a green girl on her first job. Trapped. Everything she had worked for, gone. Her sister would be lost, and there would be no redemption for Audrey.

Footsteps crested the top step, and she couldn't stop a panicked breath.

His expression changed, although her panicked mind and the darkness wouldn't allow her to read his face. The footsteps paused at the door, and the telltale sound of the knob turning caused her breath to lodge. The door rattled as the person on the other side tried to open it.

Someone had locked the door. Stephen? The person on the other side of the door retreated. Back down the steps, back across the foyer. Back to find the key.

Stephen continued to stare at her, his warm body pressed into hers. One thigh lodged between her legs.

"What—" She licked her suddenly dry lips. "What are you going to do?"

He didn't move, keeping her trapped beneath him, his lips mere inches from hers. His breath caressed her cheek. "I suppose I should take you to the magistrate."

She refused to let the tears fall. "I suppose so."

He swore and rolled off her. Reaching for the tinderbox on the desk, he lit a lamp. Audrey pushed herself into a sitting position and glanced at the open window. She might be able to make it.

"You won't make it," he said as he leaned against the desk and crossed his ankles.

She crossed her legs, mimicking his relaxed posture. A slight smile appeared before he shook his head, and his face was unreadable once more.

"Who ordered you to steal the documents?"

"No one."

"It's not too late to make that visit to the magistrate."

"No, it's not."

He studied her and moved closer. "Aren't you afraid of being sent to prison?"

"I'm terrified of being sent to prison," she said quietly.

He arched a brow and stalked a circle around her. "You look quite calm at the possibility."

She was quaking inside, but years of surviving on the streets had been an effective teacher for masking emotions and expressions. Sometimes it made the difference between life and death. Such was the case at the moment.

"Would you rather have tears, Your Grace?"

"No, but knowing you are sincere might not make me regret my choice to let you go."

Her heart thumped in her chest. "You are letting me go?"

"No."

Audrey kept control of her tears and pretended to examine her hands. She had to stop thinking there was hope.

"Then what is your intention?"

"We'll discuss that later. I will call for you tomorrow afternoon for a drive in the park."

Her head snapped up. "What?"

"A drive, in the park. Don't try to run, don't try to hide. I will find you." His tone turned hard.

Surely he had gone mad? "You trust me to wait for you in my house?"

He looked irritated, but whether it was with her or with himself, she didn't know. "Yes. I don't think you can run, or you would have done so already."

Cold seeped into her bones. She had never been this far behind an adversary in plotting. Then again, her fate had never felt so much out of her hands before.

She stared at him mutely. Footsteps echoed below once more.

Stephen crossed his arms. "You have thirty seconds to decide."

The footsteps ascended the stairs again. This time there would be no stopping the person from entering the room.

"I will meet you for a drive in the park tomorrow," she said hurriedly.

He held her gaze, and her breath lodged in her chest. The footsteps hit the top step.

"Good. See you then."

Audrey didn't wait for more. She leaped to her feet, raced across the floor, and dove through the open window. She landed roughly in the bushes and barely registered the raised voices from above before she sprinted down the street and allowed her tears to fall.

Chapter 5

"Mr. Maddox. How nice to see you."

Stephen Chalmers entered the small town house promptly, not a minute later than the time his morning note had indicated. His smooth voice wound up the stairs and through Audrey's insides.

She waited at the top of the landing, out of sight of Chalmers, but with a good view of Maddox. Maddox shuffled his feet and exchanged pleasantries. Best not to leave him alone with Chalmers for too long. At best he would make a fool of himself, at worst his loose tongue would get them a one-way trip to the hangman.

Audrey grimaced and ran back to her room. Having to share information with that poor excuse for a man went against every natural instinct and acquired skill she possessed.

She grabbed the ridiculous-looking reticule sitting on the dresser. The woman Travers had hired to clothe her had proclaimed the gaudy accessory the height of fashion. The height of stupidity, more like.

Audrey hurried back to the landing, not wanting to consider why she had taken so long with her toilette, and was now carrying the absurd bag. Dressing well for the execution or the executioner?

"Audrey isn't feeling all that well today. I'm not sure she's up for receiving visitors much less a drive in the park." Her stepfather was doing his own thinking again, which was not a good sign. A nasty crimson brightened his already ruddy cheeks.

"Nonsense," she announced brightly, descending the stairs. "It's a lovely warm day, and the fresh air will do me wonders." She held out her hand and curtsied. "Your Grace."

Stephen flashed a wicked smile and took her hand to his lips. "It would be any woman's fondest wish to look as beautiful as you do now. Like a perfect spring bloom."

The only thing blooming was the warmth spreading through her body. Unwanted heat stole into her cheeks. So he had dropped the hard, cold demeanor of the previous night and was back to playing the charmer? She could deal with that. "Shall we be off?"

Chalmers grinned, and Maddox looked overset. What else had the two men been talking about? At the moment, she needed to hurry Chalmers out before Maddox did anything stupid.

She again cursed Travers for saddling her with Maddox. He had claimed it was to maintain appearances. Appearances? She could have played her part without her incompetent stepfather in the mix. No, Travers had done it to keep Maddox in line. And also because Travers knew she loathed Maddox almost more than she loathed him.

Stephen said a cheerful farewell, and they left Maddox, ruddy and sour-looking, on the front step. Audrey passed her reticule from one hand to the other, trying not to think about where the looming carriage would take her. She trusted this incarnation of Stephen Chalmers less than the determined law enforcer she had met the previous night.

Stephen helped her into the curricle and directed the horses into the lane. "I thought we'd ride through the park and talk. Is that acceptable to you?"

"Yes." Anywhere but prison was acceptable. She examined the passing scenery and tried to edge closer to the side of the carriage seat. The seat was not nearly large enough to escape contact. She could feel the heat of his body as if it were a magnet.

He chatted about innocuous events and shared amusing stories that had her smiling unwillingly. She had no choice but to accompany him; if she encouraged him, perhaps he would let his intentions slip.

The park was nearly empty. A few artists sketched, and several nannies pushed strollers. Stephen threw the reins to his tiger and assisted Audrey from the carriage. The servant took the ribbons, and the vehicle rumbled down the street.

"I thought we might walk through the garden, then to the lake."

Knowing that Stephen was obsessed with plants and botany, she replied, "Well, if you had skipped the gardens and gone straight for the lake, I might have become suspicious. As it is, now I am left thinking that the only reason you *invited* me along was to have an excuse to explore the gardens."

He smiled. "You are a good excuse. The best I've had in a long time."

"You haven't had me yet, Your Grace."

"In one respect I *had* you last night, Miss

Kendrick." He leaned toward her, and his breath tickled her ear. "In another respect I look forward to the pleasure of having you."

"Don't bet on it."

"There are few bets I lose."

She muttered under her breath, unwilling to be goaded into a further response.

They entered the gardens and were met with a profusion of colorful flowers and intriguing fragrances. The plants were artfully arranged and presented, care being given to the placement of each color and variety.

Determined to play her part, Audrey pointed to one of the leafy plants near the entrance. "What is that plant called, Your Grace?"

"That is an Adder's Tongue."

"You are fond of those."

Stephen smiled. "Been poking through my town house recently, Audrey? That explains the disappearance of my favorite shirt and trousers."

Audrey's face reddened. She had almost stolen a pair of trousers from his London house last year. It would serve him right for her to mention why.

"I don't know what I'd do with your clothes, but I'd have Grimmond count your silver if I were you."

A look of surprise crossed his features. "I suppose it shouldn't shock me that you know my butler's name. But if you knew him at all, you would know he counts the pieces each week. The man has an unnatural obsession with my property and propriety."

"He does seem rather rigid, but isn't that the way with all butlers?"

"Grimmond aspires to rigidity. Luckily, he has me to add a little color. Or disorder and mayhem as he calls it."

A beautiful pink bush decorated one side of the path, and Audrey rubbed the petals between her fingers, letting the blossom fall from the tips. Stephen watched her touch the petals and shifted.

"That is a rhododendron."

"It's beautiful."

"Yes. But then everything in this garden is."

He was watching her. Audrey's breath caught in short bursts under that look. After their encounter last year he had been a constant presence in her thoughts. To have those bright green eyes suddenly focused on her was unnerving. That he couldn't remember their encounter was little consolation to her overly active imagination. He turned his head, releasing her from his hypnotic stare.

"That blue explosion over there is bugleweed. And these colorful vines are clematis. This is one of my favorite times of year."

He launched into a discourse on the different types of plants and flowering shrubs around them. She noticed he had an affinity for the more prickly varieties. The lecture should have allowed her to recover, but the passion he found in the subject and study of all things green enveloped her. To have a tenth of that passion directed toward her . . .

She stopped her wayward thoughts and gave herself a mental shake. *Bad Audrey.* She couldn't allow herself to forget who he really was and ignore the actual situation. Stephen paused and looked at her. She gave him a half-hearted smile and promptly stumbled over a hedge.

Stephen caught her, pulling her back onto the path and into his arms. Without thought she wrapped her arms around his waist to steady herself. Their bodies tensed at the contact, and his arms tightened briefly before he took her hand in his and tugged her along.

She almost stumbled again. Pull her hand away? Let him keep it?

Her thoughts were flying in all directions as she tried to make sense of the moment. Meanwhile, Stephen was totally in control and whistling as they continued down the garden path.

"What are you doing?"

He looked at her in amusement. "Walking with

you to the lake. We have reached the end of the gardens. Did you want to circle back through?"

"No, no, continuing on to the lake is fine." Dammit, he had known that wasn't what she meant. Why did stupid things always come out of her mouth around him? It never happened to her around anyone else. This malady occurred only around Chalmers.

Chalmers would undoubtedly start some inane banter to swindle her of her secrets, or worse, start up his passionate plant dissertation and seduce the words from her. Better to take matters into her own hands. The direct approach might work to her advantage and keep her from trouble.

"What do you want from me, Your Grace?"

"Call me Stephen," he said, with an amused smile.

She cocked an eyebrow. "Why did you invite me on this *outing*, Your Grace?"

"Isn't that what men are supposed to do? Ask a beautiful young lady to the park?" Stephen plucked a yellow wildflower from the side of the path and offered it to her. "Bring her flowers?"

Audrey accepted the bloom in her free hand and twirled it in her fingers. Smooth, handsome, charming and all too sure of himself. "We both know you aren't courting me."

"We do?"

He sounded so surprised that she dropped her carefully cultivated mask and gave him a pointed look. His lips curved into a devastatingly languid smile, and he took the flower from her grasp and tucked it behind her right ear. His fingers scalded the tip and lingered as he smoothed the wayward tendrils that had escaped from her loathsome bonnet.

His expression became intense. He traced his fingers under her ear, down her cheek, and sensuously along her jaw. He tipped her chin up and started to lean forward, and, God help her, she felt his pull and leaned into him too.

Crash.

A rabbit came skittering into the path, a skinny fox hot on its heels. Both animals screeched to a halt and appeared startled to see humans. They abruptly turned and scampered in opposite directions. The rabbit was safe this time.

Audrey looked at Stephen. His body had gone alert at the first sound. She was reminded of the previous night, her body trapped beneath his. He had looked like he might kiss her then.

And he had nearly kissed her again. Why?

She had been half-joking with the thought of

him seducing her for information. But it didn't seem so far-fetched now.

She pulled away and clasped her hands together. He was a peer of the realm. Handsome, wealthy, and intelligent. He could have any woman in London, and he knew it. And she knew better than to fall for it.

He smiled, but on further inspection, she saw the tension in his eyes. The duke wasn't as carefree as he appeared.

"Shall we continue on to the lake?" His voice was light, and had she not glimpsed the tension, she would never guess him affected at all.

She nodded, not trusting herself to speak. He held out a hand, and she placed hers lightly in his. Self-preservation had allowed her to survive to the ripe age of twenty-two with only one unfortunate stint in prison, and even that hadn't been due to capture. Even if she was unlucky with cards, she knew when to hold them.

She had to rid her mind of thoughts of last year and Chalmers's vulnerability. The thoughts that made her mind try to disregard the hard and dangerous man that he really was. Laying herself mentally and emotionally bare to any man, especially Chalmers, would be sheer folly. She could try to recover her faith in humanity after she and Faye stepped onto a distant shore.

Thankfully Chalmers kept silent. They walked into the clearing, the lake sparkling in the summer sun. Audrey lifted her face to the sky and allowed the rays to warm and calm her. A fence enclosed one end of the lake, and they walked to it in silent agreement.

Leaning against the fence, Audrey turned to Stephen. "So Chalmers, what's it going to be?" She deliberately used his last name instead of his title.

He lifted a brow. "Whatever do you mean, Audrey?"

She tugged her bonnet. She could still feel the path of his fingers running beneath it and down her face. "We both know what's happening. Why pretend ignorance?"

"I confess I haven't the faintest idea what is happening."

She picked up a rock and tossed it into the lake. It took one bounce and sank into the blue depths. "I'm sure the game was invented by you. You are toying with me. Don't."

He bent down, picked up a stone, and dropped it into her hand. It was the perfect skipping stone. How irritating.

His easy smile returned. "No toying? That removes half the fun of a game. I suppose the next thing you'll want is for us not to play at all. And that would truly disappoint me." His eyes were hot and lazy.

A hot swirl rushed through her, and she looked away. She sent the flat stone skittering across the water. One, two, three, four bounces. Satisfied, she looked for another, avoiding his gaze. He held one out for her inspection.

Another perfectly shaped stone. Lord, he was irksome. She grabbed it and sent it flying. Five bounces. She wiped her hands on her skirt before thinking better of it. Oh, what the hell. One game she didn't have to play with Chalmers was the society game. The man knew who and what she was.

She jumped onto the railing and swung her legs. "So? Why did you bring me here?"

He leaned against the fence, only inches to her left. "To enjoy the beautiful weather with a beautiful woman?"

"Is that always your excuse?"

"Only when it's warm."

She continued to swing her legs. He continued to stare at her in silence. His eyes were like the bright emerald stones she had "liberated" on her first job, unnaturally green and disturbing. She tipped her head back and closed her eyes. Better to avoid looking into those fathomless depths.

The sun felt wonderful against her upturned face. If he wasn't going to arrest her, she might as well enjoy the day. Maybe she could avoid looking into his eyes for the rest of their visit.

"Why do you think I brought you here?"

She kept her eyes closed. "To get me to confess to some horrible crime and throw me into Newgate?"

"Have you committed any horrible crimes lately?"

"No, just boring, tedious ones."

"That doesn't sound like much fun. Perhaps you should retire and try something else."

His arm brushed her leg, and she nearly lost the thread of the conversation. "I hear pirating is quite exhilarating. I'm not sure about the food, however."

"A few weevils never hurt anyone."

She had to restrain a smile. She risked another glance. He looked solemn, but his eyes were twinkling. She sighed. It would be much easier to have him trying to drag her to Newgate. She didn't want to joke with this man.

"Chalmers, what do you want?"

"To discover what you're plotting."

She fought to control her emotions. "Why? Can't we continue to play that lovely evasive game where you send some inept man to chase me?"

"Hmm . . . I think my men would take offense at that statement." He strode a few feet away and picked up a stone. "Besides, you know they will eventually catch you."

She snorted. He tossed the stone. Six bounces. Damn.

"And then where will you be, Miss Kendrick?" He drawled her last name. "I'm not sure any of my men would be willing to turn the other cheek and escort you to the park."

"Which doesn't explain why you have. As to your men catching me, we'll wait to see if it happens."

"*When* it happens."

"We'll see." She tried to sound nonchalant, but she was tense. He had already caught her. Why he hadn't sent her to prison was the question.

The whole scheme was too high-profile, too risky. She sent a silent curse in Travers's direction and uncurled her fingers from the railing.

She masked her inner turmoil with a deceptive calmness. "Shall we go, Chalmers? This has all been terribly exciting, but if you aren't going to arrest me, I must get back to my stepfather."

He walked back to her and circled her waist. A war of emotions flicked in his eyes as he paused before lifting her down from the fence.

They walked in silence. She wondered what he was thinking. Her own thoughts were muddled as she tried to assimilate the newly dropped barriers.

The bright bluebells swayed gently in the warm breeze, winking at her as she walked by. She had just initiated a challenge to the cat.

As they exited the park, Stephen's servant brought the curricle around. Stephen assisted her into the vehicle, and she resumed the role of being a lady. It was almost as if the last few minutes were but a dream.

"Have you seen the *Bachelor's Torments?*"

Audrey saw his grimace. "Are you tormented, Your Grace?"

He smiled reluctantly. "Bedeviled. But I meant the play."

"I haven't been to the theater in a long time."

"Good. We'll attend this evening."

She turned to him. "Pardon me?"

"It has had a successful run for the last few weeks."

"And?"

"And you are going to accompany me, simpleton."

"Simpleton? Who is the simpleton here? I never said I'd go to the theater with you."

"No, but your stepfather did."

So that's what they had been discussing. That explained the wild look in Maddox's eyes.

Stephen was waiting for her response. She could refuse. She didn't have to go to the theater with him. It would be stupid of her to accept, actually. But that internal voice, the one that had found her stroking his face while he was unconscious, the one that had caused her to lean into him in the gardens, urged her on.

"Very well."

Stephen clinked his glass on the library table. He had let her go. Again. He had let her go simply because of the look in her eyes. The look in her soul.

He should have brought her in for questioning, the type of questioning that usually made criminals stumble over themselves to provide answers to anything and everything. It was a normal part of the justice system and necessary for maintaining law and order.

He could have learned the identity of the man behind the rumors. Could have learned the entire plot and ended it in one fell swoop.

He stared broodingly into the brandy snifter, then lifted and swallowed a good portion of the expensive amber liquid. He hadn't been able to take her in for questioning. The look in her eyes hadn't let him. It wasn't just normal fear that he had glimpsed there, but a deep, keening cry of the soul.

What or who had put it there?

He grimaced and slammed the glass back on the table. That nagging question refused to be stilled. He had been mulling it over and over in his mind since last night. He shouldn't care about her, dammit. She was a criminal, and that should be enough.

And by all that was holy, he was romancing her. Oh, it had seemed like a good idea this morning. If some previously unknown weakness for women thieves had permeated his conscience, then why not use his second-best skill to wheedle the information?

His plan had started so well. She had been befuddled by his attitude. When he had eased in a bit more, she had willingly followed, returning his quips and matching the conversation. Everything had seemed so easy. And then it had all gone awry.

What had caused everything to go bloody wrong, he had no idea. One moment he was the seducer, the next he was drowning in her soft blue eyes. Icy, dammit, her eyes were ice-cold. How had they turned that soft blue?

Stephen tossed down the rest of the brandy. And now they were attending the theater. He had asked her to the theater. He just couldn't afford to be distracted by romantic notions. It was just one more opportunity for a knife thrust in his gut, wielded by a beautiful woman with soft blue eyes turned to ice.

Why had she promised to accompany him to the theater? Not that she had much choice, but it was just one more opportunity to be sent on a one-way trip to prison by a handsome man with deep green eyes.

Her scalp on fire, Audrey slapped the hand of her maid away. "Sarah, that's enough. Fetch my dress."

Sarah frowned. "You should add some curl to your hair, miss."

"Is that what your yanking is supposed to accomplish? It will never curl properly. How many times will you try to force it?"

Sarah sniffed and quickly coiled Audrey's uncooperative hair into a semblance of style, pinning it to her head. She grabbed the pale blue gown and forced Audrey into it. It was time to sit her maid down, maybe with her arm pinned behind her back, and have a little talk. The girl had been hired by Travers a week past, and her insolent attitude was wearing thin.

Only the manners she learned from the tutor Flanagan had hired stopped her from teaching the girl a lesson now. "Sarah, go down and inform Mr. Maddox that I will be with him presently."

As soon as Sarah's footsteps retreated, Audrey removed a floorboard, withdrew her specially made garters, and slipped them in place. She flipped one of her knives, testing its balance, and slipped it in the leather-and-lace sheath on her right leg. The hall clock chimed. She quickly encased the others while cursing the short sleeves of the dress. She grabbed her favorite hairpin and slipped it into the coil on the back of her head.

She checked her reflection in the cheval glass. She was ready.

Audrey stepped heavily on every loose riser on the way down the steps, causing irritating creaks. The noise annoyed Maddox to no end.

"Girl, get in here."

Someday. Someday one of her knives was going to slip from her hand.

She entered the study. "Is something wrong, Maddox?"

"Go back and change. I'll make your excuses. Travers won't like it. He won't like you going out at all." Maddox was standing behind the desk holding a letter opener. A note lay open on the desk.

She shrugged and moved forward. "Is that all you have a care for—what Travers likes?"

He glared at her and pulled the flat side of the letter opener across his palm. "Remember your task."

"I know my task." She picked up the split missive. "Travers will cope. At this juncture, he doesn't have much choice in the matter."

"No, I ain't gonna allow it. Being with the duke is too risky." Some of the accent he had worked so hard to extinguish came through. Very upset then. Audrey nearly shook her head in exasperation.

"You ain't goin' with Chalmers."

She gave him a steely gaze and leaned forward. "Don't think you can suddenly act like a real father, Maddox. It doesn't work that way. Besides, you're the one who instigated this farce."

He assumed the pouty look that used to work so well on her mother and whined. "Now Audrey, you know what needs to be done. Stop trying to befriend the duke."

"I am not trying to befriend the damn duke. How many times do I have to repeat that statement? What part of it do you not understand?"

His eyes narrowed. "Don't sass me, girl. I'm still stronger and larger. It's not too late to take a strip off you." He unconsciously fingered his right forearm. The scar was a lasting reminder of the final time he had ever tried to whip her. Her thirteenth birthday, the day she had taken control of her life.

Well, to a certain extent. She wasn't exactly living a free-and-clear existence at the moment.

There was a knock at the front door.

She lifted the message from Travers and tossed it in the fire grate. In his stupor, Maddox would have probably left it lying around for one and all to read.

"You're not going. I'll tell him so right now."

Audrey didn't respond; she waited several minutes, then followed him into the hall.

Chalmers was leaning nonchalantly against the door, but he straightened and smiled when she entered. Maddox looked desolate. In contrast to Chalmers's healthy, lightly tanned complexion and devastating smile, Maddox was sullen, his face blotchy and red.

"Good evening, Your Grace," she said.

Chalmers stepped forward and took her hand. "Miss Kendrick, how lovely to see you."

Maddox halted Audrey's progress by grabbing her arm. "Your Grace, I cannot allow Audrey to travel without a chaperone, and I'm afraid I'm too ill to attend."

"Not a problem, Maddox. The Marchioness of Angelford is accompanying us. She is waiting in the carriage."

An unholy spark lit Maddox's eyes, but Chalmers brushed further conversation aside as he smoothly freed Audrey from Maddox's grasp and tucked her hand into the crook of his arm. "Good evening, Maddox. I hope your health improves."

Although the mention of their female companion produced a mixed reaction in her, Audrey smiled at Maddox's suppressed rage at being outwitted. They stepped out the door, down the walk, and to the carriage.

The carriage that held Lady Angelford.

Audrey held no love for the ton, but did Chalmers truly find it amusing to parade his mistress around town? Wasn't the rule that you produced an heir and a spare before taking lovers? The Angelfords had barely been wed a year, and she was already traipsing around with someone other than her husband?

With Chalmers's good looks and charm, he

probably had a trail of women scattered throughout England. One in every shire. Each waiting with open arms for him to return. Audrey felt the irrational anger surge through her. He could take his seductions and play false with someone else. She had no intention of aiding him in his illicit liaison with his best friend's wife!

"I feel a megrim coming on, Your Grace. Perhaps your driver could drop you and the marchioness off at the theater, then return with me?"

"No." The blasé way he uttered it set her teeth on edge.

"In that case, I refuse to enter the carriage."

"Why?"

"Listen here, Chalmers, I'm not going to act as a screen for you and your tart."

He gave a short burst of laughter before hiding it behind a cough. "I'm sure James would be quite displeased to hear his wife referred to as my tart."

He opened the carriage door, and she peered inside. The interior was empty.

"I thought you said—"

"I lied. Shall we go?" There was a trace of laughter in his voice. Once again she was surprised by this unpredictable man.

She narrowed her eyes but was secretly relieved. Relieved she didn't have to face the charming woman from whom she had stolen. Relieved that she wouldn't have to be an accomplice in an illicit relationship.

Her relief was short-lived. If Chalmers hadn't invited her as a screen, why had he invited her? Her pent-up nerves and righteous indignation changed into awareness and anticipation.

Stephen was awaiting her answer. She nodded, and he handed her up and inside. Settling himself across from her, she was struck by how different he looked from a year ago when they had been together in a closed carriage. Alive and healthy now, versus pale, unconscious, and near death.

Stephen smiled. "Guess it is just you and me."

Her skin tingled. She was alone with him in a dark and luxurious ducal carriage. Alone. And this time he was alert and dangerous.

"And by the way, Calliope has never been my mistress."

Audrey was taken aback by the comment. "Maybe not now, but she lived in your house. I saw her with you, even disguised as she was."

"You saw me with Calliope? You were watching me? How delightful." He winked and she almost kicked him. "In any case, it was an act."

"Why would someone act as a courtesan?"

He shook his head and smiled. "You'll have to ask

her. She may choose to tell you. I think she likes you."

"Uh, right." She was just glad that Calliope wasn't his mistress now.

Why did she care? That way led to a bad train of thought. In fact, best to not think of—

Chalmers switched sides so that he was seated next to her.

"What are you doing?" She screeched.

"I hate riding backward, don't you?"

"No. Here, let me ride on the other side."

He rested his legs up on the other seat and crossed his ankles. "No room."

He gave her a lazy grin and tilted his head slightly toward her.

A tingle of awareness coursed through her when he looked at her like that. It was as if she was the only woman in the world, and it was hard to think of much else. The faint moonlight highlighted his blond hair and wicked features. Why had he really sought her out? It wasn't to pay court. That thought was as much a farce as the one they were about to see on the stage.

In her experience all men were duplicitous; Stephen Chalmers was just craftier at hiding it.

He touched her hand. "Your skin is cold." He took her hands between his large warm ones, rubbing the tops with his thumbs.

Craftier at hiding behind ingratiating smiles and tingling caresses. And what tingling caresses they were. His hands lingered too long on her body, fingers stroking the underside of her arm and skimming her sensitive wrists. His thighs kept contact with hers.

It was both a relief and a disappointment when the carriage slowed to a stop.

Stephen made no move to rise. Their eyes met, and unexpected warmth surged through her. "Why did you agree to come to the theater tonight?"

"Pure folly."

He laughed deeply, and the carriage door opened. He exited and raised his arm to help her down. "Good. The title of the afterpiece has folly in it. Must be strange good fortune. Perhaps tomorrow night we might attend Covent Garden and see what title to label the evening."

She took his hand and stepped onto the street. "I'm not sure that is such a good idea, Chalmers."

His hand squeezed hers and tugged her forward. "Nor am I."

She tucked her hand into his arm as they made their way toward the theater entrance.

"No, I retract that statement. I think it is an excellent idea."

She snorted. "Of course you would."

"Where is your sense of adventure, Audrey?"

She turned to him, a biting reply forming, when she saw the glint of metal. Audrey shoved Stephen forward, following him to the pavement and landing roughly on top of him. A shot echoed through the night, and the crowd began screaming.

Chapter 6

Pandemonium erupted. Ladies screamed and ran for shelter. Two carriages careened, knocking over a flower stall. The horses reared, spooked by the noise. In one fluid motion Stephen rolled them out of harm's way and tugged Audrey to her feet.

"Come."

There was general chaos as people scattered in all directions, but Audrey saw the burly figures steadily working their way toward them. Stephen must have seen them too because he pushed her to the side of the building, blocking and protecting her.

Stephen already had a pistol in hand and was peering around the side of the building. People continued running down the street. Screams echoed from scared patrons and street dwellers alike. Another shot rang out and wood splintered above them as Stephen wrenched his head back.

A determined look on his face, he grabbed her hand and sprinted toward the nearest side street. She kept pace with him but cursed her soft slippers all the same.

There was no need for him to keep holding her hand, but she didn't fight it, allowing him to keep the physical contact. His warm hand felt good. She hiked her skirt with her free hand as she ran, pinned the dress layers with her arm, and reached under to grab the nearest knife. Stephen looked back and grinned.

He pulled her into a darkened doorway halfway down one street and tried the knob. It was locked. He fiddled with the latch for a few seconds before it clicked open. Not bad. The man would make a decent thief. He pulled her inside and locked the door.

Her immediate panic in the darkened room was stilled by logic. The room was small but not overly cramped, and there was a small window overlooking the street. Stephen drew back the shade slightly. She peered over his shoulder, watching a familiar face creep past the window. What the hell was he doing here? And had he seen her in the street?

"You know who they are." It was a statement, not a question.

She hesitated only a second before whispering, "Some of them."

He leaned against the wall of the small room. "Which one of us are they after?"

"Isn't everyone after you?"

"Only your cronies. All my people are chasing you."

She shrugged although her body was tense. "I'm not the one with people shooting at me."

"No, but it could be arranged."

"I'll keep that in mind, Your Graciousness."

The sound of the knob being jerked caused Stephen to pull back against the wall and aim the pistol toward the door.

"Ye see anything?" a deep voice yelled down the alley.

"Nah, damn blighters got away," said the voice on the other side of the door.

"Who was the girl?"

"Some fancy tart. Let's go. Damn cold tonight, and I'm not freezing me stones off looking in the dark. We'll finish this another night."

Audrey smirked. Fancy tart, was she? Good to know her identity wasn't totally exposed.

Footsteps echoed down the alley and back to the

main streets. Stephen and Audrey maintained their silence for a few minutes in case the men returned.

Stephen leaned a shoulder against the door. "Fancy tart? So you're not working with them?"

She shrugged. "If I wanted to kill you, you'd already be dead." Not that she had ever killed anyone, but he didn't need to know that detail.

He smiled. "You're no longer working for Flanagan?"

"What do you know about Flanagan?" Her voice had more bite to it than she had intended, but he looked amused.

"He's a crook. Names his people after mythological characters. Runs a crime syndicate throughout England but keeps his people close at hand. And he is not as hard as he would have people believe."

"If you only knew," she muttered. But he had it right.

"You no longer work for him, do you? Your trail was cold for a year. Why return?"

She raised her chin, but didn't reply.

"If you no longer work for Flanagan, for whom do you work?"

"No one."

"Did you miss the adventure? Run out of money?" She didn't answer.

"No," he continued, "this entire escapade is not

your style. You wouldn't be so easy to catch."

She narrowed her eyes and stood motionless, but he moved to stand in front of her and she tilted her head back to look into his shadow-lined face. He spoke softly and ran a hand down her cheek. "Why are you taking these risks, Audrey?"

His warm voice seeped into her soul, and she found herself answering, "I have to pay the price."

"What type of price?" He stroked her cheek again.

Her voice cracked. "Not that kind."

"What then, money? What do you need?" He moved closer and continued to stroke her cheek.

"Not your money." She moved away, angry with herself for allowing him to befuddle her.

"I didn't offer my money."

She chose not to respond and straightened her skirt.

"Come, Audrey, let me help you." She blocked his seductive, silvery voice from her heart. She had heard that tempting song before, from others.

"The alley is empty. We should go, Your Grace."

She tried to pass him, but his arm shot out pinning her to the wall. Solid warmth trying to heat her perpetually cold skin.

"I could make you tell me," he murmured into her hair, his warm breath tickling her neck.

She was saved from testing his theory when he

released her and peered through the window. Satisfied the alley was empty, he held the door open. She slipped through and hastened back in the direction of the theater. She stiffened as a tall man stepped into the end of the alleyway. She reached for a knife, then recognized the handsome, brooding features and well-tailored clothes.

"Roth, how did you find us?" Stephen asked.

"I followed the mess."

Stephen smiled.

Roth spared her a glance that spoke measures. He was here to protect Stephen. In those cold eyes she had seen herself reflected and condemned.

Must be trying to have so many people concerned about your welfare.

Or comforting.

No, trying definitely. She didn't want or need anyone looking after her.

Roth led them to Stephen's carriage, and they entered without incident.

Roth sat opposite them staring out the window. Stephen tucked a blanket around her legs. She was tempted to throw it off, but its welcome warmth enveloped her. She left it on.

It was a silent trip back to her house. She avoided looking at the brooding golden-eyed man who had joined them.

The carriage door opened, and she accepted Stephen's assistance to the front door. He leaned down, and her breath caught. He stroked her cheek, sending fire into her belly. He exhaled, murmured something that sounded like "I must be mad," and then he kissed her. A light kiss, almost a teasing caress.

He pulled his head back and stroked her cheek again. "When you are ready to let me help, you know where to find me. Good night, Audrey."

The footman opened the door, then Stephen was gone.

She stepped into the house feeling more on edge than when they'd been shot at an hour earlier.

Stephen leaned into the squabs as the carriage rolled rhythmically down the street. His fingers still carried the feel of her cheek. Soft and smooth.

Something told him that she wouldn't have stopped him from deepening or lengthening the kiss. That piece of insight would make the next encounter all the more interesting.

"You're asking for a knife in your ribs." Roth watched him from across the carriage.

Stephen smiled. "Perhaps."

"You have responsibilities now, Stephen. It's not just about you anymore."

Stephen's smile faded. "Don't think I've forgotten it. Bloody title. I would have wrung my cousins' necks myself if I had known they'd leave me to this. At least I would have some pleasure out of the whole affair."

Roth raised both brows. "Most people envy your turn of fate."

"Fools."

Roth snorted. "When the Duke of Marston finishes feeling sorry for himself, let me know. Meanwhile, I'm thirsty."

Stephen glared and tapped on the trap, instructing the driver to head to White's.

As soon as they were seated at the club Roth said, "We need to talk about Audrey Kendrick. You're the one who discovered she was Hermes and that the wild thief Icarus was her sister. And now you are toying with her, or God forbid, courting her? Did your brain get left behind in the Thames?"

"No, Roth, my brain is functioning very well. I know this girl. I've studied her for weeks in order to prove my suspicions."

"And?"

"And she's hard as stone, but not rash. She's the planner, the plotter, the mastermind. Not the fiery brash one. The other one would probably take my head first, ask questions later. This one? She's methodical. She figures the angles before making her moves."

"*Then* she'll take your head. Sounds like a mere difference in timing."

Stephen chuckled. "Roth, you worry too much."

"And you, my friend, don't worry enough. You're too cavalier about the consequences"

"What better way to find out more about why she is here than to insinuate myself into her affairs?"

"What better way to end up in the Thames than to insinuate yourself into her affairs? Listen, she looked lovely both tonight and at the Taylors', and she has acted the perfect part of a lady." Roth leaned forward. "*Acted*. She's a hardened criminal. Possibly a killer."

Stephen swirled his brandy, watching the liquid coat the glass. "We don't know that. All we know is that she was one of Flanagan's Olympians. The only crimes attributed to Hermes are thefts."

"Very large thefts."

"Well, there you have it. Very large thefts is all."

Roth stared into his wineglass. "Ever since you determined the identity of Hermes you haven't behaved like yourself. The bloodlust is gone. Some other kind of lust in its place."

Stephen grinned. "She is rather beautiful for a thief who a month ago I had pegged as pock-marked, bucktoothed, and male."

"Beauty only makes her more dangerous. She's a thief. No different than any of the others. No different than the street thugs twenty years ago."

Stephen gripped his glass but said nothing.

Roth sighed. "I know I don't want to hear this, but what is your plan?"

"It's loose. She has a plan for me though."

"Lovely." Roth shook his dark head.

Stephen had caught a fleeting glimpse of something in her eyes before she had been able to mask it. Audrey hadn't looked scared when the men had passed by their hiding place. She had looked irritated.

"She saved my life."

Roth narrowed his eyes. "Tonight?"

He nodded. "Pushed me out of the way of the initial round of gunfire."

"Interesting. I wonder why? Better for her to let you die."

"That's the rub, isn't it? Why'd she save me when she would only gain by having me out of the way?"

Roth leaned back. "Hmmm. And you don't think it was a ploy to earn your trust?"

"Could be, but I doubt it. The action was too

spontaneous. But as I said, she definitely has a plan." For good or ill, it suited him just fine. Better to be good, but he couldn't count on her. Not yet, perhaps not ever.

He ran a manicured finger along the rim of the glass. He wanted to trust her. Needed to trust her. And that was odd. There were few people he trusted in life. And here he was, defying logic, rebelling against his own mind, wanting to trust an admitted thief. A criminal. But logic be damned. There was just something about her that was familiar. That made him feel he had nothing to fear from her. There was an indefinable feeling of rightness when she was by his side.

"I know I'm playing the part of the mother hen, but for God's sake be careful," Roth said.

Stephen finished his drink. "We've been hunting Audrey Kendrick for years, albeit believing her to be a man named Hermes. Who would have thought the fleet-footed thief would be a woman?" He set the glass on the table. "Crafty, deceptive, a trickster. We make a good match. The game must be played."

"This isn't a game, Stephen."

"Sure it is. Always has been."

"Games tend to end badly in our business."

"So they do. But life would be quite dull if everything went according to plan."

"According to someone else's plan, maybe. But you have always wanted things your way. All of us do. Just remember that Audrey Kendrick seems to be cut from the same cloth."

"I will. In the meantime, I need you to track down her sister. I don't have much information on her whereabouts—she disappeared around the same time as Audrey. Whereas Audrey reappeared a few weeks ago, no one fitting her sister's description seems to be active in the London underground. Since they work together, it is odd. Something worth checking into."

Roth nodded. "I will ask around tonight. Did you recognize any of the shooters tonight?"

"Yes. Leonard Peters, as amazing as that is. Seems to have shown up to finish the job he started last year."

"Interesting. Learn anything?"

"Audrey knows him."

"That makes sense; they both worked for Flanagan at one time. I'll ask around about dear old Leonard tonight as well. With his ornery disposition and degenerate reputation, he shouldn't be too hard to track down."

They set a meeting time for the next day, and Stephen strode back to his carriage. Roth was right. Stephen knew that even for his own nature he was behaving recklessly. He had never felt so invested in any of the others he had hunted, be they men or women. Why Audrey?

He dismissed her beauty. He had been around too many beautiful women to have the outer surface affect him. No, it was the layers beneath that were interesting. And he had just begun to peel them away. He had just skimmed the surface, perhaps two layers deep. Quickness, humor, intelligence, and irreverence. Superficial qualities, but he had a delicious hint of what was to come.

He couldn't stop himself from trying to touch and expose the layers any more than he could stop himself from trying to put an end to her illegal activities. For some reason, he cared too much on both counts.

One of his men was waiting near his carriage and handed him a note.

Stephen scanned the note, and his mouth tightened. Was he getting his wish, or was this a sign of things to come? In any case, there would not be a peaceful ending to the night after all.

Maddox was waiting for her. He had probably been peeking through the window. She tried to brush past him, but he blocked her way.

"Travers expects you to meet him."

She gave her stepfather a withering look. "I read his dictates. You left his note open on the desk for anyone in the household to read."

"I told you not to sass me, girl." He was having more trouble keeping his cockney from springing up. Her mother hadn't been able to see what lurked beneath the carefully cultivated façade. She had married him in grief and under false pretenses.

Audrey balled her fists and clenched her jaw so tightly it hurt. "And I told you not to speak to me unless it was important. Do you have something of import to say?"

Maddox's face reddened, and his large fists were clenched as well, but he remained silent.

"Good, then get out of my way. I have to change."

She stepped around him and walked steadily up the stairs. Maddox cursed and slammed the study door. Gone to drown his rage in some cheap liquor. She hoped he choked on it.

She stripped her garments and pulled on her favorite shirt, coat, and trousers. Men's garb. Fitting, what with four different men trying to dictate her life. Her only freedom came with donning their clothes.

She finished dressing and slipped her knives into place. She gripped the steel covered by the fabric at her wrists. Tonight was like any other.

The door to the study remained closed as she walked past and onto the street. Good. One man down, three to go.

Flanagan said he would leave her alone, that she had earned her freedom. But no one was ever truly freed from Olympus. She would always run into old acquaintances or someone looking to use her. Now that her identity was common knowledge, she would never find peace in London. Only new borders would provide that for her. America.

She picked up her pace.

Travers needed to be dealt with and Faye freed. Everything hinged on the plan she had set in motion. After completing the last set of tasks, which should give her enough time to locate Faye, she would take care of Travers. Perhaps with a nice large boulder tied to his feet as she pushed him into the river.

And then there was Chalmers. Where he was going to fit was anyone's guess. Every preservation instinct told her to carry out Travers's orders without involving Chalmers. If she wasn't careful, she would have an even more dangerous enemy. His reach was longer and stronger than Travers's. Although Travers aspired for more, he was still a middleman, whereas Chalmers had been at the top prior to gaining a dukedom. Now the Duke of Marston was nearly untouchable. And his calculated charm and lazy air hid the formidable man beneath.

People passed her on the street, men and women leaving for various pursuits. As she neared the more commercial area, the houses diminished in size and grandeur.

She made her way to the Green Man Tavern, a perfect place to meet. Not in the fashionable district, but not far enough away to be in the dregs. There were enough unsavory types to give the place flavor, but the aura of danger was designed more for the young bucks deciding to spend a night on the "wild side" of town.

There was considerable coin to be made taking the naïve men of the town around the city on faux adventures. She had trafficked in it herself for a short time before quickly becoming bored. Fleecing innocents offered no sport, and she had always felt slightly dirty the short time she had engaged in it. The richer and tougher meat of the ton tasted infinitely better and paid more handsomely.

And besting Chalmers would taste the best.

She pushed the tavern door open and through the smoke located Travers in the back corner. She walked to him, skirting two men on the verge of a brawl and around tavern gals carrying trays and plying their wares.

She sat next to Travers, choosing the lesser of

two evils—sitting next to him rather than exposing her back.

"So, what am I doing here?"

"I'm wounded, Audrey dear. Isn't my pleasant company reward enough?"

"No." She wasn't going to play Travers's games. A voice in her head said she was playing Chalmers's, but that was different. He was different. He was worth every move of the chessboard.

She pushed the thought aside and focused on Travers. "Now what do you want?"

"You, of course. But for tonight I will settle for some shipping documents. And a copy of the seal used."

"Where?"

"The documents are somewhere in the house of the merchant I've had you watching. He and his wife are out for the evening, the servants as well. You should have no trouble."

Audrey nearly said, "No trouble, just like the last time," but she kept her mouth shut. She hadn't told Travers that Chalmers had captured her. Something told her to keep that fact to herself.

"Well?" he said.

"Why do you want them?"

"To create my empire, of course."

His empire. Right. "The assistant to the Exchequer conquers all. Going to make Daddy proud, are you?"

Travers grabbed her arm tightly. "For as much leeway as I give you, you are incredibly stupid in how you choose to use it."

Audrey pressed one of her knives into his side. "And you are incredibly stupid to touch me. Release me. Now."

Travers did so. He laughed unpleasantly. "I will have to break you of that nasty habit, my sweet. I choose to let you carry those tiny blades around, but someday I'm going to find all your secret hiding places and enjoy removing each and every one of them."

She rubbed her arm, mentally washing his filth away. She always felt the need to bathe after being in his presence. The way he looked at her. His ambitions, each scheme bigger than the previous. Not caring whom he hurt.

It was her cardinal rule never to hurt innocent bystanders. Darkness lay at the end of that path. It also, more often than not, led to capture. Marks were well researched because they were the targets. You knew whom you were up against at all times, and who in their families might avenge the monetary loss. Bystanders were unknowns and most often innocent besides. Audrey always made sure to target only those who deserved it. Those who reminded her of Maddox.

And Travers was no innocent. With him, no one was safe. She knew someone else was pulling his strings, but that didn't lessen her dislike of Travers's actions. The danger was so incredibly high. The risks multiplied with each new assignment.

She wanted to cry with the frustration of it. Instead she said, "You still plan to go through with your shipping scheme?"

"Maddox talks too much."

"Then you shouldn't have drawn him into this."

Travers narrowed his eyes but answered her question. "Yes, we mean to go through with it. And you'd better support me. It is only a matter of time before things fall into place."

"We? Who else are you working with?"

She saw fear pass over his face before masking it. "That, my dear, is none of your concern."

"What will the Exchequer say if he finds out that you've been tampering with the shipping schedules and the cargo manifests and profiting from the illegal merchandise you've been unloading? He would be highly embarrassed and angered, and you would be going to the scaffold faster than I."

"And why would he find out? My plan is perfect.

And if he finds out, well, accidents are so common nowadays, something you should remember."

"One thing makes sense. If you want to get to the top, the only way you are going to accomplish it is by accident."

Travers gripped his tankard. "I told you to hold your tongue."

"This is a dumb plan, Travers. I know you have debts, and, due to your unfailingly stupid desire to unseat everyone that has wronged you, you have formed alliances with some vicious people, but you are in way over your head. All it takes is one mistake, one person to plant the seed of doubt, and everything will fall to pieces around you."

"In that case, perhaps I'll be forced to eliminate everyone who knows the plan."

Audrey forced her muscles to relax, but her knife was in hand if Travers moved an inch.

Travers snarled. "Why so tense, Audrey? Worried that your sharp tongue has finally gotten you in over your head?"

"Go to hell."

"Ah, I believe we are already there. Let's enjoy it, shall we?" Travers toasted her and took a drink. "My partnerships with the 'vicious people,' as you called them, are ingenious. I will be rich, powerful, and untouchable. Mark my words, in five years I will be Prime Minister. And then, my dearest Audrey, *you* will be begging for my favor."

A young serving girl splashed a tankard down before Travers, her bountiful breasts nearly popping from her dress as she pressed against him. Travers threw her a coin and shifted his gaze back to Audrey. The serving girl brushed seductively against him, but pouted upon receiving no encouragement. She grabbed the coin and flounced from the table.

Travers took a drink and smiled. "I only tell you these things because you are now mine, Audrey Kendrick. I own you and your sister."

Audrey chose to ignore his words, as they only made her think violent thoughts. She noticed the serving girls whispering among themselves and eyeing Travers. He only needed to crook a finger. She didn't know why they couldn't see beneath his handsome, aristocratic features. She could barely stomach looking at him; it was like seeing a petulant monster hiding behind an ill-fitting mask.

Travers was a second son of a viscount, with an ego not quite large enough to overcome his feelings of inadequacy. He believed with every ounce of his being that his birthright had been stolen. And he made everyone pay for the theft.

Attracting his attention was one more sin she could lay at Maddox's feet. Maddox, who always needed money and had arrived in London furious that he could no longer claim guardianship over Faye and Audrey and touch their amassed monies. So instead Maddox had figured out another way to make money off them by selling their identities to Travers. Dear Lord how she hated Maddox and Travers both.

She tamped down the feeling and forced a smile. Let him believe her cowed by his bizarre designs for power. "I understand the shipping interests and the Exchequer plot, but what about the watch?"

"The watch is a personal item. It is mine."

"Somehow I doubt that."

His eyes narrowed. "It's mine, and you will get it back for me."

"So, does your partner know about this side project of yours?"

Fear passed over his face. He waved his hand, trying to act nonchalant. "This is no concern of . . . of my partner's."

For a second she had thought he might divulge the man's name. Although she wasn't quite sure if she wanted to know. Sometimes knowledge was dangerous. "You still want me to steal it then?"

He gave her a look that said, "Of course."

"Then release my sister from Newgate, or no deal."

"There is no 'deal,' don't you understand? I repeat, you are mine to do with as I will. All will happen in good time." His voice trailed off as his dark eyes devoured her.

She again felt the need to bathe. "No. There is no way you will convince me. And if you touch me, I will cut off whatever body parts make contact."

"Even dressed as a boy, you are breathtaking when angry, my sweet. But do remember in which part of Newgate you were housed. A word from me, and your sister will be hanging from a beam by the Old Bailey."

Every muscle in her body clenched. "You wouldn't do it. You have to know you would soon follow."

"Perhaps. But I am willing to take the risk. Are you?"

Audrey stood and said nothing. She didn't trust herself to speak.

"Dr. Smith will be by in the morning. You'd better have the papers in hand. Faye's release in a few days depends upon it."

She took a couple of even breaths. "You will release her then?"

"As long as you do as promised. I'm not a monster, Audrey." He opened his eyes wide, but couldn't quite wipe the smirk from his face. "If you would only agree to my plans, everything else would go so much more smoothly."

She turned to leave, but his parting words caused her to pause. "Oh, and Chalmers is being taken care of. He shouldn't bother you for a good while."

She whipped around. "What are you planning?" Travers lost his smile and narrowed his eyes at the edge in her voice. She realized her mistake immediately and tried to sound offhand. "I just want to make sure his friends don't rush in and retaliate against me."

Travers looked slightly mollified, although the corners of his eyes were still crinkled in suspicion. "Just an unfortunate accident. Nothing that he won't survive. He will be ripe pickings when we need to use him. See you in the morning, my sweet."

Audrey turned and maintained a normal pace through the tavern. She pushed through the door and walked a block before bending down behind a tree to catch her breath. She felt as if she had raced across the English countryside. Stupid, stupid. She couldn't care about Chalmers. And what was more, she couldn't let Travers know she did. Stephen would become another Faye, to be used against her. Except in his case she had a feeling Stephen wouldn't survive Travers's wrath.

Faye. She had to get her out of Newgate. Bile rose in Audrey's throat at the thought of entering the prison, but somehow she had to manage it. Travers was deceitful and unpredictable. She couldn't wait for his next promise to release her sister and next threat to hang her.

Audrey pushed herself to her feet and began walking. The merchant's house was just down the street. She would steal and deliver the papers. She had to allow time to find and release Faye. Time to figure out how to get out of this mess and away from Travers's madness.

Audrey increased her pace. She rapidly passed houses and celebratory groups; none of the drunken revelers took notice of an undistinguished boy on the street. A hack whistled as she approached an unremarkable West End house. The hack disappeared down the street, and all was quiet.

Slipping around the side of the house, Audrey removed her picklock and opened the back door. Somewhere inside were the shipping documents Travers needed in order to reroute the cargo.

Audrey walked into the main hall. Good thing the merchant and his wife were gone for the evening, because she had no idea where to find the papers. She rifled through the drawing room quickly. She tried the merchant's office next. Not in the desk. Not on the shelves. The only item in the hidden desk compartment was a lightly braided, feather-soft whip. And the portly man had looked so stodgy. Some humor returned, and Audrey smiled as she replaced the implement.

She made quick work of the rest of the first floor and headed for the stairs. The master bedroom was the next most likely place. She checked the hallway clock. Plenty of time. Still, she quickened her step.

Audrey opened the door to the master bedroom and stopped. A cold rush of panic started in the center of her chest and spread outward, freezing her lungs and throat. Stephen Chalmers was lounging in a chair facing her and reading from a sheaf of papers.

"Good evening, Audrey. I expected you sooner."

How had she not seen the light?

"The heavy hallway rug blocks the light so well, don't you think? I had to experiment several times to make sure."

She automatically looked at the Aubusson rug. It was indeed thick.

"But you went home." Her throat was dry and scratchy, her brain a second slower than usual.

"And so did you."

"What are you doing here?"

"Reading. What are you doing here?"

Some spark returned. No one had jumped from the closet to arrest her. "Looking for something to read, actually. What have you there?"

She couldn't sense anyone else in the room. She casually walked to the window and peered through it. No one waiting for him on the street.

"A few boring shipping documents."

If it was just the two of them, she had a chance for escape. A slim one, but it was a chance nevertheless. She would still be a fugitive, but she'd be free. She would have another opportunity to figure out a way to save Faye and flee the country.

"Audrey, you look as if you're readying for a fight."

Her muscles had tensed, and she was indeed reaching for one of her hidden knives.

He sighed. "I'm not here to fight with you or arrest you. I could have had you the other night, and we both know it."

"Then why didn't you?" Her heart beat a mad thump in her chest. Her hand was only an inch from one of the short blades.

He shrugged and languidly stretched his long legs forward, leaning back in the chair. "I didn't feel like it then, nor do I now."

"But you hate criminals."

His features tightened momentarily, but he regained his lazy air. "If you'd like me to catch you, I can." He scanned her slowly, and his gaze made her heart thump in an entirely different rhythm. "It would undoubtedly prove exhilarating."

"Chalmers, if you're not going to arrest me, then what do you want? And why are you here?" She let her hand drop to her side. She seemed to be asking those questions a lot lately, but no one seemed to care what *she* wanted.

"I'm trying to answer that question myself."

He rose slowly and walked toward her. She stood still as he tucked a stray lock of hair into her cap. "What do I want from you, Audrey?"

She held her breath. A tight feeling inside echoed the stroke of his fingertips. The warmth of his hand urged her to step to him. She stayed in place.

"What's going on, Audrey? You've never been this careless before."

"I'm spending all my time these days dodging you."

"Yes, but dodging me by yourself. Where's your sister?"

A streak of alarm shot through her and the urge to bolt manifested itself. "I don't know what you're talking about, Chalmers."

He studied her and lightly drew a finger across her cheek. For the second time that night, she felt as if he could seduce her merely with a caress.

"You'll tell me."

She closed her eyes, then he was gone. She heard his footfall on the stairs; he made no effort at stealth.

Why had he let her go again? What did he know about her sister? There was no getting rid of Chalmers. He would just keep popping up in unlikely places. She had no choice now but to involve him in her plan. At least if he worked with her, she could somewhat control him.

She looked at the papers stacked where he'd left them on the chair. With reluctance, she walked over, lifted them, and read the top document. They were the papers she sought. She had known it as soon as she'd seen them in his hands.

How had he known she would be here tonight? What game were they playing?

Chapter 7

❧❧

Stephen finished writing the note to his superior, explaining the papers he had switched the night before. It had been a near thing. He had arrived only minutes before Audrey, and it had taken all of his acting abilities to maintain a casual air.

His orders were to discover who was behind the changed cargo manifests, schedules, and routes. Who it was that was allowing illegal goods onto the docks. Someone crafty enough to ask the right questions, and someone with the right connections to gain access to the information. It had to be someone in an important position.

That person was using Audrey to gather and change information. Stephen was using Audrey to make sure she gathered the wrong information.

Whoever had hired her wouldn't know the difference in the switched shipping papers. Stephen had painstakingly changed the information, making sure all of the new information looked valid. In two weeks the villain would be forced to show his face at the docks to inquire about one detail. Or *her* face, he amended. He would never again underestimate or overlook women as suspects.

In two weeks this mess would be over—for better or for worse.

"Your Grace, Lady Stinson and Lady Appling are here to see you. I seated them in the parlor."

Stephen sighed and stood up. "Grimmond, we are alone. Stop calling me 'Your Grace.' "

The butler raised a brow as Stephen walked toward him. "I will bring tea to the parlor, Your Grace."

Stephen tweaked the butler's coat, skewing it slightly from its impeccable position. "Thank you, Grimmond."

A martial light appeared in Grimmond's eye, but the loud rap of a cane in an adjoining room produced a smug expression on his face and seemed to forestall his usual retort.

"Have a good meeting with Lady Stinson, Your Grace," he said, the smug look still evident.

Stephen sighed again as Grimmond walked

from the room in a stately manner. He knew why the two ladies had come. He might as well get it over with.

The ladies were silent as he entered the library. Lady Stinson's hawkish gaze was piercing, but he gave her his best smile and nodded to Lady Appling.

"How lovely of you two ladies to stop by."

"Marston, we're here to talk about matters of importance." Lady Stinson rapped her cane.

Stephen reined in the grimace over hearing his title. He wondered if he would ever grow accustomed to it.

"And what serious matters would you like to discuss, dear ladies?"

"Your predecessor promised seasons for his three cousins, Meg, Mary, and Margaret. I want to know your intentions."

Stephen raised a brow. "I have no desire to marry any of my cousins, no matter the distance of the connection."

Lady Appling pressed in front of Lady Stinson, her lashes fluttering on colorless cheeks. "Well, you'll have to marry eventually, and you can't do better than my sweet Margaret."

Lady Stinson sent her sister a scathing glance and rapped her cane on her left foot, causing Lady Appling to recoil to the corner of the settee. "Or my Meg or Mary." She turned back to Stephen. "The point is, what are your intentions as to honoring the gentlemen's agreement between the seventh duke and our families?"

"I will, of course, honor it, Lady Stinson. I see no reason to change the arrangement as long as I don't have to attend any fittings."

Lady Stinson looked down her nose, a quite impressive feat as her nose was somewhat prominent. "Your levity in this matter is misplaced, Your Grace. I want to be reassured that the girls will have their promised seasons."

"They will."

Some of the tension ebbed from Lady Stinson's shoulders. "Excellent. You were always a good sort—should have been sent to us after your parents died. We wouldn't have shuffled you around the countryside."

Stephen stiffened but continued to smile.

"Looks like you are finally over your wanderings, though, and may I say I'm glad. Good to see you take the reins and steer the family in the correct direction. Too many poor decisions in this family recently." She leveled her gaze at him. "I'm expecting you to avoid that path."

"Your vote of confidence warms my heart, Lady Stinson."

"Good. We will leave you now, Your Grace. Thank you for receiving us."

Lady Appling recovered her composure and smiled becomingly as she trailed behind Lady Stinson.

He had seen Lady Stinson's free hand knotted in her skirt. She hadn't been sure he would honor the promise. He took no offense; pride was the only thing holding Lady Stinson together. Her husband had lost their wealth at the tables, and Stephen had always admired the lady's pluck.

Not, he shuddered, that he would want her as a mother-in-law. He had spent a small amount of time in her presence during his "shuffling," as she called it, although never in her household. Luckily he had ended up with a distant cousin of his father's, the late Viscount Canfield. The viscount had been a much-needed mentor, and Stephen had become fast friends with his oldest son, Brandon. Running wild with Brandon over the estates had saved his sanity. The memories brought a smile to his face. He needed to pay Brandon a visit soon.

Lady Stinson would never have afforded him the freedom allowed in the other houses. He had never spent time in her household, as his other relatives had been afraid that Lord Stinson would drain his inheritance, a well-founded concern.

Lord Stinson wouldn't be able to touch the money Stephen would give to the girls for their seasons. He would talk to Logan, the Marston solicitor, about setting up an account manager to communicate directly with Lady Stinson.

Stephen glanced at the clock. Another hour until Logan arrived. He rubbed his hands together and headed for the conservatory. An hour to be Stephen Chalmers and not the Duke of Marston.

Audrey wiped a hand across her dusty cheek, the excitement from a job well done still humming in her veins. She threw her tools on the rug and placed the bundle on the bed. She unwrapped the cloth to examine the papers within.

The beautiful impressions of the seals and signet rings were stamped on each page. Each stamp a verification by its owner to follow through with the directions on the page. Obtaining papers and seals was usually a mindless task. Only Travers's separate assignment was proving troublesome.

It was the one item she might be able to bargain with once Travers told her its location. Travers had talked about it in a voice heavily laden with desperation.

She sighed heavily. Travers would never let them

go, and it was time she reconciled herself to that fact. It was time to execute a new plan. ·

She chewed her bottom lip as she carefully stowed the papers in the floor hollow she had created. Chalmers had offered his help. Perhaps she should have Flanagan stage an attack on her and appeal to Chalmers's protective instincts?

She needed to talk to Flanagan in any case—might as well see if he had any useful information before formulating a plan. In saving Chalmers the night before, she had tossed her lot in with his.

Saved him yet again. She seemed to be forming a bad habit.

She washed, dressed, and made her way to St. Giles. Places where people like her belonged, not in wealthy Mayfair houses like Stephen Chalmers's.

Someday maybe she could forget her past, someday when she was on a new shore with a new identity and a new outlook on life. But not today. Not as she made her way through the winding and twisted streets. Not when she knew which ways led to dead ends and possibly the ultimate dead end. Not when she knew exactly the paths to take.

She marched right into Flanagan's "office," having no trouble getting past his security.

"I want you to stop the attacks on Chalmers."

She paused. "Or Marston, or whatever people are calling him these days."

"Nice to see you too, Hermes, my dear."

She grinned and sat. "Fine. It's nice to see you, you old goat."

The deep wrinkles around his eyes creased, but he didn't smile. It was about as close as he came, though, which was a good sign. "I see you are in fine fettle. Wasn't sure what to expect with all the rumors circulating."

"What have you heard?"

Flanagan waved her question away. "Why do you want me to stop the attacks? Chalmers has it coming, even if it's not on my orders. S'truth, the orders didn't come from me. There are lots of rumblings about big rewards for taking out Chalmers. A couple of men have split from our ranks to do so. They itch to deal with Chalmers, Angelford, and Roth. Damn if those three don't cause all our trouble." He gave her a knowing glance. "And I would retain my best people if Chalmers were out of the picture."

She winced. Flanagan always saw more than she wished. "I know. But it's damn stupid of the men who attack them now. Last year after the attack on Chalmers at the river, half of the blighters who participated were captured or killed."

"S'truth, all but one. Leonard." Flanagan spat.

"I need you to use your influence to stop the attacks."

"Was wondering when you'd work up the mettle to come here and ask for my help. Demanding is more your style, but that's what made you such an asset."

She took her pride in hand. "I need your help, Flanagan."

"Why does it matter to you? Wouldn't it be better to be rid of him?"

"I need him."

Flanagan surveyed her for a few seconds, all the while pulling his long mustache. "You and Icarus left Olympus, so the job won't be free. This Travers bloke probably already knows about us if'n he contacted you." He gave the mustache another tug, and his eyes creased in his near smile. "You wouldn't be in this bind if'n you hadn't left."

She continued to look at him, not twitching a muscle in response. She wasn't surprised he knew about Travers or the situation. Flanagan was nothing if not an information hound and hoarder.

"You're a hard one, Hermes. Always have been, always will be. But you know the rules. What's in it for us? I have to settle the boys down somehow.

And just so you know, I can only settle the ones under my influence."

"One hundred pounds."

"Five hundred and not a crown less."

"Three hundred and not a pence more."

"Deal. Now you want to tell me about Icarus?"

Audrey moved in her chair. "She's in Newgate."

"Heard the rumors. Didn't want to believe it myself. This Travers bloke is the cause?"

"Yes. He put me in there long enough to get a taste, to know that nothing would stop me from freeing Faye. The bastard reworked the papers—he's blackmailing at least two of the guards, paying off ten others, possibly more."

Flanagan pulled his mustache. "A dangerous man."

"He is using some of the men from O'Leary's ring. I recognized a few of the thugs."

"O'Leary's gone missing."

"I doubt he will be found. Keep your back to the wall, Flanagan. Someone dangerous is behind Travers. Whoever it is will make a play at the first opportunity."

"I can handle things. If'n he tries, he'll be fodder for the mudlarks."

Audrey nodded, but worry still gripped her.

Worry for the bear of a man in front of her. "See that you do."

"So what you planning to do about Icarus?"

She leaned back. "Travers says he will release her in a few days."

He eyed her. "But you don't believe him. What about going in to get her?"

Ice swept her insides. "That's my plan."

Flanagan nodded. "Saw your stepfather in your rented house."

Her lips tightened. "He's not the problem. Merely a fly to be swatted."

"Don't underestimate the devil, Hermes. Never a smart thing to do."

"Don't give undue credit." She waved a hand.

"You always were a smart one. But don't overlook those under your nose, or you'll get a pistol in your belly. Johnny made that mistake."

Audrey stood. "I'll have the money to you soon."

"I know you're good for it. Luck, Hermes. You know the way out."

She walked past the two guards, who stepped out of her way, still holding their heads in their hands. She didn't know them very well. Flanagan had been actively recruiting, and many of the faces were new. She watched an older man cuff a boy who was practicing his pickpocketing skills. The boy turned in her direction, and she recognized him as the boy who had picked her pocket in the market.

"Even a dullard'll feel that. Now try again."

The boy's face was eager as he tried again and was once more cuffed.

She wondered what Flanagan was doing for initiations these days. She and Faye had received the dubious honor of raiding Carlton House. One pair of George's trousers, a handkerchief, a snuffbox, a wax seal, a piece of poetry written by the King. They had been given a list of items and had not been allowed out of the mansion until everything on the list had been collected.

They had searched nearly every room in the house, hiding from guards and guests and running from room to room, collecting items, waiting to be caught. It had been a nightmare. She could still remember the wide-eyed look of her then-nine-year-old sister—a sort of wild shock tempered by youthful excitement.

Those first few years with Flanagan would have been excruciatingly difficult even without a little sister to worry about. Faye, her only link to her parents, her only responsibility in a world tipped upside down. Her one true friend, her one true weakness.

Audrey maneuvered through the streets, eager to leave the section of town that held too many bad memories. The boy tried two more times to pick the man's pocket before she finally turned a corner and they disappeared from view. Even in defeat the boy's face had been lit with eager determination.

She shook her head. It was a strange feeling to see another's excitement over becoming a criminal. She remembered the fear from her first time picking a pocket. Seeing the hangman's noose. Seeing people she knew hanging from it. Seeing them dead in the street. Seeing Johnny, her friend and partner, dead on the floor, blood trailing from his mouth, death overtaking his once bright eyes.

Audrey quickened her step. Those images no longer haunted her waking moments, but she sometimes woke in a cold sweat, the feel of a braided rope chafing her neck.

The ugly scar on her side was a vivid reminder of what one could expect on the streets. Yet excitement always lit the faces of those starting off in the business. Moving up the ranks kept a body fed and clothed. And there was prestige and honor in being a member of certain gangs. Flanagan's was one of the best. His gang provided an opportunity for those with little to carve a life for themselves.

She had been born to a wonderful, caring family

with means. And then she had been forced to the bottom of the cesspool and made to scrape her way back up. It had been a living hell.

Sure, there had been moments of fun, of jobs gone well, riches collected or nabobs given a well-deserved fleecing. There had been exhilaration the first time she knew without a doubt that she was one of the best. She had celebrated, then Flanagan had cuffed her, reminding her it was only a job, and the next one would probably leave her dead.

There were moments of camaraderie among the different groups, Flanagan's, O'Leary's, and the other rings. But it was an artificial feeling, superficial and tenuous. Every day was a new challenge, a new threat, a new death. Death was part of the game. Part of the life. Inescapable. The friend you hugged while dancing and drinking ale was the same soul you laid to rest a week later.

Never get too close. Never make friends, only contacts. Never get personally involved. Those were the rules, and they were implacable. She had learned them the hard way.

She was stuck with Faye. Her sister was the one person in her life she couldn't keep out. She would keep Faye safe and never let another in. It was as simple as that.

She continued south, lost in thought. She could

keep Chalmers out. Emptiness lay beneath that charming façade—there was no depth. If she could just convince herself of that . . .

Audrey looked up, and Newgate Prison wobbled in her vision. She could smell the unwashed bodies, the decaying odor of spirits long dead. Whether it was real or dredged from memory, she had no idea. The rats, the confined cell, the greasy hands. She retched in the street, but felt nothing, as if she was detached from her own body.

People passed by, no one offered a helping hand. They just stared straight ahead. Good. She wouldn't have helped them, either. Her hand shook as she wiped it across her mouth.

Dear Lord, she would have to go back in there to find Faye. She had to see if her sister was still alive.

She forced herself to walk past the prison, everything inside her urging her to run.

Johnny would have whipped the gang into a frenzy, calling for them to charge into the prison and rescue Faye. He would have had no plan, no organization. Yet he had always managed to convince people of his outrageous ideas, until Flanagan unfailingly had to cuff him in the noggin to silence him.

Johnny had been able to charm all with his bright green eyes full of mischief and . . .

Audrey stopped. Johnny's eyes hadn't been green. They'd been . . . they'd been . . . brown?

It didn't matter—her friend was gone. She grabbed a lamppost and shook the image of Stephen's eyes from her mind.

She walked toward Mayfair. Travers had said he was going to remove Chalmers from the situation. But how was he going to do it? And could she use Chalmers in the meantime without Travers knowing? She needed to put her rapidly developing plan into action.

Stephen's lazy grin appeared in her mind. Never get too close. Never make friends, only contacts. Never get personally involved.

Johnny hadn't followed the other rule of the game. Never trust anyone.

Audrey moved toward her target.

She wouldn't forget.

Chapter 8

"**W**hat do you mean there's no money, and the estate is bankrupt, Mr. Logan?"

The lanky man shifted his spectacles. "The funds are gone, Your Grace."

Stephen leaned forward in his chair. "Cousin Vernon was wealthy. I never saw any sign of excess."

"The seventh Duke of Marston implemented a total redesign and redecoration of the various estates. He incurred very large expenses and did not spend his money wisely."

Stephen tapped an impatient finger. He vaguely remembered Vernon talking about redecorating the primary seat. "I would have heard if Vernon were having trouble."

Logan shook his head. "Not to speak ill of the

dead, but the seventh duke was not very good with figures. I doubt he even truly realized the extravagance of his expenditures, and he was not willing to be guided. I attempted to speak with him about it many times and was always rebuffed. There is also one large gaming debt to his name."

"Who holds the marker?"

"The Earl of Bessington."

"And the redecoration was done mainly to Marston Manor?"

"Yes. Although, a number of the other properties were updated and renovated as well." He listed five.

"How much did he spend?"

"Two hundred thousand pounds."

"The estate should be able to handle that."

"Not if a number of crucial investments failed as well. Unfortunately . . ."

Stephen gave an ironic laugh. "Well, at least that means no money needs to be spent on the lands. We'll just have to live off the year's income."

"Well, you see, that is also a problem. While the residences have been maintained, the tenants' properties have not. Many of the buildings need repair and updating. The tenants have become angry about their conditions and lazy in their output."

Stephen gripped his pen. Damn Vernon. Spending money on trappings and not his people. "How much is needed for this coming year?"

The solicitor listed exorbitant figures for all of the entailed estates. By the end of the recitation, Stephen was in a state of shock.

"I can't believe it is that bad. There are at least two properties, Fieldstone and Pimont's Park, that should be producing enough money on their own to pay for the rest."

"Yes, but they have been poorly managed. The duke refused my guidance and insisted that his own men run both estates. Look at the figures here." The solicitor pointed to two unbelievable deficits.

Stephen digested the information. The dukedom was utterly devoid of funds. Which also meant there was no money for his cousins' debuts.

"This is unbelievable."

"I didn't believe it either, Your Grace. I dismissed the stewards immediately upon the discovery."

"Why was I not informed about this before?"

"The duke kept the books in his office. Didn't trust anyone. He was a very secretive man. It has taken nearly this entire time to locate the books and understand his notations."

Stephen frowned. Vernon hadn't been secretive. He had been indulged, yes. The excesses sounded like Vernon—to a point. But secrecy? Overspending?

"That doesn't sound like Vernon."

"Had you seen him recently, Your Grace?"

Stephen shook his head. "No, in the past few years I have frequently been out of the country."

The solicitor nodded. "He changed, Your Grace. Something caused him to be secretive and wary. Please ask your aunts or your staff here in town."

"I confess I haven't moved into Marston House yet."

"It's only two weeks now since you've assumed the title. And there are many matters requiring your time."

But only one matter that truly interested him. And she would probably steal everything else he had.

"How many years have you served the family, Mr. Logan?"

"Going on thirty, Your Grace."

"Vernon passed on three months ago, then Thomas became duke. Did Thomas know about the monetary situation?"

"Most of it, Your Grace."

Stephen sighed. Suddenly the accidents that had taken his cousins' lives looked more suspicious. Had the weight of the debts been too much for Thomas? "How much do we need for operating costs next year?"

Logan named an outrageous sum, and Stephen

nodded tightly. "Am I to understand there is no way the estate can generate even a quarter of that amount?"

"Yes, Your Grace."

"How long before we earn the necessary income?"

"With good management, maybe five years."

"Five years is too long."

"Yes, Your Grace."

"Any suggestions?"

Logan hesitated. "Just the normal, Your Grace. Selling unentailed properties, borrowing the funds, or raising more income."

"I'd rather raise the income," Stephen said dryly.

"Speculation, trade, marriage, all the usual options exist."

"Lovely." Stephen sighed again. "That's all for today, Logan. I need to digest my impending trip to debtors' prison or Australia."

Logan hesitated. "Will Your Grace be visiting any of the estates in the near future?"

Stephen shook his head. "I won't be able to leave London for an extended period for at least a month. Too many matters here need my attention. And since the money problems have been kept quiet, we needn't worry about the creditors knocking yet. I'll send some funds to the tenants in the most desperate need, then figure out what to do for the rest."

Logan nodded, and Stephen could have sworn a look of relief crossed the man's face. "Why do you ask?"

"If it is permissible to you, Your Grace, I'd like to personally undertake an audit of the entire dukedom. Possibly see if there is anything we can improve or if there are errors in the books. I'm quite embarrassed by the situation really." And he looked it.

"Proceed with the audit. It will be a relief to have someone look into the task until I'm free."

Logan nodded. "Thank you, Your Grace. I will do my best."

He turned to leave, clutching the books in his arms.

"Mr. Logan, leave the books here tonight. I'd like to glance over them quickly."

The man turned. "I'll need them to conduct the audit."

"You can pick them up in the morning. I will leave them with Grimmond if I'm not available."

Logan bowed and shuffled from the room. An odd man, but Stephen would withhold judgment

129

until he talked with him a few more times. Still, something was strange, and Stephen wanted a closer look at the books all the same.

His mind whirled. The estate was in debt. Extreme debt. What was to be done?

Stephen rested his chin on top of his hands and stared at the closed ledgers. First the responsibility, now the indebtedness. Three weeks ago he had been free and rich. Well, rich by most standards. Now he was yoked and poor. His own liquid assets wouldn't cover half of the operating cost of the entailed estates for the next year. He had put most of his available money into land. The land wouldn't pay off his investment for another few years.

He had also invested in a few shipping ventures, but they were still at sea, and no one knew when they would return. None were scheduled to return for the next few months, and with the problems that plagued the shipping community, if any managed to return, it could be more than a year.

He rubbed his chin on the back of his knuckles. He had just promised Lady Stinson that all three cousins would be given seasons. The cost of one season was outrageous. The cost of three was, well, three times the outrage.

He could finance their seasons using his own

savings, but that still didn't solve the estate and long-term financial problems.

Damn this whole title business. He shook his head and sat back. He needed a diversion, something to take his mind away.

He withdrew a piece of paper, and started a list of options. Roth would be pleased with his industry, no matter the slight mockery Stephen was making of his situation.

Number one, sell all unentailed properties. He estimated a figure and made a column to the right, filling it in. He made a third column with the anticipated date of payoff. He could probably sell the properties at a loss within the next few months. He entered that total into the column.

Number two, wait for shipping ventures. At half of the possible monetary reward the estimated cost was generous, but he entered it anyway. One needed a bright hope somewhere. Since he was being optimistic, he gave it six months.

Number three, use his own funds. He knew that amount and entered it. Date equal to the present.

Number four. He chewed on the top of the pen. Did he really have to write it? Did he really want to list it as an option? Stephen sighed for the third time.

Number four, marry an heiress. Estimated

amount, dowry covers operating cost, income enough to keep estates alive. Estimated date, anytime.

He winced. Even seeing it on a ludicrous list, that one hurt.

He continued the numbered list with other options like taking up a trade and becoming a merchant, but the estimated dates were far in the future. To complete the rapidly degenerating catalog, he added begging and running to the Continent. Heck, even running to the Americas. Or jumping off a bridge. They were all options, and one had to be thorough before making an informed decision. He was feeling a bit more sarcastic than usual.

Stephen smirked at the last option. He had lived through his last leap off a bridge, so that might not be a solution after all. Although one couldn't always count on having a rescuer.

Roth's voice irritatingly echoed in his mind. Responsibility. He looked at the list and began to cross off possibilities until he was left with the first four. The first three combined might give him enough. The fourth definitely would.

He looked at the massive ledgers sitting on his desk mocking him. Conspiracies screamed through his mind. But was he trying to convince himself that he wasn't in trouble by falling back on the old habit of looking for villainy everywhere? Or were things really bad? He hadn't seen his stuffy cousin in a long time—but Vernon couldn't have ruined the estates that badly, could he?

He would talk to Bessington first and settle the gaming debt. That, at least, was a tangible thing. Then he'd figure out the rest.

The window jiggled. Stephen turned in surprise as Audrey Kendrick hoisted herself up and over the sill with ease.

"What the hell are you doing?"

She stood and brushed her trousers. Trousers that clung to her in all the right places. What was she doing crawling through his window in those things?

"I'm here to see you."

"What's wrong with the front door?"

Her brows puckered. "I didn't feel like using it. And I'm not dressed properly."

"Keeping in practice for this evening's activities?"

She gave him a dark look. "Listen, Chalmers, I don't have time to chitchat with you. I came to offer—"

There was a knock at the door. Audrey dove under the desk.

Grimmond entered. "Your Grace, the Earl of Bessington is here to see you."

Stephen tried to hide his surprise for the second time in the same number of minutes. "Send him in, Grimmond." Grimmond left to get the earl.

Audrey squeaked. "Send him away, you lunatic. I can't stay under here."

"Then you should have come the proper way."

"Chalmers, I swear I'm going to—"

Stephen saw the list of options and shoved it under the desk and into her mouth as the visitor entered.

"What a pleasure it is to see you, Lord Bessington." Stephen said as he reached across the desk to shake hands with the distinguished-looking earl. "I was just pondering a visit to you myself."

"Ah, yes. Probably about the same matter."

Stephen motioned for Bessington to be seated. Audrey beat his toes with her fist.

He hid the jerk of his body behind a cough. "I was just informed that my late cousin, the seventh duke, had an unfortunate turn at the tables with you."

"He did indeed."

"Do you happen to have the marker?"

"I do, but that is not what I was hoping to discuss today."

"Splendid. But all the same, why don't I take the marker from you now and get it settled."

Bessington fished the marker from his pocket and handed it to him. Stephen looked at it and raised his brows.

"Fifteen hundred pounds? Is that all? I was led to believe it was significantly higher."

Bessington shook his head. "No."

Relief cascaded through his body. Perhaps all of Logan's figures were off. He was going to have a bloody fun time burning his list of options in the fire grate as soon as Bessington was off.

"The thing is, Your Grace." Bessington hesitated. "I bought a few of Vernon's outstanding debts."

At the look on Bessington's face the list was once more dry and whole in Stephen's brain.

"I see."

Bessington shifted. "Your cousin and I had an understanding. He was about to propose to my daughter, Clarissa. Things were going to change, Vernon promised me. I hold the strings to Clarissa's income. And then the riding accident happened."

Dread coiled in Stephen's gut. He knew exactly where this conversation was heading.

Bessington pushed on. "Clarissa's dowry and income are substantial." Bessington named the figure, and the coils of dread knotted. "She's a good girl. Not yet had a season, the next one would be her first. Can't deny her the first few balls, but an early marriage in the season would be encouraged. In exchange, upon signing the betrothal documents I'll advance you the sum necessary to keep the estate afloat until the wedding. And after the wedding I will consider the debts repaid."

Lord, he didn't know whether he was hot or cold. He fought both sweat and chills.

"That is a very generous offer, Bessington. Let me think it over." He wanted to add that the offer was very close to blackmail, but he knew better than to antagonize someone before he was ready to destroy him.

Bessington nodded. "Going to have a lot of offers for Clarissa, but I know she will like you much more than she did Vernon and all the other swains as well. You have a good lineage and a distinguished title. We will be making a very good match."

Stephen nodded mechanically, already planning the first bit of research into Bessington's affairs. "Yes, that would be true."

Stephen forced some small talk, then Bessington was on his way. Bessington could be acting as a noble, aristocratic parent. Everything he had said was true. The match would be flawless. He had seen the chit. She was a lovely girl. Everyone would exclaim it was the match of the year. Everyone but Stephen.

Today hadn't much put him in the mood to be amenable to blackmail. His intuition was saying that something didn't ring true, and he was going to discover what.

Sharp teeth bit into his leg.

"Ouch!"

"He's gone, let me out!"

He moved his chair back as Audrey pushed her way out from under the desk. His list was crumpled in her hand.

"Here let me have that back." He tried to snatch it from her, but she scooted around the desk.

"Interesting reading, Chalmers. Sounds like you need some blunt. And quickly too."

He frowned. "Give me the list, Audrey."

"So what's it going to be?" She scanned the options. "Jumping off a bridge? Why is it crossed off? Sounds like a good one to me."

He growled and moved toward her, she darted to the other side, keeping the desk between them. "Uh-uh, Chalmers, I don't think we're done just yet."

Audrey looked down again, number four on the list leaping toward her. She had overheard the entire conversation with Bessington. A conversation she'd rather not think about.

"Well, along with your first three options, being hired for some side work could provide you with enough to cover the costs of your failing lands."

Stephen shook his head and leaned into the desk; she couldn't read his expression. "No, I fear you will see me leg-shackled to some whey-faced debutante."

The thought bothered her more than a little.

"Why did you come through the window?"

"Are you really going to marry an heiress to save your lands?"

He shrugged. "It's the way of things among the ton. But, it's not my first choice as you can see." He motioned toward the list, and she looked down.

Next thing she knew it was out of her hands and she was spun and trapped against the desk. Damn but he moved quickly.

"Chalmers, let me up." His legs were inside of hers so that she was nearly straddling him. The heat from their joined bodies sent warmth shooting straight to her face.

"Why did you sneak through the window?"

"I told you, I felt like it."

He leaned forward and pressed her farther into the desk. "Not good enough."

"I considered your offer of help." Audrey was nearly breathless.

"Good. We can get to that in a minute. Why'd you come through the window?"

He moved his hips, and she felt the lower portion of her body catch fire. But his words registered through the haze. "You're a tenacious piece of—"

He slipped his hand into her trousers, and she gasped in outrage and from the tremors that shot through her body.

He stepped back with her papers in his hands. He had removed them from her waistband, that rotten bas—

"What's this?"

"Dammit, Chalmers, give that back."

"Fair is fair, Audrey. Now you'll have to earn it."

"You are a rat bas—"

"Did anyone ever tell you what a foul mouth you have? Really, a lady shouldn't speak thus." His mouth twisted into a lazy smile.

She fisted her hands and glared at him.

"What was this offer you were going to tell me about before we were interrupted?"

"I have a mission to undertake."

"And what? You came to turn yourself in first?"

"No, I need your help."

"My help?" He quirked a brow, but the lazy smile remained.

"You did offer it yesterday. Twice in fact."

"Yes, but I don't plan on taking up any illegal hobbies to do so."

"No illegal activities. It doesn't even involve stealing." She crossed her heart.

He looked doubtful.

"Well, not really," she said defensively.

His delicious mouth turned up. "Let's hear it."

"I need access to a certain place." She paused and brushed a piece of lint from her trousers. "I need you to give me access."

"So you can steal something?"

"No, so I can *recover* something that was stolen from me."

Stephen observed her. "The mission documents are in here?"

She nodded, and he shuffled through the pages. They were still warm from her skin. His fingers tingled at the contact.

There was a map located in the middle of the stack. The aged parchment had lines and symbols drawn in dark ink. It was a map of Newgate Prison. Stephen felt a stirring of interest.

A determined smile appeared upon her face. "I will pay you extremely well, with both money and information."

"That's very generous of you. It seems quite against your nature. What are you looking for and where?"

"I'll tell you when you need to know."

He looked at the map again. A scan of the rest of the papers showed detailed accounts of twelve men. He didn't recognize any of the names.

"Not illegal, you say? Looks like you are trying to break someone out of prison."

She gave him a tight smile and pointed to his list. "Do you want the job or not? You aren't going to get the information otherwise, and based on these, you could sure use the extra money."

Stephen considered her. She was wound as tightly as she had been the two nights he had caught her. Why was she exposing herself to him now? He could have her arrested on pure suspicion and she knew it.

"You can consider me a tentative participant. I'll need to know the full details and full amount you will be paying me before I make my decision."

She looked relieved.

"However, you have to promise to forgo any illegal activities while working with me."

"Deal. If you uphold your end of the bargain, then you never need see me again, Your Grace. I will disappear and never darken your door again."

An unidentified flash ran through him. "You are leaving?"

"Yes, when this is done I will bother you no longer."

He felt that nothing could be further from the truth, and he did the only thing he could think of—he began a campaign.

Audrey breathed deeply. He had agreed. The tentative part was something she would worry about later.

He advanced toward her, rolling his sleeves, a lock of hair falling into his face. So male, so alive, all glistening and golden. There was such a deep hammering in her chest, she thought her heart might beat its way right out.

"What are you doing, Chalmers?"

"Sealing our deal."

A flurry of half-formed thoughts flew through her brain. "Uh, right." She thrust a hand toward him.

He grabbed her cold hand and pulled her toward him. His lips swept hers, and the half-formed thoughts scattered completely under his warmth.

He deepened the kiss, and she leaned into his

heat. What would it be like to be loved by this man? To be in his arms every night? A taste of it, that's all she craved. Just a taste, like a forbidden sweet.

She found her back against the wall and wondered where she had found the strength to move. He pressed into her, and she was sucked into the swirling heat he promised. His hands were in her hair, teasing. The forbidden delights. The oh-so-easy pleasure.

But he broke the kiss with a groan and laid his chin on top of her head.

"I'm not sure if this deal will be tormenting or fantastic, but it will not be boring."

He pulled away, his bare forearms brushing against her neck and making her shiver.

"When do we begin?" he asked.

She pushed upright and retrieved her papers with a shaking hand. He raised a brow, but didn't take them back.

"Soon. Perhaps tomorrow. I need to gather a few more pieces of information. Will you be ready?" She was pleased to find her voice steady and strong.

"Yes. It might help if you shared everything with me though. I can be of more help than as just a key turner."

He reached over and tucked a dislodged piece of

hair into her cap. She couldn't think well this near to him, she needed to get away. She scooted to the window.

"I will talk to you later, Your Grace." And with that she disappeared through the window.

Stephen watched her disappear, then jotted down the names listed in her packet along with all of the details he had read. He would make some inquiries and see what was going on. He smiled. She had come to him, just as he had hoped she would.

At least from this angle things were looking up.

Chapter 9

Audrey entered her rented house and put a shaking hand to her forehead. He had agreed. He had agreed, but at what cost she did not yet know.

"Audrey, my dear, is that you?"

She closed her eyes and clenched her fists. Releasing her fingers one by one and inhaling deeply, she straightened and walked stiffly into the drawing room. Travers and Maddox were lounging in the chairs.

She glared at Travers. "What are you doing here?"

"Why, is that any way to talk to your benefactor? Have a cup of tea with us." Travers motioned her over. Maddox's tea must have been at the bottom of the bottle of whiskey he was tipping.

"No, thank you. I need to change my clothing and leave again."

"No hurry, dear. There has been a slight change in tonight's plans. I need you to attend Liddendock's costume party. There are some papers there that you need to retrieve."

"What papers?"

"St. John's."

She gritted her teeth. She had hoped the St. John task would come later. The viscount made her nervous. "Why tonight?"

"Because he is meeting with his contact and plans to spend the night at Liddendock's. The papers will be in his room."

"I need the particulars. Who is St. John meeting and when does the meeting take place? What if I get there too late?"

"Don't bore me with such trifles, my dear. Those are things for you to worry about."

She smiled, baring her teeth. "Fine. Then give me my invitation."

"I've placed it in your room. Interesting decorating choices, although a bit sparse for my taste." He smirked, and she could imagine him pawing through her things.

"Stay out of my room, Travers."

She walked from the room, and his soft laugh followed her.

Audrey perched on her bed and looked around her room absently. Travers was correct. Her room reflected a spartan existence. She displayed very few personal possessions. A woman on the run couldn't be encumbered with material objects. She heard the front door slam and felt a spasm of relief. Enough thinking about the cretin's observations; she needed to concentrate on the bigger picture. Travers and Chalmers were tools to get her sister back.

There was a knock at the front door. Audrey waited, but no one answered. The knock sounded again. She trudged down the steps and opened the door.

A liveried man stood on the steps and handed her a note. "For Miss Audrey Kendrick, from the Duke of Marston."

Audrey looked over her shoulder, but no one seemed to be around. She took the note and thanked the man's timing. If he had appeared while Travers was in residence, Travers would have snatched the note. Who knew what he would have done then.

She read the note. Chalmers was inviting her to

accompany him to Liddendock's party. She chewed her lip, fingered the note, and pondered her alternatives. Attending the affair with Chalmers would complicate her plans. But how could she gracefully decline, then appear at the gathering on her own? She knew he would identify her, and that would create a greater problem since she was supposed to be working with him now. What was his motive? The timing of his request and Travers's dictum seemed too coincidental.

She looked at the servant, who was awaiting her response. "Tell His Grace that I will be prepared at the specified time."

The servant nodded and took his leave. Audrey watched him leave and retreated to her room to sort through her jumbled thoughts and plans.

She sprawled on her bed and mentally played scenarios until her maid entered the room to help her dress.

Audrey had many costumes from which to choose. Looking through her wardrobe she pulled out a white chiton and decided to attend as the Goddess Diana. She draped the gown over one shoulder and tied a gold filigree cord at her waist. A quiver with arrows completed the outfit. The quiver contained a secret compartment designed specifically to conceal anything she might "pick up." Her maid styled her hair in a partial upsweep; a white ribbon trailed through the design, the ends of her hair dripping down her back. She tilted her head to the side. No loose-flowing curls, but it was a classic Greek style all the same, and for once the maid was agreeable. Their private talk had improved the girl's attitude.

After the maid left, Audrey lifted her skirts and strapped her knives in place. It was a damn nuisance to be without sleeves. She heard the footman open the door, lifted her gloves, gold mask, quiver of arrows, and bow, and headed downstairs.

Stephen was dressed as a flamboyant highwayman, with a flowing cape, jaunty hat, and wicked mask. There was an appropriately dashing air about him. He smiled when he looked at her. "The huntress? How appropriate."

He slid a hand down her arm and clasped her hand.

"You look ravishing. Or ravishable. Which would you prefer?"

Her heart beat a different rhythm when he was near, and his words caused the odd staccato to intensify.

"I think I'll go with ravishing for the moment."

"Well, in that case, I reserve the right to change your mind." A flurry of thrilled bumps raced up her arm as he lifted her hand to his arm and trailed his fingers over her knuckles.

She thanked the skies that no one was there to observe either her reaction or their departure together. Maddox must have taken himself off to some gaming hell, and Travers had not returned. The footman and the maid would probably make a full report to Travers, but she would deal with that later.

She peered at Stephen. He was such a hard man to read, constantly hiding behind his winks and grins. Her thoughts were bittersweet. Just a few more days, and she would never see him again.

He whispered in her ear, "Liddendock's parties are a bit racy."

The warmth of his breath caused a shiver. "I know. But the partygoers will be much more interested in their own pursuits than in me."

"Nobody likes a person who doesn't participate."

She frowned. "Well, I'm not going to participate in their sordid affairs, so we'll just have to be unobtrusive."

"The Duke of Marston, unobtrusive? Never."

"Come now. No one even has to know it's you."

She sensed his smile and wanted to throttle him.

Of course they would know it was him. The ton wasn't brainless when it came to social intrigue. Only when it came to everything worthwhile.

"Wonderful. I suppose that means I'm your strumpet for the night."

"What a lovely offer. I accept."

"That wasn't an offer!" She lowered her voice. It had gone high. "That wasn't an offer, and you know it."

"I think it was an excellent offer. And I've already accepted."

She fingered the fabric concealing the steel in her garters. "I'll take you apart piece by piece."

"Sounds delicious."

Fortunately, the carriage pulled up to Liddendock's town house before she had a chance to respond. The carriage door opened, Stephen took her hand and helped her navigate the drive. A number of guests were enjoying the warm night and frolicking outdoors. A lusty buccaneer was chasing a scantily clad Cleopatra, and a gaudy Helen of Troy was accepting a thousand launched offers to join her for the night. A highwayman, a beggar, and a bard were actively engaged in the bidding and fondling.

Standing at the entrance, laughing heartily at the antics of his guests, stood Lord Liddendock. When

Stephen and Audrey approached, his attention shifted. "Ah, Marston, welcome. And who is this lovely creature?"

His appreciative eyes focused on the low-cut expanse of her bodice.

Stephen raised her wrist and kissed the inside in a feathered caress. She shivered and a tingling began in the pit of her stomach.

"Diana, this is our host, Lord Liddendock."

Liddendock reached out, kissed the back of her hand, then trailed his tongue upward to her wrist. As if an adder had struck, she snatched her hand back. Liddendock frowned momentarily, and Audrey tried to cover her distaste with a smile, but it was a grimace at best.

Stephen pulled her close to his side. "She's new to such pleasures."

Liddendock brightened. "Ah! Maybe you will be interested in some of the later entertainment in that case."

Stephen smiled blandly. "Perhaps."

Audrey fumed until they were beyond Liddendock's hearing. "That dirty old sot," she growled.

Stephen burst out laughing as he escorted her inside. "Careful, my dear. Our host may not appreciate your honesty."

The room was overcrowded. There were people

everywhere. Stephen snatched two glasses of champagne and steered them toward a man dressed as Robin Hood. Audrey looked at the insipid and giggling Maid Marian standing to his side. There was no way she was going to waste a moment's conversation on that woman.

Audrey spotted St. John across the room. He was one of many men dressed as a pirate. St. John had a streak of silver through his dark hair, which made him easy to recognize. She surveyed his associates and blanched when she met the eyes of a very sober Travers. Travers was appropriately dressed as a demon, and although he was chatting with St. John, he was staring directly at her. She sipped her champagne and turned away. There was no need for the footman or the maid to spread the tale of her escort after all. The sooner she could get the papers the better.

Robin Hood was waving his hands, agitated about something, and Stephen was trying to calm him down. Taking advantage of his momentary distraction, Audrey ran a hand down Stephen's arm and excused herself. He shot her a warning glance, but Audrey slipped away and followed a maid balancing a tray of champagne flutes. As the maid stepped into the hall, Audrey intercepted her.

"Pardon me. I was wondering if you could help me with a problem."

The maid balanced the tray and took her measure. Audrey slipped a coin from her pocket and clasped the maid's hand.

The maid smiled and put the coin in her own pocket. "What can I do for you?"

"The man with the silver streak in his hair, Lord St. John, do you know which room is his?"

The maid nodded. "Lucky for you I do. Top of the stairs, turn right, and it's the fifth door on the left."

"Wonderful. Thank you." Audrey turned, but the maid put a hand on her arm. Audrey flinched at the contact but smiled politely.

"Other ladies have asked after his room. Lots of competition for that one."

Audrey thanked her again and returned to the ballroom. St. John was a notorious womanizer. The better for her—his penchant for debauchery would keep him occupied downstairs.

When she returned, Stephen lifted her hand and kissed it again. He had a mischievous look, and she frowned at him. He didn't release her hand, but led her to a gaming room.

"I figured you could win me some money while we are here."

"Why *are* we here?"

"Some polite socializing. Establishing a partnership. That sort of dastardly political maneuvering. Hopefully it won't tarnish your reputation too much."

She purposely trod on his toes, but her soft-soled shoes did no damage. He wanted to see her play, did he? Well, he'd be in for an unpleasant surprise.

They were welcomed at the hazard table, and Stephen gave Audrey the dice.

She threw the dice. Lost. Threw them again. Lost. After three more rolls Stephen grabbed the cubes from her. He rolled back-to-back winners and recouped the money she had lost.

"It's time to move on. You are a terrible hazard player."

"You never asked me if I was good."

"Well, I give you points for consistency. Are you able to roll anything other than a two or three?"

She grinned, and couldn't explain why she suddenly felt happy. Her luck at the tables had always been a sore spot. "I have the worst luck with dice."

"Are you any better at cards?"

"Not much," she said cheerfully. He laughed, and a spark of light burst inside. Her lack of gaming skills had been the bane of their ring. She was a dismal gambler. She had no luck with cards or dice, and the others had forever been disappointed in her. Unbidden memories diminished the ray of light, but a spark remained.

Stephen brushed a soft kiss on her cheek. "I wish I knew what dark thoughts flash through your mind."

Before she could say anything, his hand grasped her cold one. "Let's socialize."

He led her into the hallway. A few couples were scattered about, and Travers and St. John stood talking near the library door. Two women drunkenly danced, spinning each other in the middle of the hall.

Stephen caught one of the women as she careened into him.

The woman grabbed his shirt and suggestively slid herself up Stephen's front as she regained her footing. "Welcome to our hall." She ran a hand through his blond hair and twirled a lock in her fingers. "I think I've found a more surefooted dancing partner. And one with all the right equipment."

Stephen disentangled himself and set her to St. John's side. The woman pouted but clutched St. John's waist.

St. John smiled at Stephen and greeted him. They appeared to be friends. Travers gave a tight nod. He turned to Audrey. "I don't believe I've had the pleasure of meeting your lovely companion."

Stephen paid Travers's show of temper little attention and Travers's eyes narrowed even farther. Stephen introduced her as Diana, and Travers's hand slithered over hers. He gave her hand a painful squeeze, and she schooled her features so as not to flinch. "Such a virtuous goddess to appear among such debauchery. One would think you would seek more tranquil places."

She summoned a smile. It hurt. "Sometimes one has to traverse hell in order to reach heaven."

Stephen was not smiling. Travers released her hand and turned, ignoring her completely for the rest of the conversation. This gave Audrey a chance to survey the hall. She'd have no better time to steal into St. John's room. Travers's thinly veiled hint implied that he would keep them both occupied.

Audrey excused herself to the ladies' retiring area and stepped down the hall, made a few turns, then casually walked up the stairs.

She tried to still her racing heart. This was a routine job. She had a perfectly secure place in her quiver to stash the papers. Stephen would never know.

A gaggle of women dressed as various Greek goddesses walked past her as she cleared the top step. Her luck was holding. If anyone asked about a Greek goddess, they would say they had seen her descending the stairs from the retiring room.

Audrey followed the maid's directions and turned right. The fifth door on the left was locked. She removed one of the arrowheads and pulled out her picklock key.

The lock was not a challenge, and she had it open a few seconds later. She entered and closed the door behind her, relocking it to give her precious time in case someone tried to enter. Papers were stacked neatly on the dressing table. If her luck held, she'd be back downstairs before being missed.

She sifted through the papers until she found the ones Travers had demanded. Something about smuggling activities in Cornwall. She took the outer covering off of the quiver and rolled the papers inside. Snapping the cover back on, she slipped it around her shoulders and walked toward the door.

She froze as she watched the knob turn beneath her fingers. The only good place to hide was inside the wardrobe. The dark, closed wardrobe.

She didn't have time to consider her decision or to face her fear when the door opened. Flattening herself against the wall behind the door, she held her breath and prayed. Maybe the person would leave before she was discovered. If not, she would have to incapacitate the intruder or feign an interest in a liaison.

A man stepped into the room and closed the door. Audrey's breath let out in a whoosh when she saw him.

Stephen stood in front of her, his arms crossed. "I really wanted to believe you."

"I can explain."

He shook his head. "What is Travers to you?"

"Nothing, I just met him."

"I don't think so, Audrey." He lifted her hand, and looked at her wrist, where one of Travers's fingers had strayed. His face was angry. "A man you barely know doesn't leave marks when he touches you." He smoothed a gentle finger over the bruise. "The new assistant to the Exchequer and I are going to have a few words before the evening is through."

"No, Stephen." She snatched her hand away. She was a fast healer. If he had only waited a few more minutes, the angry red marks would have disappeared. "You are mistaken."

"I don't think so, Audrey," he repeated, and stepped closer, sliding a hand into the back of her hair and pulling her closer. "Why are you here in

St. John's room? What message passed between you and Travers? Are you robbing St. John under his orders?"

"No." In all respects Stephen was getting too close. She stepped back, and his warm hand fell away. "I got lost on the way to the retiring room. The ladies must have meant the fifth room down the left hall."

"Audrey." His voice was soft. "What did you take?"

"Take?" She sputtered indignantly. "I got lost—"

"You're telling me that you accidentally ended up in St. John's room after conveniently seeing that he and I were occupied? Is that your story?"

"Yes, it was an accident, and no, there was no 'conveniently' about it."

"You asked for my help, but I wonder if this isn't all some elaborate ploy in your grand theft scheme."

"No! How can you say that? I'm here because you invited *me* here tonight, not the other way around."

"You dishonored our agreement. You agreed to stop your illegal activities."

"Yes, as soon as our plan is set into motion. But it hasn't yet begun." Her voice rose marginally.

"So now you are arguing semantics? You know

damn well what I thought. Why should I trust you now?"

"My word is good."

"You haven't proven that to me yet."

"Damn it, this plan was put in motion long before our agreement."

Stephen latched on to the statement. "What was in motion? What are you doing?"

"Nothing!"

"For once, can't you be honest with me? Even when you are caught, you continue to lie."

Audrey was horrified to feel tears prick the back of her eyes. "I—, I—, I can't."

His eyes softened a bit, and he stepped forward. The look in his eyes further pricked her tears, and she felt herself stepping forward too.

Loud voices traveled down the hall and stopped just outside of the door.

"Hurry."

Stephen grabbed her, opened the wardrobe, and threw her inside. The tears instantly transformed into panic. "Stephen, no, wait—"

He flung himself inside and pulled the doors closed just as the door to the room opened.

She was trapped. The walls were too close, too close.

"No, no, I can't breathe," she gasped.

Why wouldn't anyone help her? Couldn't anyone hear her scream? No one to help you, no one to ever help . . .

Audrey was making confusing sounds. Her voice was barely a squeak. But with two people standing outside their hiding place Stephen couldn't take the chance of their being discovered.

He reached out a hand in warning as she continued to mutter incoherently. She was cold and trembling. Stephen had the feeling that if he could see her eyes, they'd be glazed over. He gathered her into his arms. She shivered and whispered "breathe" against his shoulder. Time stood still. He lost track of what was happening outside the wardrobe until she relaxed against him.

"Oh, that feels wonderful," a female voice sighed.

Stephen nearly groaned. St. John had taken no time in bringing one of the willing women to his room. He just hoped they were quick.

The noises from the bed amplified as the woman explicitly told St. John what she wanted him to do. No docile miss there.

Audrey's arms twined around his neck, and she pressed herself against him. His body reacted from the contact. Nothing like some good old-fashioned torment to cap the day. He massaged her back, making low, soothing noises. There was no way the boisterous couple was going to hear them even if he and Audrey started chatting about the weather.

"Yes! St. John, more!" The four-poster bed was bouncing and slamming as it connected with the wall.

A cramp formed in Stephen's neck from bending over. Audrey's mouth pressed against the hollow at the base of his throat, and the cramp moved south. Her lips trailed the pulse at the side of his neck, then up and under his chin. Every part of his body and brain was on alert. He was already hunched over in the small space, and he only had to lower his head an inch to claim her lips.

His lips descended to meet hers. The first light kiss blazed into an inferno as their mouths fused. The smooth texture of her lips and her eager movements were driving him crazy. He lifted his hands to her nape and tried to be gentle. He wanted to devour her.

"Oh, yes, oh, more."

The voice was a cry inside his head and outside the wardrobe. Audrey's hands moved down his shirt and his moved down her back. The cries became incessant. Each word was punctuated with a bounce of the bed off the wall.

"My gads! Oh! This . . . is . . . the . . ." The woman sang a little note. It broke through the haze of sex that was descending upon Stephen, and he buried his face in Audrey's hair to stifle the urge to continue. Her hair smelled of jasmine. He had to again remind himself not to take her in the wardrobe while another couple lay just outside.

The rustle of skirts and laughter penetrated the silence that had descended.

"Again?" A voice twittered.

Stephen felt like banging his head against the door. He willed St. John to leave. It was probably a waste of mental energy, but he was going to go mad if he had to stay in the wardrobe with Audrey's soft curves molded against him. To his surprise, the viscount said something in a voice too low for him to hear, but the woman twittered again, and Stephen heard their footsteps leaving the room.

Stephen sent up a silent prayer of thanks.

Seconds after he heard the room door close he tentatively opened the wardrobe. The room was empty. He stepped out and drew Audrey after him.

Her eyes were wary, but there was something else there. Something positive.

She smoothed her hands down her costume and pinned some fallen tendrils of hair. When she spoke, her words were directed to his shoes. "Thank you."

He lifted her chin and stroked her cheek. "We'll talk later."

She nodded, and they headed for the door. No one was in the hall. He relocked the door, took her hand, and they descended the staircase to rejoin the party.

Travers was standing at the bottom of the stairs, but merely inclined his head and walked away. Stephen clenched his fist. He would deal with that ego-driven bastard just as he had in the past.

But first he had to figure out what was going on.

Chapter 10

❦

Audrey checked herself. Her panic had sub-
sided, but the wild emotional remnants
remained. Ever since being thrown into that rat-
infested prison, she had troubles with dark, confined spaces.

Chalmers had calmed her down. Helped her get
through the blind terror. She owed him, yet when
the time came, she would be forced to betray him.

Audrey looked at the marble floor tiles. Never
had she abhorred her life more.

"Audrey?"

She looked up. "Yes?"

"I'm going to get you a glass of champagne."

Anguish flowed through her at his kindness.
"Thank you."

Stephen walked toward the refreshment area, and Audrey saw Travers watching her from the veranda. She walked toward him. Might as well get part of this mad mess over with. She made a display of showing him her quiver as she removed the papers.

He turned and shoved them into his jacket.

She was feeling maudlin and sarcastic. "No 'Good job, Audrey'? 'Nice work getting those documents'? Or, 'How are you tonight, Audrey dear?'"

Travers turned and yanked her closer. He gripped her wrist in the same spot he had previously marked. "What are you doing with him?"

Audrey tried to pull away without creating a scene. A few couples were sauntering along the terrace and into the gardens. "It's a long story, you ass. Now let me go."

Travers narrowed his eyes. "You had better be nice to me. I'm the only thing standing between you and a dank cell. Chalmers will never help you."

He looked over her head and dropped her wrist. Audrey followed his gaze.

Stephen was moving swiftly and purposefully toward them. He shoved a man out of his way. Fury painted his features.

Travers gave a mocking little bow, but anger

seethed from him. "This is your fault. Stay away from him or your sister will suffer the consequences." He slipped into the garden hedges.

"Where is he? Is he in the garden?" Stephen made to move past her, and Audrey had to put a restraining hand on his forearm. His eyes connected with hers, and she felt a rush. He really was acting like her rescuer.

She snatched her hand back, scorched. "He's gone. It was nothing."

"Nothing, eh?" His eyes scanned the bushes before returning to hers. His voice was edged with steel. "What is Henry Travers to you?"

She wanted to say, *A monster, a jailer and a cruelhearted bastard*, but instead said, "A garden pest, nothing more."

"You have a past with him."

"No. We are only recently acquainted. But to cut him would be rude."

Stephen's eyes narrowed. "Since when have you cared about being rude?"

Audrey shrugged, still feeling tense. "Wearing a gown makes me feel nicer."

He stepped back and looked her up and down. "Me too."

"Wearing a gown makes you feel nicer?"

"Only if you are in it too."

She fanned her suddenly warm cheeks. There was nothing to be done about Travers at the moment. Her secrets were unraveling at an alarming rate. "Would you care to go inside?"

Stephen scanned the dark foliage one last time, then offered his arm.

The action had become a bit rowdier inside. The attendees were feeling the effects of the free-flowing spirits. A knight lurched toward Audrey as one armored kneecap tangled in the other. Stephen plucked her out of the way, and the knight went crashing to the parquet floor.

The knight grabbed the hem of her dress and awkwardly pulled himself to his knees. Audrey tried to snatch the material from his hands, but the man swayed and lifted the hem from the floor, attempting to peer beneath. A startled gasp escaped her as she whacked him on his uncovered head. He thumped to the floor.

Stephen chuckled and pulled her through the crowd. The onlookers lost interest in the drama and left the knight prone on the floor.

Stephen was still laughing when they reached the front door. "You looked so outraged. And at a debauched party, no less."

"He was trying to peer up my dress!"

"I'm sure he will have sweet dreams of it."

His eyes were still warm as they glanced over her in that familiar way. She suddenly felt emboldened.

Audrey lightly tapped him on the arm. "Sweet dreams, you think?"

Surprise shone briefly in his eyes before he moved closer. "Definitely."

"How can you be sure when the theory hasn't been tested?" Dear Lord. She was flirting with him. The rush of emotions over the past hour must have muddled her mind.

He considered her. He started to respond, when Liddendock interrupted.

"Off so soon, Marston?"

"Afraid so."

Liddendock gave her a waggle of his thin brows. "She must be something special to take you away so early. Looking forward to better making your acquaintance, madam. Perhaps another day?"

Audrey leaned into Stephen, and he put an arm around her waist. "Mmmmm, perhaps."

Liddendock leered. "Capital. Night then."

Stephen and Audrey escaped through the front door and waited for the carriage to be brought round.

As soon as it arrived Stephen helped her inside. Audrey checked the window shade to make sure it was still cracked open a bit.

"How long have you been scared?"

The muscles in her back tightened. "I'm not scared."

"Is it dark spaces or cramped spaces?"

She pressed her lips together, but there was no denying it. "Small, dark spaces."

"And yet you still find the nerve to crawl about other people's rooms. Rooms you're unfamiliar with. Rooms usually dark and airless."

"Don't patronize me, Chalmers. I do what I must."

"I'm not patronizing you, Audrey. I'm amazed is all. I've known fierce men who won't do what you do after experiencing a time in the hold or a cell."

She jerked her head. "This is a childhood ailment."

Her eyes had adjusted to the dark and she could see him shake his head. "No. If it were a childhood problem, you would have either overcome it or you would not put yourself in situations that would cause it to occur."

"Maybe I enjoy discomfort."

"Maybe. And maybe you are desperate."

Audrey snorted. "I'm desperate, all right. Desperate for this carriage to stop so I can vacate it."

"When did it happen?"

"I became desperate about two minutes past."

He ignored her comment. "Did you get accidentally locked in? You can't have been in jail, I would have heard of it. And it is hard to imagine someone keeping you locked up."

Bitterness swept through her. You couldn't hear about something if a false name was used. "Yeah, I was accidentally locked inside a storage shed."

Silence met her statement.

She yanked the shade all the way down. She was horrified to feel weepy.

Stephen's voice was soft. "Where did they hold you?"

"Oh, stuff it, Chalmers." She leaned her head against the back of the cushion. His understanding tone was giving her a headache and prompting waterworks in her eyes.

"Tell me, Audrey."

The soothing voice of temptation.

"Newgate."

"Oh, Audrey." He sighed. "Why do you do it? Why do you break the law?"

Emotion boiled in her. Hatred for Travers, loathing for Maddox, anger at Flanagan, irritation at Faye, resentment of Stephen. "What do you mean, 'why'? I'm a thief. It's what I do. What I was trained to do. It's all well and good that you can raise yourself on your moral pedestal, but some of

172

us have to worry about where the next meal will come from and where we will sleep."

Stephen's voice lost some of its nectar. "Come now. You don't expect me to fall for that old song? You probably have more money stashed away than I do. I have it on good authority that you've stolen enough to be quite wealthy."

Her lips tightened, and her face went white. "You have all the answers, Chalmers, don't you? Why bother asking any questions?"

"So, you're telling me that you can't do anything else?"

"What's it to you, anyway? Take your power and title and go play with your friends in Parliament. Go make up rules for the rest of us, while you remain above them all."

"So you've lumped us all together in the same pot and called us stew?"

Her eyes narrowed, but she held silent.

"I'll tell you what my problem is. When I was eleven my parents were killed by street thugs. They were left to die in the gutter. Murdered for fifteen pounds. And the villains ran free, escaping into the maze of the Seven Dials." His tone was conversational, but a steel edge lay beneath.

"That's a good story, Chalmers." Pride and bitterness held her straight. "I suppose you hunted them down and punished them justly once you were old enough."

"Yes, I did." His voice was soft again, but cold.

"Thus began Stephen Chalmers's great vendetta against the rogues of society. The wretches in the gutter. The beggars on the street."

He didn't answer.

"And what type of stew are we?"

He turned to the window, tugging the shade up. "Lawbreakers."

"Ah, so the woman who steals a loaf of bread to feed her hungry son, should she be thrown into Newgate?"

He shook his head, but didn't turn back. "What about the baker she has stolen the bread from? What about his family? Or maybe he is wealthy? Does that make it better? Easier? I would give her the bread myself. But stealing is against the law, and laws are in place for a reason, Audrey. Society is a pact between its members."

"Well I didn't sign up for this society. Where was my say?" Her face was hot. Her palms hurt from her nails digging into them.

He pushed away from the window and looked at her for a long moment, then sighed and reached forward to tuck a strand of hair behind her ear.

"Yes, where is your say? Would you value it even if you had it? It's hard being responsible, so much easier to be a member trotting along."

She didn't pull away. She wanted to lean closer. Even through all the anger, all the pain, she desperately wanted to lean closer. "Only if you are a valued member."

"Yes."

He pulled her onto his seat, and she didn't protest. She was running across a ragged rooftop, and if he were to let go, she would surely fall. As long as he held on she was safe.

He smoothed her hair. "I'm sorry you were in prison."

A tear slipped from her eye. She was thankful he couldn't see it. "Thank you."

He lifted her chin and kissed her. Gently this time, unlike the frenzy of the kiss in the wardrobe. His lips softly pulling hers. Coaxing them open. Something blossomed inside her chest. Like she had raced across London, but without the associated pain.

His hand was gentle on her neck. Skimming and stroking the area where her neck met her hair. Her whole body relaxed against his. Stephen could wash away the pain. He could keep her warm. Always.

She broke contact and rested her head against

his shoulder. He rubbed her arm, as if understanding her need for withdrawal. His action only made her feel more alone.

She needed some perspective. There would be no always. Not with this man. She needed him to save Faye. She could not risk needing him for more. The plan was straightforward. In the end she could have no relationship with Stephen other than one of cat to mouse.

Their path was clear as day. She needed to get her head out of the soft, comforting clouds that were muddling it.

The carriage pulled into the drive and in front of his house. Stephen offered his arm, and they walked into the house. It felt good to be back on sturdy ground.

"Would you care for a drink?"

"Yes, that would be nice."

They walked into the library and Stephen poured brandy for himself and Madeira for her.

She sat on the comfortable couch and sipped the flavorful wine.

"Audrey, maybe we should talk."

She fiddled with her glass. "What do you want to talk about?"

"How did you become a thief? You are gently bred. Your words and actions speak for themselves."

"Good actors can fake breeding very well."

"Yes, but I don't think you are faking it. When in distress your speech is impeccable, with no signs of a street accent."

She hesitated and watched the liquid swirl in her glass as she twisted it. "My mother and father were gently born."

"What happened to your parents?"

She pushed away from the couch and walked to the window, drawing back the heavy velvet curtain.

He persisted. "Maddox is your stepfather."

Audrey grimaced and let the shade fall. "My father succumbed to a fever. My mother married Maddox, but died soon afterward."

"How long between their deaths?"

"Not even two years."

"How old were you when your mother passed?"

"Ten."

"Where did you live?"

Audrey felt restless. She walked to the desk. "Not a week after burying her, Maddox moved us to London."

"And?"

"And what?"

"Maddox left you, didn't he?"

"No, he didn't leave us."

"How did you end up with Flanagan?"

Audrey stared into the liquid in her glass again. It didn't matter if he knew how she had grown up—at the end of their partnership she would be an ocean away. But it was still a hard admission. "He bought us."

Silence greeted her statement.

She restlessly twisted the glass again and watched as the edges of the liquid clung to the sides before slithering back into the pool.

"Your stepfather sold you?" There was no shock in the statement. Stephen had to know it happened all the time.

"Yes. He would never have just left us. There would be no money in it."

"He sold you to a criminal and left?"

"Flanagan was better than the alternative." She remembered the woman with the heavily rouged lips and aged eyes that her stepfather had also approached. And the terrified feelings she had prompted when she had looked the girls over. Thank the Lord Flanagan had bought them. But oh how she yearned for the innocence of the girl she once was. The girl who hadn't understood any of it.

Stephen lightly touched her hand, and she was surprised to find him at her side. His eyes were angry, but not at her. His anger on her behalf was . . . nice.

"Where is your sister?" he asked in a soft tone.

"She's still in Newgate." The admission wasn't as wrenching as she expected. Something had changed. Instead of just needing his help, she now wanted his help.

"You want to free her." It was a statement. "That is why you have a map of the prison and the names of the guards."

"Yes." She knew that showing him the guards' names had been a calculated risk. It was a sure bet he could list them for her right now.

He straightened. "I had my suspicions. I checked the registry and didn't see your sister listed."

"We weren't being held under our given names." The bitterness clutched at her.

"Who put you in there? Travers? I wouldn't have thought the lackwit had the skills or connections."

Audrey looked at him sharply. Stephen's off-hand comments revealed a great deal about why Travers hated him. To be so dismissed was galling.

"No, it doesn't matter who put us there. I will give you all the information you need after we rescue my sister."

"Someone went to a lot of trouble to coerce your cooperation. Sounds like someone we need to worry about."

She was struck by the use of "we" in his statement. "Well, then you know it is obviously not Travers."

Stephen picked up a pen and twirled it. "I suppose it could be." He shook his head. "We grew up together. He is a distant cousin. After my parents died I was shuffled between relatives. I lived with his family, the Canfields, for a few years. A number of their properties border the Marston holdings, land separated by the family in the past, before his branch of the family was given a title as well. Henry was always a nasty kid, trailing behind his brother, Brandon, tattling and getting everyone else into trouble. Never could keep up with all of us though, as hard as he tried. And he was such a malicious child that no one wanted him to."

Warning bells sounded in her head. They grew up together? Distant cousins? Dear Lord. She put Travers's reactions into context and realized her extreme danger. Travers would move quickly after seeing them together tonight.

"You look like you could use some air. Come into the conservatory, and we'll discuss your plan."

She nearly gasped for breath as he opened a set of doors at the end of the library. Cousins? Focusing on the doors and not on the buzzing in her head, she followed him from the room.

Extending back through two sets of open windows was the most amazing space she had ever seen. Audrey drifted, momentarily awestruck, into Stephen's private sanctuary. Small gas lamps lit the space. The shadows of the night lent a magical air. Something about the room calmed and allowed her to tamp her panic.

She was overwhelmed by the variety of color and smell. Here in the midst of a city teeming with waste and grime was an oasis of paradise. The room was part conservatory, part study.

"Do you like my refuge?"

"It's magnificent. I haven't seen anything more beautiful."

The room was a marvel of brick and glass, beautifully upholstered sofas, and a profusion of flowering plants. Although grand, it was lush and relaxing. Lolling hydrangeas lay across the Italian marble floor, and an abundance of variegated flowering clematis and wisteria vines framed the windows and doorways. Baskets and planters of geranium, petunia, lobelia, fuchsias, and impatiens were placed artfully throughout the room. She remembered the names from their park visit.

"I added it after my uncle passed on. My uncle on my mother's side, no relation to the Marston side of the family."

Strange-looking tools dotted the workspace. She

remembered their walk through the park gardens and his explanations on the different species. He already looked more relaxed as he walked through the room, in the midst of his passion.

She needed a break from thinking about Travers and Newgate. She pointed at the sofa in the corner. "That's an odd-looking settee."

"I commissioned it from a German furniture maker who designs settees and sofas for comfort."

She noticed the blankets at the side. Did he sleep here? She continued her examination. A small spiral staircase was tucked into the corner. Stairs to his room?

"So what do you do with all of these plants?"

He smiled. "Study them. Grow them. Write about them."

"Write about them? What, in a diary?"

"No, I contribute to the *Botanical Register*."

Audrey had vaguely heard of the magazine. She had never been too interested in foliage except as a place to hide. "How long have you been doing that?"

"Since its inception." When she continued to stare at him, brow raised, he added, "Seven years. Ridgeway pulled me over from the *Botanical Magazine*."

"Isn't that a form of treason within your community?"

He laughed. "No, the *Register* has full support."

"So is that what makes the difference?" she murmured the question, but saw him tense.

He seemed to fight with himself, then shrugged, letting her comment go. She was vaguely disappointed.

"We are trying to form a Botanical Society in London. Trying to convince George to have it in Regent's Park."

"Perhaps in thirty or forty years when they finally complete the blasted thing. You're going to be waiting a long time, Chalmers." She touched a leaf. "Although the park does have promise."

"Regent's Park isn't open to the public."

She shrugged. "Guess you are right."

He shook his head. "No walls keep you out. So, when do you plan to go to Newgate? How do you plan to gain entrance?"

Audrey tried to keep Travers's reaction to her breaking her sister out of prison from her mind. "You can get us in."

He nodded. "Yes, but I can't just stroll back out with your sister in tow."

"No, but my first goal is to locate her and assess the situation. If there is any way to bribe the guards, that would be the best plan. I have profiles on most of them. Their vices, bad habits, and a few dirty secrets. I'll use those if I have to."

Stephen touched a large leaf on one of the plants. "I thought you said there was going to be nothing illegal?"

"My sister was locked in there on wrongful charges. She isn't even listed under her real name. Nothing about her imprisonment has been legal."

"Although you both have stolen enough to be in there a hundred times over."

Audrey pressed her lips together. "But not this time. We left the business last year."

He surveyed her. "So tomorrow we take a tour of Newgate, locate your sister, and plan from there."

A hot current of fear ran through her. "Yes, tomorrow would be best. Early morning. I'll give you money, and if we can't bribe anyone, then you will keep it as part of your fee."

His eyes narrowed, but he nodded. She had the feeling she had just insulted him, but that was the least of her worries now. Travers and Newgate. She had to avoid Travers tonight and somehow live through the visit to Newgate in the morning.

"We will have to leave early in the morning."

She worried her lip, still thinking about the other problems. She nodded absently to his statement.

"Might be best if you stayed here."

He walked to the door and called for one of the footmen. A man appeared at the door, and Stephen told him to have the servants ready a guest chamber.

She looked up. Staying here would be the best option. Travers could even now be prowling through her house. "I need different clothes for tomorrow. I can't go like this."

He looked at her costume and a smile lifted his lips. "Are you sure? I bet we could bring your sister out easily using you as a distraction."

He closed the door and walked toward her. Or stalked toward her, it was hard to tell.

"I suppose we could alter your garment." He trailed a finger through the shoulder strap and followed the flow of the material down her side, lightly brushing her breasts. "But it might take all night." He traced the sash with his fingertips, then ran his fingers up her arm.

Her heart urged him to continue, while her brain screamed to stop.

"I'm not sure there is enough material."

"Oh, there is plenty of material to keep us busy." He reached into her hair and loosened the pins. Tendrils fell down her back as each pin was removed. The slow pace of the movements made each brush of hair a wicked sensation. He slowly pulled the ribbon from her hair, the satin whispering against her skin.

His lips lightly caressed her neck, soft as the satin had been. "You should never rush a masterpiece."

He didn't stop touching her, just the barest of touches with his lips, his fingers feathering her skin. She started to touch him, but he stepped away, looking down at her. His lids lowered, his eyes burning beneath. "Advice I should follow."

He touched the strap of her gown once more. "You can borrow one of the maid's dresses. I'm sure Grimmond will find it odd when I ask, but a day barely goes by when he doesn't find a request from me odd."

She bit her lip and moved away from him, wanting nothing more than to bury her head against his chest. "I will see you in the morning then. Good night, Stephen."

"Good night, Audrey." He ran her satin ribbon through his fingers. She could feel his eyes on her as she left, but nothing more was said. She walked as slowly as she could manage to her room.

Remember the mission. Remember the rules. Remember the pain, Audrey.

But nothing could help the ache that had started in her heart. She tugged the edge of her costume; it had started to chafe more than her skin.

Chapter 11

~~~⟨✦⟩~~~

Morning light seeped through the shades as Audrey watched Stephen dip the nib of a quill into an ornate inkstand. An assortment of steel and gold pen points was splayed across the table. Flashes of light reflected from the mother-of-pearl onto the walls as he twirled the pen, his brow creased in thought. He had said the series of notes would be their secondary plan if something went wrong.

Feeling uncomfortable from studying him for so long, she wandered around his library. If a man's wealth was measured by the quantity of his books, Stephen was extraordinarily blessed. Two long mahogany-paneled walls were filled floor to ceiling with shelves of leather-bound volumes. A fireplace dominated the exterior wall, and huge windows on each side bathed the room with light. It was grand, yet because of the wide variety of trailing plants and hanging baskets, unpretentious and relaxing.

She touched a book by Voltaire that she hadn't yet read. She skimmed her fingers across others on the shelf and sighed. To possess so many books . . . And he was supposed to be in debt.

It was all unreal. Considering the previous night's escapade, she had awakened remarkably refreshed. Stephen's housekeeper knocked then entered, arms laden with durable garments. Audrey changed into the dowdiest brown serge that was cut in the most unflattering lines. The dress hung from her slight frame. The serviceable garments made her feel invisible and comfortable in the morning light. Useful. More real.

She touched another volume and turned to find Stephen watching her. An imperceptible smile curved his lips. He looked down and picked up the list, as if not wishing to be caught staring. She found the thought comforting. She was not alone in her confusion.

"Are we ready to leave?"

He nodded. "Yes. Cook packed several berry

scones for us to eat on the way. Gather your belongings and let's be off."

She tied the unremarkable bonnet in place. One thing to be said for servants' garb, it was practical. Not quite as comfortable as her custom outfits, but more serviceable than dressing as a lady.

Stephen walked to the door, but Audrey found her feet rooted to the floor. She grimaced and awkwardly pushed forward. If he noticed her struggle, he was gracious enough not to mention it.

They entered his carriage and headed east. Her stomach started churning, and her legs felt weak. Perhaps she should eat something. In her current condition, she doubted she would have enough energy to exit the carriage and stand on her own feet.

She dug a scone from her pocket and chewed on it. Her throat was dry and coarse. Swallowing proved difficult. She finally managed to force the pastry down, but her legs, at odds with her throat, felt watery. What was wrong with her?

Stephen was assessing her agitation. "It's nerves. Try not to pay them any attention."

She drew herself up in the seat. "I don't get nervous, Your Grace. Cautious, yes, but not nervous."

"So you say. Forgive me if I don't believe you. It is not a sign of weakness to admit anxiety."

"Dammit, I'm not nervous."

"So you say."

"Chalmers, so help me—"

"Are you certain you will remember the way once we're inside?"

Audrey sat back and closed her eyes to visualize the passage. Her legs still felt buttery. "Yes. We were housed next to those facing the noose. It's just a short walk from there to . . ." Memories turned ugly, and she gripped the homespun skirt.

He reached across and kneaded the muscles in her neck. "Is that why she isn't under the Matron's guard?"

"Yes, we weren't held in the women's quarters. They were too nice for Tr- . . . for our purposes."

"That's going to make our task more difficult. Only prison staff and the Ordinary are allowed there. And neither of us is going to pass for a guard or the chaplain. I will have to work around that. You just need to identify the cell."

She cleared her throat. "I can do that."

"Good." He continued to rub her shoulder blades until the carriage pulled up in front of the cold, imposing structure.

Audrey took a deep breath and securely grasped Stephen's hand. Stepping onto the cobblestones confirmed that her legs were going to buckle. She stumbled, and Stephen supported her until she found her footing.

He didn't look at her as they walked toward Debtor's Door. She was glad he was with her. His reassuring presence and understanding was a blessing, but for their plan to succeed, she needed to pull herself together and concentrate on the task at hand.

She couldn't rely on him for everything. It was essential that she play her part. Luckily her part was best played as a meek, weepy-eyed maid.

She averted her eyes from the scaffold and concentrated on placing one foot in front of the other. She looked at the stone wall construction and focused on the colors and grit, and not the imposing façade. Stephen exchanged a few words with the guards, and they were admitted.

Audrey paid little attention to what he was saying. Her normally perfect memory saw only flashes of faces and flares of light. Features wobbled in her view, and she stumbled into Stephen's back. He ran an encouraging hand down her arm. It was so quick that it looked like he was gesturing. But it allowed her time to still her racing heart and regain her bearings.

The prison interior was much the same as she remembered. A dark, dank place with neither light nor heat. A familiar face walked past and as a matter of course, she ducked her head. She doubted she would be recognized. She barely resembled the girl who had been imprisoned here. The thought didn't stop her knees from knocking.

From a distance, cries of pain were audible. Everything around her was growing dim. For once her fear was too strong for chastisement. She felt an instinctive urge to flee. She looked up into Stephen's face and saw his lips move. He gently shook her, and the rest of him became brighter.

"Diana, we are going to be admitted. We have very little time, however. Are you ready?"

Something in his voice caused her to snap back, both mentally and physically. She straightened. Faye was somewhere below, waiting for her. "Yes, Your Grace. I am ready."

He nodded, and the man to whom Stephen had been talking pocketed some coins. Stephen must have bribed him. In doing so, he too was breaking the law. Why was he doing this for her?

They walked down the hall, and she hurried to keep up. Time was short, that she understood. Stephen had mentioned that he hoped to arrive during the guards' shift change, hence their early arrival.

They walked for what felt like forever down into

the belly of the cold beast. She shut out the sights and smells and focused on Stephen's back. People wailed and called out, but she ignored their cries. She couldn't afford to let them in and break the fragile grip she had on her panic. The panic was throbbing beneath a layer so thin she felt every step she took would shatter it.

"Up ahead is where ye will find the unforgivables. Ye have ten minutes before the change of guards." The henchman shuffled off. As soon as he was out of sight Stephen touched her hand.

"Quickly, Audrey. Which way?"

She allowed her senses to open. The shock reeled her back and he gripped her hand.

"Audrey, I can't lose you now. Remember our role here. You aren't nervous, remember?"

She looked into his eyes and nodded. "I remember."

Holding tightly to her lifeline, she looked around. Walls, bars, hands gripping bars. That was familiar. Wailing, dirt and slop buckets, urine and body odor. That was familiar too.

"I need another minute."

He nodded, but she noticed the tension etched in the corners of his eyes.

She looked at the floor and the walls. The pitched dirt and grime. The stones inset in . . .

"Down that corridor," she said.

She walked to the right, and Stephen maintained her pace. She didn't release his hand. Direction started to return, and she made a few more turns before coming to a very familiar area.

She ran to the bars of a cell, nearly dragging Stephen in her frenzy.

"Faye! Where are you?"

She poked her head between two bars, straining to see. Then between two more, not finding a familiar face in the grime.

"Faye?"

"She's not here."

Audrey looked toward the voice. A bedraggled man with long, matted hair was shackled in the corner. Tension and panic threatened to choke her. "Where is she?" Audrey croaked.

"She's been gone for several days now. Men came and took her away. She was drugged something fierce."

Yes, she would have had to be for anyone to transport her feisty sister without losing a limb in the process.

"Do you know where they took her?"

The man shrugged. The other prisoners were barely paying them any attention. "No. Do you got any food?"

She started to shake her head before she remembered her other scone. Fishing it from her pocket, she tossed it to the man in the corner. The other prisoners perked up and looked at the small bit of food like ravenous beasts. Tears pricked at her eyes. She remembered that feeling very well.

Stephen tugged her hand. "We need to go."

"What if she is in another part of the prison?"

He squeezed her hand. "Do you believe that?"

She looked at her feet. "No. She's gone."

"I'm sorry, Audrey." He said it softly. She nodded, and he tugged her toward the exit.

Leaving Newgate proved faster, but it was as much a nerve-wracking experience for her as entering. Faye was gone. Relief and terror vied for prominence. At least Faye had been released and hadn't spent the last few days in those evil cells. But if Faye had been housed there, they could have freed her.

Travers could have her stashed anywhere. And with anyone. She could be in a much worse situation for all Audrey knew.

Travers had lied. That wasn't a shock in and of itself, but if he had lied about Newgate, it was a possibility that Faye wasn't even alive. No, Audrey wouldn't even consider that possibility.

Stephen lifted her into the carriage and pulled

her on his lap. Her entire body was shaking as the carriage began moving.

It didn't seem fair. She and Faye had quit last year. They had stopped their illegal activities, tried to reform and lead a quiet life. But they seemed destined never to find it.

Stephen rubbed her back, but she felt empty inside. She felt powerless. Her normal defenses were falling apart around her. Nothing would ever work out, nothing was the truth. She despised the victimized feeling that was coiling around her, but her protective walls had taken one too many assaults.

"Where do you suppose they've taken your sister?"

"I don't know." Her answer was hollow.

"Who has her?"

"Travers has her somewhere." It just didn't matter anymore if he knew. None of it mattered.

"Telling me helps more than you realize."

She stared at the door panel. "That's good."

He gave her a shake. "I know you're upset, but snap out of it. You won't help your sister this way. Be happy that she isn't in there."

Audrey bit her lip and looked at him. "I am happy she isn't in Newgate. I just don't have another plan now that she's not there."

"Well, I told you last night that Travers's family has properties bordering mine."

Audrey focused on his mouth and some feeling came back into her limbs. "You did. I just didn't think about it other than being concerned you knew each other."

"We're going to have a long talk about dear Henry Travers on the way to the country tomorrow."

She studied his face, only a few inches from hers. "Why are you helping me?"

"Because."

"That's not an answer."

"I'm helping you because I want to." He looked irritated.

"And you think you know where Faye could be held?" Her world had somersaulted. The shock was still interrupting something in her brain. Everything had turned upside down. Stephen had somehow taken charge, and she felt as if she were flopping in the breeze, witless.

"No, not for certain, but Travers has a number of properties. He owns places in remote areas that he could easily stow someone without attracting undo attention. One is in Buckinghamshire very near here, about a day's ride. Fieldstone Manor, one of the ducal estates is next door." She saw him grimace. "Actually, this trip will serve dual purposes for me."

"To determine what is wrong with your lands?"

"Yes, I have only been to the estate a few times, and those were many years ago. I don't know what I'll find when I arrive."

"I can definitely be of assistance." Color was returning to her cheeks. She was regaining her spirit.

He raised a brow.

"I've been to Fieldstone a few times. To your property, not Travers's. I had never met him before this year. But I know your estate well."

He gave a short laugh. "How's that for a partnership. I'm helping to find your criminal sister, and you are helping me inventory my estate using the knowledge of your criminal past."

She studied him. "Sounds like a fair trade to me."

He returned her gaze as the carriage stopped. "Let's hope it turns out well for both of us." He moved to the door. "It's important that I meet with a few of my people before we leave. You are welcome to stay in my town house if you need."

"No. No, I need to make my own plans." She moved toward the door. "I will return in the morning."

She knew he wanted to say something more. But they both sat in silence.

As the carriage slowed, Stephen nodded to her. "I will see you at dawn tomorrow."

Audrey turned and nearly ran from the carriage.

Stephen watched her go, then returned to his town house. He didn't know what to say to her anymore. She reminded him of his favorite plants—hardy and invincible one moment, delicate and vulnerable the next. She was all of those things, but somewhere in between was the real Audrey, and he desperately wanted to find her.

He sent a scheduling note to Logan. He planned to inform the solicitor in person that he would be traveling to Fieldstone tomorrow to inspect the properties. Stephen had considered not telling Logan, but gauging the man's reaction to his announcement would speak volumes. Stephen would ascertain if his suspicions were true.

He prowled through the library and absently examined the volumes on the shelf as Audrey had done. He had never been fond of ton living, and now it was thrust upon him. In the past, he preferred to remain a gentleman on the fringe of society, able to come and leave as he pleased and responsible only to himself.

He walked to the window. He was perplexed. Now he didn't know what he wanted. Of course, he didn't want to be in debt. But to be alone no longer held the joy that it once had. He had been steadily changing over the past year. James and Calliope's happy marriage had made an impact on him. They reminded him of the happiness his parents shared, an aberration among the ton.

But his parents' love hadn't been enough to sustain them on earth. He smiled at the foolish thoughts of a young boy, but emotions rarely followed a logical path. It was becoming more difficult to hide behind the façade.

A couple strolled down the street, a young boy and girl at their sides. He didn't want a typical ton marriage, and if his suspicions proved true, then he didn't care what anyone said, a ton marriage wasn't his only choice.

Logan cursed for the second time in his fifty-five years as he stumbled down Stephen Chalmers's steps after their meeting. This new duke was too perceptive by far. Things were spinning wildly out of control.

Thirty years of doing his best for the Dukes of Marston and it boiled down to dirty secrets and blackmail. He headed to Bow Street. It might not be too late to salvage things.

But he needed to make sure he was covered first.

With shaking hands, he jotted a note and handed it to a young boy on the corner. *We have a problem . . .*

"What's this all about?" Maddox grumbled as he slid onto the tavern bench.

Travers rolled the bottom of his glass in a circle on the table. "We have a problem."

"Yeah?" Maddox grabbed the serving girl and ordered her to bring him ale. He turned back. "What problem?"

Travers grimaced at the man's lack of finesse. If it weren't for Audrey, he wouldn't put up with the fool across the table. "It looks like your dear step-daughter has betrayed us. She was with the Duke of Marston last night."

"Yeah, so what? Sounds like your problem, not mine."

"No, Maddox, all of my problems are now your problems." Maddox snorted and Travers smiled unpleasantly. "I wouldn't be so quick to dismiss the issue. I know for a fact the Hendrix brothers are looking for a man who owes them a considerable amount of money."

Maddox's laughter ceased, and his face blanched. Travers examined his perfect nails. "Nasty business they are in. Did you know that the bodies of the last men who crossed the brothers weren't identified for weeks? They had to find all of the pieces first."

Sweat dotted Maddox's forehead. "These men, um, who are they looking for?"

"Seems that the man they are looking for gave a fake name and address. Good thinking, but not brilliant. All it takes is a description of the man and a few hints."

The serving girl appeared, and Maddox snatched the mug from her hand. "So what do you want from me?" His hand shook and ale sloshed onto the table.

Travers moved his pristine sleeve out of the way. To what depths had he sunk to be conversing with this buffoon? He smoothed his cuff. A foolish question; he had always done what needed to be done. "I want you to talk to your stepdaughter."

"She ain't gonna listen. Damn girl has a wicked tongue and a more wicked reach with those knives. You talk to her—you seem to rein her in proper." He fingered his arm and took another drink.

"And then what would I need you for?"

Maddox paused and lowered his mug. He finally seemed to understand. "Fine. I'll get her to see reason." He moved his shoulders as if gearing up for a fight.

"I don't want you to beat her. Use . . . incentives. You can even use her sister Faye as an enticement."

"Don't know nothing about Faye."

"She's all tied up. A pig in a poke." Travers smiled at his own joke.

Maddox looked confused, but that was neither unusual nor unexpected. "What?"

"Nothing. Listen, I want you to—"

"Sir, a message for you."

Travers looked at the boy who had run to their table. He took the note, and the boy hopped on one foot waiting for a reply.

He read the note, gripping it more tightly as he read each line. He didn't usually shoot the messenger, but by God he was damn tempted. The boy seemed to sense his irritation and scooted back a few inches.

He turned to the boy. "Get me paper, pen, and wax."

The boy ran to the bar, and Travers traced a furrow in the tabletop with his finger. He had to stay focused—he couldn't lose everything now. His partner would kill him.

The boy returned, and Travers grabbed the writing implements and scratched out a few lines. *Gather the new recruits and meet me in an hour.* He sealed the wax with his ring and flipped a coin to the boy, who snatched it and the note and ran off.

Maddox raised his brow inquiringly, but on seeing the wrathful expression on Travers's face, said nothing. Travers stretched his tight fingers, then curled them. Stretch, curl, stretch, curl.

When he felt calm enough to speak he said, "What can you tell me about Audrey's dealings with Chalmers?"

Maddox snorted. "The bloke has been damn near courting her. Came by the other day to take her to the park, then the theater."

"What?" Travers's rage built. "Why didn't you tell me?"

Maddox shrugged. "You didn't ask, did you? Besides, I ain't your damn slave."

Travers reached across the table and grabbed Maddox by the lapels lifting him off his stool. He had to restrain himself from slamming his fist into the man's nose. *Cap the anger for now*, he said to himself. *Funnel it later*.

"Well, you are now my slave. I want accurate nightly reports from you and those worthless servants I hired."

Maddox avoided his eyes. Ah, so he had thought he would get in trouble if he told. That explained things better. He could use Maddox's fear to his advantage.

"Yeah, whatever." Maddox slugged down his drink, but Travers could see the panic building in the man's body.

Good, he could forget about Maddox for a moment and concentrate on the more pressing problem. Travers jerked his knee up and down, a bad habit when he was in a rage. His toes absorbed the shock. A band of fear laced through his anger. By now Chalmers had to know about his involvement. He had been surprised to hear that he was packing to go to the country, but the note made everything clear. And that was dangerous. Audrey was going to be very, very sorry that she had crossed him. He was done being patient with her.

"The two of them went to Newgate to free Faye today. And Chalmers is leaving for a trip to the country in the morning." Travers gripped his tankard tightly. "She has thrown her lot in with Chalmers, has she? We'll see what Chalmers has to say when she is arrested for murdering his solicitor."

He laughed and began to focus his anger and fear. "Yes, poor little Audrey is about to be thrown into prison for real this time. And she's going to be begging me to save her."

Maddox looked at him as if he had lost his mind. "Thought you needed her to complete your tasks, or plans, or whatever it is you're doing."

"Oh, she will complete the tasks." He would make certain of it. "If she doesn't—"

Another messenger appeared at their table and handed him a note. The boy took off without awaiting a reply as Travers opened the note. It was Audrey's handwriting.

You will have your long-lost item soon.

He laughed, a bit of euphoria lacing through the rage and fear. The power of it was exhilarating. "She will complete her tasks indeed."

He laughed again, but the pitch was abnormally high. He cleared his throat. "Clever girl. She will complete them better now than she could have before. And Chalmers is going to be very sorry he got involved with her. Very sorry. I could not have asked for more."

But Audrey still needed to be punished for her insubordination at Newgate. Having her spend a little more time in prison would curb her independence before he graciously made it up to her afterward.

There was no need to inform his partner about these latest developments. It was time for him to take charge. The fear left him. Audrey would steal back what rightfully belonged to him, then he could pin everything on her if need be.

Oh, how good this plan was starting to feel. Maddox looked at him as if he had lost his mind. Travers decided against sharing the latest bit of information. Having Maddox work on Audrey would be an amusing interlude while he waited for the finale to explode in Chalmers's face.

Chalmers was the interloper who had taken everything of his. Just like his own brother had, the two of them thick as thieves, always the ones who had everything and everyone's attention. His mother and father had had no room left for anyone else. How he despised them all. How he would show them all.

Chapter 12

It was late when Audrey returned to her town house. She had avoided it for most of the day. Walking around town, visiting Flanagan, and talking to some of the street informants had neither settled her nerves nor helped her solve any of her problems. Flanagan had people searching for Faye, which made her feel marginally better. If she couldn't find her, he probably would.

That Flanagan was assisting her was not as surprising as she would have found it a week ago. Some crazy happenstance was causing her to have more faith in people, and she couldn't quell the urge to trust. That in itself was dangerous.

Ever since she had learned about the relationship between Travers and Chalmers, something had felt out of place. The piece of information she had unearthed earlier had been both interesting and daunting. If her suspicions were confirmed, then life would be getting more complicated soon.

Meanwhile, Maddox was out for the evening. Probably gaming again and getting them in deeper trouble. Audrey was relieved he was gone. She pulled out a case to pack for the journey. Her riding habit and a few dresses should be sufficient for a few days. She and Stephen wouldn't be gone long, and traveling gear was the most important.

Light feet padded down the hall, and her maid opened the door. She took one look at the case and narrowed her eyes. "Are we going somewhere?"

"No, *we're* not," she stressed. "But I'm leaving for a few days."

"Master Travers won't be taking well to your leaving."

"No? Well, I'm sure he will recover."

The girl gave her a sour look and left, no doubt to pen a note to her master.

Audrey finished packing and realized how hungry she was. One dry scone was all she had eaten today. She foraged through the kitchen, finding cooked meat, bread, and cheese. As she ate, she thought about the plans for the next few days. She was juggling many loose ends. If any of them came crashing down, she was going to be in greater trouble.

The front door slammed, and a voice bellowed her name as she finished her last bite. She wanted to avoid Maddox if at all possible so she cleaned up and gingerly opened the door.

Maddox stood belligerently in the foyer, blocking her path. "The maid said you're going to the country tomorrow. What for? Everything you need is here in London."

Audrey tapped her toe in irritation. "No, I have some things to take care of in the country."

"Travers is not going to like it. He's already in a fit about you and that duke fellow."

"Travers is perpetually piqued. He'll recover."

"Not this time, he won't. Never seen the man so angry before. Got something against that duke. You'd better mind yourself, gal. And if you can't mind yourself, well, then, I'm to do it for you."

She narrowed her eyes. "Heard you are in trouble again. Been gambling with other people's money? You should watch who you mark, you never were any good at staying away from the big boys' tables. And when you play with the big boys, you're bound to lose."

Maddox looked angry, but his eyes were wild. They focused on her with a wheedling smile.

"You'll give me the notes to pay them back. I'm in charge of this operation after all. I need some blunt to keep it running."

"I'm not giving you a pence, you weasel."

"Why are you such a grouchy wench? One would think you'd have gotten over yourself by now. That thief fellow didn't cuff you enough."

Her nails dug into her palms. She had avoided this conversation since setting eyes on her stepfather again. Anger shoved past her carefully constructed dispassion.

"Our 'schoolmaster' cuffed us plenty. Isn't that what you told all our family friends? That Faye and I were at school? And how was that trip to Italy that you took while we were at *school*? Did you manage to pay off the men who were after you then?"

"Audrey, I was just trying to keep the two of you safe. I came back for you, didn't I?"

"Yes, three years later you returned. Interested in the money we could make you again. I never did ask whether you intended to use us as your personal thieves, or if you'd planned to sell us once again to the highest bidder." She was breathing hard. "Which was it?" She bit out.

"It's not like life was rough for you. Damn, girl, you'd think I was some two-bit pimp. I didn't sell you to the madam, did I? I sold you to a fellow that would keep both of you in line."

"You're not supposed to sell people!" She shrieked. She had held it all in for so long. "You left us in hell."

He shrugged. "I was sold as a child. I turned out just fine. That's the way of things. And you're free now, so quit complaining."

"It shouldn't *be* the way of things, you ass. What the hell is wrong with you? Did *you* like being sold?"

"That's what happens to children on the street."

"We weren't on the street." She ground each word. "And we had money and friends. Two things you know nothing about."

He shrugged, and she felt like throttling him. He had wagered all their money, and when he had sold them it had effectively cut them off from any friends. Buyers didn't just let their acquisitions run off to find a new family.

"What did you intend, Maddox, when you came back three years later? We were no longer children. What were you going to do with us?"

All traces of pleasantness disappeared from his eyes. They were dark and a bit wild again. "Hadn't quite decided that. Would have had to see how much you were worth."

Cold rage settled in her gut. Audrey drew a long finger down her right forearm. "Too bad you never had the chance."

Maddox unwittingly grabbed his scarred arm. "You bitch! It's time I taught you a lesson." He lunged toward her. She stepped aside and put her foot in his path. He tripped headfirst into the bookcase, fell to the floor, and was still.

Her hands were shaking as she walked over to make sure he was breathing. He was. She couldn't stay in the house and wait for Maddox to recover—she might do him more harm, and she had promised her mother on her deathbed to protect their family. And even though Audrey didn't consider Maddox part of the family, her mother had, and for that reason alone Audrey wouldn't harm him. She looked at his crumpled form. Well, she wouldn't harm him any more than necessary.

Audrey walked to her room. Protect him? No, that part of the promise had been completely negated the day he had sold them to the streets. So what if he had been sold as a child. As if that somehow made it acceptable. He had made a choice and had chosen greed over right. She knew that no matter what position she found herself in, she would never make the choice he had. Once she found Faye, Maddox would be permanently out of their lives.

Her hands shook as she placed the last of her items in her case. She was ready to juggle the biggest and most dangerous of the men in her life.

Chapter 13

S tephen gently stroked her long supple limbs and caressed her burgeoning buds. "Gorgeous."

He sank his hands deeper into her mass of curls. Slow and steady.

He arched her back and pushed in deeper.

"Almost there," he whispered.

He was so close. Sweat was beading on his forehead. She was a handful—young, beautiful, willful, if a bit clingy.

The fit was tight, and he made cooing noises as he thrust in a few inches, making small circles to allow more.

So close now. Just a bit more . . .

"Your Grace?" Grimmond called from the other side of the door.

"Please, not now, Grimmond," he snapped. He had told his butler he did not wish to be disturbed.

"You said to let you know if Miss Kendrick arrived. She is waiting in the library."

Desire to see Audrey warred with his need to finish. He looked down. He had been wooing this one for the last few days. She had just started showing signs of acceptance, and he almost had her.

He sighed. He needed to see Audrey. This could wait.

He patted the soil around her roots and sprinkled water on top. Hopefully she would stay strong for a few hours. Who knew, maybe Audrey was waiting to shoot him, and the meeting would take but minutes. In any event his blood was already heating in anticipation.

Roth was concerned Stephen would get a knife in the back. Even St. John, who was the most carefree individual in the service, had said something before Liddendock's party when they had been setting up the papers Audrey had stolen. His friends weren't mad to think so. In fact, Stephen acknowledged he was the mad one to go along with this scheme. He simply couldn't resist. He wanted the truth. He needed to know what Audrey and Travers were up to.

And he wanted to unlock Audrey's secrets. He needed to figure her out.

There was a vital link missing in the shipping plot. A key piece of information was unaccounted for, and it tickled the edge of his brain but wouldn't coalesce.

He washed his hands and strode to the library. Lingering in the doorway, he watched her stroke the spines of several books. He felt the caress down to his toes.

"Chalmers, your butler said you were busy. If you wish, I can return tomorrow."

She never turned around. He had made no sound when walking toward the library, yet she had known. He found himself smiling. "First, to what do I owe the honor of this late-night visit?"

She turned, but didn't smile. It was as if she were trying to determine if he were joking or not. Her solemn expression tugged at his heart. Someone had hurt her deeply. She looked more weary than she had this morning. It was as if she had more problems than just the hundred that had already been dropped on her head.

She visibly scanned him. "Been working in the backyard, Chalmers?"

He leaned against the doorframe. "Conservatory."

She nodded. She was clutching her reticule rather tightly.

He kept his tone light. "Would you like some tea?"

She cleared her throat. "I would love some."

Stephen nodded and rang for Grimmond.

"Yes, Your Grace?" Grimmond appeared in the door.

"Tea, please."

"Of course, Your Grace. And I put Miss Kendrick's bag in her room."

Her bag? Her room? "Thank you, Grimmond."

Audrey fidgeted. "I brought my case. I thought it easier to stay here tonight so that we could leave early in the morning."

Stephen was tortured by curiosity. She was obviously in trouble. But then again, since meeting him she was always in trouble. "Will you tell me what happened?"

She hesitated, then sat in one of the armchairs. "It is really nothing. Just old wounds I thought had healed."

"Can I help?"

She touched her brow. "No, but thank you for asking."

"Did you bring your maid?"

"No, I don't want her. She reports to Travers, and since we won't be making social calls, I can attend myself." Her voice grew frigid, and her eyes narrowed. "Afraid you'll have to marry me if we are seen together without a chaperone, Chalmers? Don't make me laugh. I won't get in the way of your heiress hunting."

Grimmond brought in the tea tray, placing it before her, thus interrupting Stephen's growing irritation caused by her words.

"That's not what I meant."

She sighed and leaned back in the chair. "I know. I'm testy, and I apologize."

His irritation vanished, and he was left speechless by her apology.

She seemed to interpret his thoughts and laughed deprecatingly. "I'm not totally devoid of manners, you know. I just don't usually choose to employ them. May I serve you?"

He nodded and watched in fascination as Audrey poured tea into the fragile china cups and passed his to him as if to the manner born.

They drank the tea in silence. Stephen hoped she would relax.

"I have no problem with your staying here."

A bit of the tension left her shoulders. "Thank you."

"Come, let's go to bed."

Let's go to bed. Audrey's heart leaped into motion. "What?"

"We need to rise early tomorrow."

"Yes, but . . ." But what?

He waited patiently for her to continue. She floundered for a response.

He took pity on her. "You go up. I need to finish some things in the conservatory. I'll see you in the morning."

Audrey exhaled loudly, not realizing she had been holding her breath. Grimmond was waiting outside and escorted her to the room she had occupied the previous night.

Her case was inside, and she removed her nightclothes. Now was perhaps her only time to search Stephen's chambers. He was downstairs, and his servants wouldn't be in this wing of the house.

She walked down the hall to his room and opened the door. She wondered momentarily why he had left it unlocked with a thief like her around, but perhaps he assumed she'd just pick it open anyway.

She poked through his dressers and wardrobe, found several secret compartments that contained nothing unusual. She was on a mission to satisfy her curiosity, and since she didn't know what he would say if he walked in, she finished her search quickly and returned everything to its place.

She felt momentarily guilty about rifling through her host's room, but changed into her nightclothes and slipped under the covers. She couldn't bring herself to turn off the light. Now that she was finally alone, she couldn't stop reflecting on their trip to Newgate. She had kept herself busy all day to avoid remembering. She had survived entering the prison again and felt stronger for the experience. But right now she didn't feel like being alone in the dark.

The clock struck half past, and she continued to stare at the ceiling. She assumed the servants had retired since no footsteps had passed her door. So why hadn't Stephen returned to his bedchamber. What was he doing in the conservatory? Some type of mad work on something green, no doubt. She whipped off her covers, slipped on a wrap, and grabbed the oil lamp.

Padding silently down the hall, stairs and foyer, she tried to jump from rug to rug to avoid the cold floors. Finally arriving at her destination, the same place where he had nearly seduced her last night, she pushed open the heavy door.

"Stephen?"

The interior was dark, and she held her lamp aloft, trying to see farther back. She wound around the plant stands and toward the back of the sweet-smelling room. A form was lying under the covers on the strange-looking sofa. She approached as silently as possible and held the lamp over him. He looked relaxed, his golden features perfect. The top of his bare chest was visible, and his arms were resting on top of the covers. The light from her lamp danced on his hair like sunshine. The world was never dark around him. She fidgeted, then turned to leave.

His hand closed around her wrist before she even realized he had moved.

"What is it, Audrey?"

She turned and saw him regarding her. Had he known she was there the whole time? It occurred to her that he might have thought she was trying to murder him. She held out the hand not holding the lamp to show him it was empty.

"I was restless and couldn't sleep. I was just wondering why you were still awake."

It sounded lame even to her ears, but she hadn't really thought through why she was seeking him out. She had just been staring up at the ceiling and decided to come.

She rushed into speech before he could respond. "Why are you sleeping down here?" She shivered.

"I sometimes stay here if one of the plants is being fussy."

She looked at the darkened workbench. There were a few leafy silhouettes, but nothing she could identify. "Oh."

"Do you need something? I can ring the staff."

"No, no." She shook her head and shivered. The cold floor seeped into her toes. "I was just having trouble sleeping." Her brain supplied the rest of the sentence, *sleeping alone in that dark room*, although she refrained from saying it aloud.

She met his eyes for a long second, and he shifted onto his side and lifted the cover. It took but a second more for her to put the lamp on the floor and scoot under the covers he had already warmed. She blew out the lamp and promptly fell asleep with her feet tucked next to his.

Chapter 14

Audrey woke slowly, feeling refreshed and ready to tackle the day. She had spent a dreamless night, the first one in a long time. Light filtered in through the windows, and she snuggled back into the warm body holding her.

It took a moment for reality to sink in fully. There was a warm, pulsing body cocooned next to hers. She rolled to her right. Dark green smoldering eyes met hers.

"Good morning." His voice was husky, but his eyes were unreadable. "Did you sleep well?"

She glanced away, unaccountably embarrassed. She had, after all, been the one to seek him out in the night.

"Uh, good morning." Her mind registered the

sunlit conservatory, a pair of trousers tossed across a chair, and the sounds of the servants moving through the house. She wanted to pull the covers over her head and expire on the spot. She was in her nightclothes and was going to have to get out of bed and walk across the entire house to reach her traveling case.

She moved her leg a bit. His legs were bare. Therefore, who would rise first and retrieve her clothing? Having often worked with men who forgot she was a woman, she was no longer embarrassed at seeing a half-naked man. But the thought of seeing Stephen in such a state made her stomach do little leaps.

She shifted to allow him to rise, but brought herself in closer contact. He put a restraining hand on her arm. "Please stop moving around. Unless you wish to sorely strain my last ounce of reserve." His voice was tense.

"Oh." She froze, then scooted out from under the covers, grabbing the blanket as cover and removing the choice of who would rise first.

Well, actually, on further inspection, he had risen first, just not in . . .

She blushed furiously. "I-I-I am just going to return to my room. I'm sure you want to get up . . . I mean leave soon."

He gave her a sardonic look, and she turned to go. His voice interrupted her flight. "You can use the circular staircase if you'd like. It comes out next to my room. I'm sure you can find your way to your chambers from there." He pointed to the staircase in the corner.

She ran for it, trying not to look back down at him lying on the sofa. At the top of the steps she peeked into the hall. No one was present and she ran into her room. She was appalled to see the time. It was nearly noon. She couldn't remember the last time she had slept that long. Changing took little time, and she found herself with nothing to do but fret.

She answered a knock at her door, and a maid announced breakfast. She followed her and saw a footman enter and retrieve her case.

Stephen wasn't in the dining room and Audrey put some food on her plate and pushed it around. She was becoming too reliant on Stephen's generosity, first in Newgate, then again last night. She needed to stop the progress of dependence.

She forced herself to eat everything she had heaped on her plate. She'd need the energy and refused to let her emotions override good sense again. At least for now. She had the feeling that her emotions, usually reined in, might be her downfall.

It would be an amusing notion if it weren't so discomfiting. She was known as icy. If any of Flanagan's men could see her now, they would laugh.

Stephen walked into the room, whistling, and served himself. "We will leave in fifteen minutes, unless you have anything else you need to retrieve?"

There was nothing she could retrieve at the moment. "No, I'm ready."

She found herself alone with him in the carriage exactly fifteen minutes later.

"We'll stop at Bailey's Inn for dinner."

"That's fine." She pretended interest in the scenery as they left the city. "Why didn't you wake me earlier? I can't believe I slept that long."

He gave her another unreadable glance. "You needed rest, and it was no problem to wait the extra few hours. I sent word ahead that we will arrive late."

"Then we won't be able to search tonight."

"Searching tonight wasn't on the agenda."

She narrowed her eyes, hoping for a fight. "Whose agenda? If we hadn't slept so late, we would have been ready to look tonight."

He leaned back and looked out the window. "Our getting attacked or killed is not going to help your sister."

"But at night we would have had the element of surprise."

He gave her a barely passing glance, as if she were nothing more than a pest. His disregard irritated her more than if he had shown anger.

"Does your nerve challenge you, Chalmers?"

He continued to look at the passing countryside, the bluebells and wildflowers swaying in the breeze. She again felt the unease of swirling emotions. She latched on to her anger as something she could control.

"I wouldn't have thought it of you. You seemed such a commanding individual at one time."

He turned to her. "Audrey, I don't know what you hope to accomplish with this tirade. Would arguing cure whatever ails you?"

She knew she was behaving irrationally, but her hackles went up immediately at his charge. "Forget it, Chalmers."

"You only call me Chalmers when you are irritated."

"Better than being called Your Grace. I only call you that when I dislike you."

A smile nearly touched his lips. "I do hate that."

She left the ambiguous comment alone. Conflicted emotions swirled through her. She looked at her hands. His smile warmed her, and although his presence drew her in, she didn't want it. Relying on people had never been a good option for her in the past, and she didn't know why that would change now. It wasn't that she didn't want to rely on people. It was just too rife with danger.

She was annoyed at how cowardly that made her feel.

"I saw you examining my books. Voltaire and Swift. Do you like their work?"

She peeked at him, but he seemed interested, not just poking fun. She nodded. "Yes. I love satire."

"You and Calliope would get on famously. Which authors do you like best?"

She frowned at the mention of the other woman, but answered his question, which started a serious dialogue about satire, religious intolerance, and the role of literature. The interchange was invigorating. It had been a long time since she had been able to talk and argue with someone who shared her interests. Interests that her gentle parents had loved.

The afternoon passed quickly thanks to their lively conversation. And as the carriage pulled in front of the country inn where they were to stop for dinner, she felt herself drowning in the spell he had cast. It had started a year ago, and the past few days were tightening the net around her.

Audrey watched Stephen speak with the innkeeper. The innkeeper kept bowing. In fact he looked like he might fall over.

Ironic how one level of society was so like another. Every stratum of humanity established a hierarchy. She was accustomed to getting what she wanted in the London underground, just as Stephen was in English society. His domain was just larger, with more respect and power. She'd had to slave to get hers, while his had come with ease and birth.

Stephen turned and walked back to the carriage. "Dinner will be ready soon. We are being given chambers to wash and rest."

Her stomach did a little flip. "Together?"

"Unfortunately, no." He winked, and her stomach did another flip.

The inn's mistress cooed over Audrey and how tired she must be, beckoning her to follow. The woman chattered the entire way.

"His Grace honors us with his presence. And yours as well, my lady. I understand you are His Grace's cousin and traveling to see a sick relative in the country? We've had a bout of fever in these parts . . ."

The woman continued on until she opened the door.

Audrey sank onto the bed and stretched her legs. A moment later her case was delivered.

The bed was soft and inviting. A short nap sounded divine.

* * *

A soft tickle worked its way from her nose to her ear. She batted it away but it returned a scant second later. She balled a fist and swung. A solid object blocked her path.

"Next time I'll know better."

Audrey opened an eye to see Stephen rubbing his chin. A feather in his other hand. She jerked upright.

"What are you doing in here?"

"Dinner is getting cold, cousin. I came in to see if you were ready to eat."

She was still fully dressed, but seeing him on the edge of her bed made her feel slightly exposed. He had watched her sleep this morning as well. She pushed him off the bed.

He slid from the bed gracefully, not landing on the floor in a lump as she'd intended.

He was still rubbing his chin, but the sparkle in his eyes was present. "See you downstairs, cousin."

Audrey dragged herself from the bed, checked that the door was locked, washed, and quickly redressed. All she needed was for Chalmers to open the door while she was naked. He'd probably just be amused.

And then she'd have to kill him and ruin everything.

A maid met her outside the door and led her to

the dining area. It was a small, intimately set room. Stephen must have ordered it. Or more probably the inn owner had kicked anyone else out of it.

"Audrey, you're frowning."

"That's because I'm stuck here with you, Chalmers."

"Then you should be smiling. All of the ladies wish they were stuck with me in a cozy setting like this."

"Then the world must be in a sad state of affairs."

"Ah, just like you then."

"No."

He grinned.

"I meant, yes, I am in a sad state of affairs."

He nodded, a serious look on his face.

The innkeeper bustled in with their meal, fawning over them both.

Audrey quirked a brow. "Yes, my good man, if you could so kindly bring us your best brandy as well?"

The innkeeper assured her he had a fine label available and hurried out.

"You like brandy?" Stephen asked.

"No, the stuff is vile. But you like it."

He showed no surprise that she knew, he just nodded. "You should try one of my favorites. You might change your mind."

She shook her head. "Even the stuff you store in your cabinet is terrible."

Stephen laughed so hard that the innkeeper's wife popped her head around the corner to see if there was anything amiss. The innkeeper brought the brandy and left them alone once again.

"Is there anything at any of my properties that you have not snooped through?"

She shrugged, but the question burned her. Yes, there definitely was.

"Eat, then we will drive the rest of the way. A few more hours is all we have left."

Audrey ate her remaining asparagus and sliced the veal.

"Tomorrow you can show me around the estate," Stephen said.

"Very funny."

Stephen put his fork down. "Actually, it has been since my childhood that I visited. My parents preferred to remain close to home, in Shropshire. And after their deaths . . . well, I was shipped around to various family members. When I came of age my work kept me in London when I wasn't serving abroad."

"Ah, yes. The infamous spy."

"That's supposed to be secret, you know."

Audrey shrugged and cut another piece of meat. "Hard to keep secrets these days, Chalmers."

"Yes, Audrey, I do agree." He gave her a direct look.

Audrey put down her fork, no longer hungry. Stephen took a sip of brandy and continued to look at her. She felt stripped of her remaining secrets. What did he know?

She picked the fork back up and moved the meat around her plate. "What are your intentions, now that you're the duke?"

Stephen grimaced. "Take my seat in Parliament, worry about my lands, bully the common folk. The regular tasks of the nobility."

Audrey couldn't resist a smile.

Stephen flexed his shoulder, rolling it back and forth.

"What's wrong with your shoulder? Old and decrepit already?"

He smiled, then made a face. "An old wound from last year."

"Did you accidentally shoot yourself? And here I thought you seemed rather graceful for a bumbling lord."

He ignored her baiting and rolled his shoulder again. "Took a tumble into the Thames."

Her heart sped up, but she covered any outward reaction by playing with her fork. "Ah, I stand by the bumbling, in that case."

"Well, it was either that or be beaten to death. I thought a swim a good alternative in that instance."

"How was your swim?" She could have kicked herself for asking. Why had she just said that?

He looked cheerful. "Don't know. I promptly blacked out. No idea how I survived. Someone fished me from death's door and tended to my wounds."

An image of wet, blond hair clinging to his forehead and the chill of his body next to hers came unbidden to her mind. The image of not having dry trousers in his size came next. She lowered her head to cover her reaction to the second memory.

The innkeeper appeared with an assortment of tarts for dessert. She snatched a lemon tart, thankful for the interruption. Her mind was still focused on her memories as she devoured the dessert.

"I agree."

Audrey looked at him, startled.

"Your reaction to the dessert showed on your face."

Audrey put the tart down slowly. Her reaction hadn't been solely to the dessert, not that he had any idea where her mind had wandered. Stephen was wheedling past her defenses. She had to put them soundly back in place.

"They are satisfactory. Eat yours, and let's go. You seem to like tarts well enough."

He lost his smile. "I allowed you to defame Calliope the other day in your ignorance, but no more. Curb your tongue."

"And if I don't?"

"Then I will make you curb it."

"Chalmers, you have an active imagination."

His eyes narrowed, and her blood heated at the dangerous intentions lurking there.

"Am I to understand that you don't think I can keep you quiet?"

"You are quick at times, Chalmers."

Stephen leaned back and popped the rest of the tart in his mouth, chewing slowly. The look in his eyes was still present, however, and her blood boiled. Memories pressed against the backs of her eyes.

She tried to calm herself down. "Quick, but definitely not up to the challenge. Why, I'll bet that—"

Said quickness was demonstrated as he leaned forward, gripped her waist, and yanked her forward. She landed facedown in a heap on his lap. He trailed a finger down her shoulder blade and curved his hand around her hip. Her breath caught, and her mind went blank. Her breasts were pressed against his thighs. Thighs that she had seen bare before.

A deep beat began just below his hand, at her center. He skimmed a finger just above her backside and up her spine. His fingers worked into the hair at the nape of her neck. He pressed closer, and she could feel the warm air tickling her skin.

His lips caressed the back of her neck, his fingers trailed a path down her spine, around her thighs, and up toward the center of the frantic heat he had produced. His fingers neared and—

He thrust her back into her chair. She knew her mouth hung open, but shock had muddled her wits.

He popped another tart in his mouth, chewed slowly, and said, "Ah, you know a dessert is good when the silence literally vibrates the air."

Fury poured through her, and she grabbed the knife on the table. The innkeeper walked into the room.

"Was the fare satisfactory, Your Grace?"

Stephen rose, and Audrey removed her hand from the knife. She listened, fuming, as Stephen thanked the man and refused his offer of lodging for the night. She thought of him reaching for her, even in his delirious state. Of the things he had unknowingly revealed about his body and the way he thought.

She'd get even with him. She'd get even before they reached his estate.

Stephen was only slightly worried. Audrey had been livid after his earlier stunt. But she had recovered quickly. They had taken to the carriage and sat in silence for the past few hours. Until the light waned she engrossed herself in her book. They were almost to the estate.

Audrey spoke for the first time since leaving the inn. "How much farther?"

"Half an hour, maybe less."

She nodded, lapsed back into silence, and closed her eyes.

He had been studying her for the past few hours, first in the fading daylight, then in the evening shadows. The way her lashes brushed her cheeks still caused an odd flutter—the same flutter that had been present while he watched her sleep last night and before dinner. He really ought to pay heed to the warnings. He was definitely thinking with his—

Her eyes popped open, and she looked at him. "I need to thank you again for the way you have come to my rescue. Please forgive me for any bad behavior. It's just that I'm not used to working with my enemy."

She put a hand on his knee, and the warning bells that had sounded when she began the speech turned into blaring screams.

She ran her tongue slowly across her lips. His body leaped in reaction. She leaned forward, which put pressure on her hand, causing it to move slightly upward. His body happily moved as well.

"Stephen, do you think maybe we can set aside our differences? Just for a few days? And really work together?"

She arched toward him and her hand continued its assent. His breathing increased, but he said nothing. Warnings bells were ringing in his brain, and other lewd thoughts were shouting from an entirely different part of his anatomy.

She slid onto his side of the carriage, her hand was now stroking the upper portion of his thigh.

"I remember what you said about sealing our deal," she whispered, her breath hot against his ear.

The soft whoosh of air was driving him crazy as she continued, "I think maybe we should seal this one too, don't you?"

Stephen moved to grab her, but the coach stopped, and she slid to her own seat, her hand trailing provocatively across his lap.

An eager footman opened the door a scant second later. "Welcome home, Your Grace."

The footman assisted Audrey as she exited the carriage, and Stephen resisted the urge to plant his feet on her backside and push.

"Your Grace?"

The footman was waiting for him to exit.

"Just a moment. I need to straighten some things that shifted during our travel."

"We can clear it up for you, Your Grace."

"Nonsense." It took all of Stephen's efforts not to snap at the helpful servant. "There are just a few things here that need to be adjusted."

Stephen took a few deep breaths and adjusted his clothing. If she thought she'd won, she was vastly mistaken.

He exited the carriage and was slightly mollified to see her hurrying into the house.

Footmen, maids, stable lads, housekeepers, and cooks dotted the front entrance. Greeting the staff took nearly an hour. The butler was explaining everything in a dry, formal manner. Grimmond would probably like him. Stephen vaguely wondered what Grimmond was going to do with all of the duplicate staff between the Marston households and his own. Stephen had tasked Grimmond with restoring order, but it might be quite entertaining to watch these two spar.

The cook asked if they were hungry. The housekeeper asked if there were any special requests. Finally, the butler, lord save him, steered him around the other servants, explaining that His Grace had estate business to attend and would surely rather meet the rest of the staff in the morning when he was fresh and relaxed.

Oh, he'd attend to business all right.

"Your cousin, Miss Kendrick, is in the Blue Room for the night. If another room would be more suitable, we can change it for her." A room with bars and locks would be most adequate, but he didn't think the butler would understand.

As they passed the Blue Room, the only closed door in the hall, the butler pointed it out.

Stephen hoped she'd have a nice night and pleasant dreams. She'd need them.

They reached the master suite, and Stephen dismissed the butler. His valet was waiting to assist him. After cleaning up from the ride, Stephen dismissed him as well. Prowling around the room, he found no urge to sleep, and realized he and Audrey hadn't discussed their plans for the next day. What if she went off on her own tonight?

He carried on a running conversation with himself. He wasn't going to go to her tonight. It would be a show of defeat. But he couldn't let her escape either. He would set a watch on the room. Satisfied with his decision, he strode to the door and opened it. Audrey stood on the other side in her nightclothes, her hand poised to knock.

Stephen cocked a brow. "Yes?"

"Um, I realized we hadn't discussed our plans." She looked him over, from top to bottom; a fine rose tinted her cheeks.

He leaned his bare shoulder against the doorframe and slipped his hands in his pockets, not willing to give her the upper hand in any way.

"So you came here to discuss our plans? Why couldn't we discuss them tomorrow." He watched her squirm and found himself enjoying her discomfort, especially after her stunt in the carriage.

"We can search tonight."

"No."

"Why not?" Her brows drew together in irritation.

"Because it's not safe. I don't know the lay of the land well enough, and neither do you."

"I know enough."

"Yes, we both know you know better than I how many pieces of silver I own, but this is different. Besides, we are tired. Be sensible."

242

Perhaps he should have left the sensible comment off; she looked even more irritated.

"I don't have time to bandy sensitivities with you, Chalmers; what I want to know is—"

Footsteps were rounding the corner, so he did the sensible thing and pulled her into the room and shut the door.

"Wha—" she sputtered.

The door started to open, and he pushed Audrey against it, closing it tight again. The action pushed his hips against hers.

The person on the other side seemed to hesitate. "Your Grace? I haven't properly put your clothes away."

"That isn't necessary. I've taken care of everything I need."

"Is there anything else you require tonight, sir?"

"No, thank you, I will see you in the morning."

His valet again hesitated. "Very well, Your Grace."

The man finally retreated.

"Well, uh, I suppose that was necessary." Audrey didn't seem to know what to do stuffed against the door. He saw the color in her cheeks and the deepened blue of her eyes.

"Mmmmm." He didn't move.

"Um, I think I will go back to my room now."

"No, I don't think so. You went to all the trouble

to come to mine, and now here you are."

He stepped a hair closer, putting his right leg in between hers.

She looked into his eyes. "Well, do you want to discuss our plans?" Her voice was a bit high.

"Yes, after that deal you promised me earlier."

"I didn't promise you a deal, I was merely—"

He didn't let her finish. Instead he crushed her to him, kissing her thoroughly. She was immobile for only a few seconds before shivers of desire raced though her, and her hands began their own exploration up his chest, around his neck, and into his hair.

Audrey pushed her body into Stephen's even as he pushed her against the door. He was devouring her with kisses, and she reveled in the assault. A voice in her head intruded momentarily, reminding her that he wasn't hers. But for a short time he could be. For tonight he could be hers.

She ran her fingers through his sunshine hair and gave a gentle tug. He responded by covering her mouth and increasing the depth and pressure of the kiss. Spirals of ecstasy coursed through her. So this is what it was to be consumed. She nearly melted down the door. Her fingers continued a path down his naked back. Strong muscles moved beneath her hands, and he responded by running his hands down her shoulder and over her breast. Her body leaped to his touch, and the bodice of her dress was suddenly too tight. Her breath came in short gasps.

The comfort of his arms, the strength he exuded was at odds with the dangerous feelings that his touch provoked. And the greedy creature that she was, she wanted it all for as long as she could have it. This was a gorgeous oasis in a deserted wasteland.

She arched against him, molding her lower body to his. He moved his hands from her breasts to her back and deftly unfastened the buttons. He stepped between her legs and feathered kisses down to her neck. She arched into him again, this time pressing herself in direct contact. He missed a button in response. Finally, the unfastened nightdress slipped downward, his lips following its path. Her breath caught as the gown reached the tips of her breasts. He pulled the fabric ever so slowly back and forth across her nipples, and she moaned aloud from the erotic sensation.

Her reaction fueled the urgency in him. He lifted her against the door, pulling her into his mouth. His free hand moved down her other breast, her side, and to her thigh. He bunched the fabric upward. The hem of her nightdress started its ascent. His mouth began its downward exploration, moving gloriously from one breast to the other. Heat zapped downward to where she was pressed against him, their hips rocking rhythmically together. The material along the side of her leg was finally freed.

He shifted a bit, putting one leg outside of hers and giving free rein to his hand.

She reached down toward him, but he blocked her attempt and pushed her more firmly against the door, taking her mouth fully in his. She threaded her hands through his hair and pulled him closer, tasting him, needing to devour him. This was exactly what she wanted and needed. To be enveloped in his embrace and made to feel like she was the only one on earth that mattered to him.

His clever fingers reached their goal, and she gasped into his mouth as he lightly stroked her. His kisses continued, and her sensitive nipples brushed against his rough chest in a rhythm that nearly ignited her. She stilled as one of his fingers slipped inside her while his thumb continued its exploration without.

He had taken control, and she could only move with the flow. One stroke, two strokes, two fingers, three strokes. In and out. Her body clenched and coiled around his fingers before exploding in a million fragments.

When her breathing returned to normal, Audrey released the tight grip on his neck, and the back of her head hit the door with a thud. But it didn't hurt. She didn't think anything could.

The draperies across the room could have ignited, and she wouldn't have been surprised. She searched his face. Stephen smiled, and his expression made her suddenly lazy heart speed up again.

She reached for the front flap of his trousers, but he intercepted her hand and lightly laid his forehead against hers.

"No, love, not tonight."

Not tonight? He had just made her feel like the most sensuous and alive woman in the world, which was not an easy feat to do to someone who had lately felt half-dead inside, and he didn't want or expect anything in return? Why? That tiny warning bell started again somewhere in her brain.

"I can see your discomfort. I can *feel* it," she said.

He didn't answer, but tugged her toward the bed. He pulled up her nightdress and redid the buttons while her mind was in denial. She wanted him. She knew he wanted her. His body was hard and ready. The tension was written all over his face. But he wasn't going to go any further tonight—she knew it, knew by the set of his features. She could seduce him, not that she had ever seduced anyone before, but she had been around the streets long enough to know how it was done. And she knew he would capitulate eventually. There was something between them that pulsed through the air.

The question was why wasn't he initiating the seduction? He had made it perfectly clear in the last few days that he wanted her.

Tonight, something in their relationship had changed. She chewed on her lip as he refastened the last button on her nightgown. Had she done something wrong?

He picked her up, placed her under the covers, and snuffed the light. Joining her there a few seconds later, he pulled her against him. Audrey fretted for a few minutes before the eventual tug of sleep and the haven of safety she always found in his arms pulled her under.

Stephen listened to her even breathing and expelled his breath. He stared into the darkness. His body throbbed and ached. Being this close to her without release was sheer torture. But he deserved it. Her confused face flashed in his mind. He couldn't explain to her why he had chosen to deny himself, deny them both, the pleasure.

Something about taking her against the door for

the first time had pulled some sense into him. He wanted her so badly, so strongly, that something in his mind had set off alarm bells to quit and not take their physical relationship further. If they made love, it was over for him. By doing so it would give her too much power over him. There would be no separation between the mission and the girl. There was barely any now. That she was going to betray him before this was over seemed inevitable. He wasn't sure how he would bear her betrayal if he allowed her to worm herself any closer into his heart. And he knew she was already pushing the barrier. It worried him more than he cared to admit.

Chapter 15

Audrey woke in Stephen's arms for the second time in as many days. She was nestled against him, and it felt good. She rotated to look at him. He was asleep, the light caressing his face.

Conflicting emotions surged through her. Stephen. Last night. Her body tingled in remembrance. But he was a distraction she couldn't afford. Her mind returned to the painful realization that Faye was still missing.

She touched his rough cheek. He stirred but didn't open his eyes. "Is it time to rise?"

She looked to the window. "Yes, I'd say it's around eight. Past time to be up and searching."

He opened a bloodshot eye. Now that he had his eyes open, he looked tired and a bit haggard.

"You look terrible."

"You look terrific."

She blushed and slipped from the bed, desire to remain cuddled safely under the covers nearly overriding the need to face the day. She didn't look back as she walked to the door. She needed to refocus. She looked into the hall and crossed the distance to her room. Hoping to find it empty, she was slightly embarrassed to find a maid waiting for her. The young woman hopped up and immediately helped her change.

The maid said nothing about Audrey's appearance or the fact that she hadn't slept in her own bed. She simply helped her change into a riding habit and pinned her hair while maintaining a pleasant chatter about the estate.

Audrey thanked her and the girl bowed and left. Too bad she couldn't steal the girl. She was a three hundred percent improvement over the maid in Travers's employ.

Audrey strapped her knives into place and checked her appearance in the cheval glass. She made sure no conspicuous bulges showed the weaponry beneath. Excellent.

Stephen was seated at the dining table when she arrived. He greeted her politely and continued to eat and read the paper. She helped herself to the breakfast buffet. She had planned on stuffing down a few mouthfuls of food, not wanting to waste time, but he seemed somewhat invested in the paper.

She peeked over, trying to read the headlines. He handed her a section without looking up. Audrey relaxed and started reading the paper, grimacing when she realized they were the gossip pages. Shooting Stephen an evil look, she read the first few snippets.

. . . VSJ fought another duel in the dawn of the third day of the month. Word has it that his opponent CF has fled to the Continent in disgrace . . .

. . . the M of A has been seen with numerous persons of less-than-genteel description. One can only guess that her dear husband has not broken her of her poor associations . . .

. . . LW has reappeared in town after the E of P's gathering and has been seen frequently in the vicinity of the B of R. Dare we speculate as to why?

. . . whatever are we to do with the handsome new D of M? He is causing a riot in the streets. Rumor has it that he is searching for a woman of means. All over town women are stabbing their husbands and young ladies are holding up stagecoaches to try and ensnare his interest . . .

Audrey couldn't decide whether to smile or

frown at the last entry. It looked like Stephen's secret was out. The ladies of the ton would be breaking down his door when he returned to town.

"Anything interesting?"

She dropped the paper on the table. "Not particularly."

He smiled, and her heart jumped. She smiled back.

A quiet cough and clearing of the throat alerted them to another's presence. They turned to the room entrance.

"Your Grace, a messenger has arrived from London to see you."

"Send him to the study."

Stephen turned to her, "If I'm not back by the time you finish breakfast, feel free to wander to the stables or browse through the house." He winked and rose. "You can reacquaint yourself with the rooms."

Before Audrey could respond, a boy walked past the room. His eyes widened when he looked at her. Not a good sign. Her heart picked up speed.

"Great." She forced a smile, and the boy skittered past.

Stephen walked from the room and followed the boy to the study. She pushed her plate forward, no longer hungry. Chewing on her lower lip, she grabbed the gossip section and scurried after them.

The door to the study was closed, and she paused in front, casting a quick glance around the hall. There was no one in sight.

She knelt on the ground, spreading the sheets in a disordered fashion. It was a feeble excuse at best, but it was going to have to do in a pinch. She leaned toward the closed door while maintaining the act of collecting the fallen papers.

The voices were muted but still audible.

"He says that you have to return forthwith to the city. Don't tip off the girl but use extreme caution."

"Did he tell you anything else?"

"The girl murdered your solicitor, Mr. Logan. The Watch and Bow Street runners are presently looking for the girl."

Audrey's heart hammered in her chest. No. She refused to be locked away again for a crime she didn't commit.

The boy continued, "There are reports that the woman stole documents and books from the man before doing him in."

"How was Logan killed?"

"Stabbed, Your Grace."

Should she run or stay?

A servant rounded the corner, and Audrey swept

the papers into a pile. She forced a smile and walked down the hall.

So what was the worst that could happen? He could kill her. He could jail her. He could take her back to the city. He could . . . what? Not care? Not be upset? Because she meant nothing to him?

She increased her pace. This was a game to him, after all. A game for the bored aristocrat.

She stumbled, but caught herself. Her breath came out in short gasps. She didn't care. This was a game to her too.

She headed for the stables, unsure what to do. A groom greeted her, and she followed him inside. She selected a spirited mare. The mare, a beautiful rich brown horse with friendly eyes, nudged her from inside her cell. Audrey shook her head. Stall, not cell.

There was nowhere for her to run. She was as good as caught—a fly in a web. If Stephen chose to arrest her, she'd never make her escape in time. His lands and woods stretched for miles. She wouldn't even make it to Travers's lands before Stephen could hunt her down. He would overtake her, bind her, and cart her to prison. No one would question a duke. No one would care.

She patted the mare's nose and stared blankly at the stall door.

"Audrey?"

Stephen stood at the next stall, absently playing with the stallion's reins. Audrey straightened her shoulders and stared back.

"Have you decided where you want to begin?"

Her heart started beating again. It was a game. Play it like a game. Her options were limited. If Chalmers wanted to play it out, she would too.

"Yes."

The reins flipped left to right. "Shall we begin?" She nodded.

"I told the grooms to make the saddle astride. Would you rather have a sidesaddle?"

"It doesn't matter. I have ridden both ways. I grew up in the country."

The horses were led out, and Stephen helped her mount. They trotted toward a wooded path, a groom on horseback leading the way.

The landscape turned into a deep valley, and small houses dotted the countryside. It was a gorgeous pastoral scene. Audrey had grown up in the country and appreciated the setting, even if she had become a rabid city dweller.

Stephen asked the groom several questions about the running of the estate, and Audrey could see his mind working. The estate looked very prosperous. There was no way this property could be in debt.

Stephen was a perfect gentleman and included her in the conversation with the groom. The cool morning turned into a bright midday as they broke from the countryside into the village.

As they meandered down the street, the villagers stared at them in unabashed curiosity. Small children ventured close to stare, and Audrey saw puffed cheeks and healthy glows. These people were in excellent health. No starving here. And yet they were supposed to be in dire need of help.

And she was supposed to have killed the solicitor? Her eyes narrowed. This was all too convenient.

There was a small inn in town. Probably not even ten rooms large, but they made their way there.

"They used to have excellent stews," Stephen confided as he helped her dismount. His hands were warm on her waist. Her heart sped up and his fingers seemed to linger before releasing her.

The groom excused himself and left them to the innkeeper, who busied himself with making the two of them comfortable.

"I confess I have been thinking of nothing as much as your lovely stew since stepping foot in the county," Stephen told the innkeeper after he was seated.

The innkeeper beamed. "I'll be back with two bowls."

A rich beef stew sounded superb after her meager breakfast, but Audrey didn't know if she could dredge up an appetite when her stomach was coiled in knots.

Stephen gave her an unreadable look. "What do you think of the estate?"

She thought it looked very nice, but she was no closer to finding Faye after the inspection. Of course she hadn't complained. She had no idea where she stood at the moment, but good sense proclaimed the ground shaky.

"I think the estate looks healthy and prosperous."

"I do too. It looks well run and in need of little repair. I'll need to look over the books."

"Oh?"

"I have copies of some of the accounts, but the full ledgers are with my solicitor. I'll retrieve them from him when I return to London."

Audrey felt a faint line of perspiration dot her forehead. She had to get herself under control. He was watching her closely. "I'm sure you will have everything under control in no time."

The innkeeper arrived with their food, saving her for the moment. Stephen started eating, and she stared at her own bowl. Might as well eat, one never knew when it would be the last meal.

The stew was indeed good, and she ended up using her bread to wipe the bowl clean. She thought a faint bit of amusement crossed his face, but the unreadable mask was back in place. She found herself hating him at that moment. She had become accustomed to his joking manner only to have it rudely pulled from beneath through no fault of her own.

"Let's ride some more. We can discuss our plans on the way."

He thanked the innkeeper and sent the groom ahead to the manor. Stephen boosted her onto her horse, and she froze as his hand lightly caressed her backside.

She didn't know what his game was, but if she could survive this experience and get him back to London, she could escape into the streets. The country was a wide trap, but the city was her domain, and she knew all its twists and turns.

If necessary, she could always fall back on her other plan. She would loathe herself if she had to resort to it, but her choices were slipping away. Last night she had felt a ray of hope. Today it had dimmed and withered away as usual.

Even the sun slipped behind the clouds to reflect her mood.

"There are numerous buildings to investigate on Travers's property. Which direction do you want to search first?"

"I don't know," she snapped.

Stephen looked at her askance. He had been trying to determine if she had heard the message and attempting at the same time to figure out how to ask. The case was becoming more and more complex, taking more twists and turns than St. John's affairs.

"Feeling snippy?"

"None of your business. I'll take care of my own problems, thank you."

Irritation spread through him. "I know why you're piqued. You overheard my conversation with the messenger."

She looked at him sharply. "No."

"How much did you overhear?"

"I don't know to what you are referring."

He couldn't remember being this irritated with a woman before. Usually women were so pliable. So happy. So docile.

"Come off it, Audrey. I know you were there. Let's get it out in the open."

"Why?"

"Because then we can discuss why someone is making false claims about you being a murderer."

There was a wary look in her eyes as she examined him for what seemed like hours. She slowly nodded. He had the distinct impression that she would rather have answered no to whatever he said.

Was there ever a woman so contrary? His mother had never been like this. She had been a nice, thoughtful, caring woman. Not a prickly, stubborn, ungrateful one. At least that is how it had appeared to have been in his young mind.

Had his parents ever fought like this? It was unbelievable that their sunny relationship had ever had any stumbling blocks. Not even in the end. They had died in each other's arms, something not even the street thieves could steal.

Stephen shook off the dark thoughts and stared at the street thief. He shook his head, no, at Audrey. "Rumor has it that you murdered my solicitor. The funny thing is you somehow carried out the dastardly deed two nights ago while I slept, then managed to tiptoe back into my bed while I slept. Furthermore, you magically disposed of the body. Witnesses saw you kill him, but no one seems to know what happened afterward."

A look of relief crossed her features. "Oh, thank God."

"You thought I believed it?"

"Why wouldn't you, considering my checkered past?"

Why hadn't he? He had automatically sought an alternative explanation as soon as he had heard the first words from the messenger, never once feeling the messenger's words were the truth.

"Because it didn't make sense," he said smoothly. After he had asked some targeted questions, it hadn't, that was true. The accusation had been carefully crafted. Only his desire to believe in Audrey had prompted him to press the messenger and reveal the discrepancies.

"So what do I do about the allegations?"

I, not we. Their relationship had quickly regressed. "Roth is concerned you will do me in."

"And what do you believe?"

"I told you I didn't believe the tale. Should I be worried about my health?"

Audrey gave him a dark look. "I don't make it a practice to kill my partners in crime."

"Then whom do you make it a practice to kill?"

"Irritating men. Be grateful you're my partner."

He smiled. "I am grateful."

Color stained her cheeks, and she moved her mare forward. "We should really be searching."

He nudged his horse into a trot. "You've made an enemy of Travers, you know."

She nodded brusquely. "Yes, I figured he was behind this. We now have something else in common, Your Grace."

The title stung, but he knew she was right about Travers. The man had hated him for years, even decades. And he knew what Travers desired. All the pieces were falling in place, and it wouldn't be long before Travers was brought down. But first he had to locate Audrey's sister. He was too nervous to put Audrey to the test if they didn't find her sister; he knew he would end the loser.

Audrey glanced at Stephen riding next to her. He hadn't believed the lies. Or was this a more elaborate ploy? She quashed the negative thoughts. She had to believe him.

A weight lifted from her shoulders. They were still no closer to finding her sister, but at least they were back on even ground.

"Let's be methodical and head south first." Stephen cantered ahead.

The mare was more spirited than she looked, and she sped off with only the slightest urging. They soared over an open valley. The wind on her face, the ground flying beneath, Audrey had forgotten how much she enjoyed riding. There was never an opportunity in the city.

A few empty dwellings and barns occupied the southern portion of Travers's property, but there were no tracks and nothing suspicious around them. They rode to the eastern portion that adjoined Stephen's property, the portion closest to the manor, and scoured the area. The sun was starting to set when they finally found what they were looking for.

"Stop." Stephen motioned to her, and she saw the small burst of smoke ahead.

They dismounted and tied their horses. Stephen removed his gun, and they crept forward. A small cottage was nestled in the trees, and a man sat on the edge of the front porch trying to light a fire in a pit. Tendrils of smoke haphazardly rose from his efforts. Audrey could see forms moving inside, but could not determine the number or gender of the people within.

Audrey recognized the man as an elder from the stews who sometimes worked with Flanagan.

Another man, this one a stranger, exited the house. "Our guests are all settled, boss. Are we supposed to just wait now?"

Had Flanagan sent someone? Or were these men working for someone else? And who were the guests? She wanted dearly to burst into the clearing and shake the answers out of them.

"The little Kendrick filly will stay put. Don't worry about her, she's well taken care of."

The elder shook his head. "You don't know her."

Cold rage descended. They had Faye. She moved forward, but Stephen grabbed her. She balked and nearly pulled away, but their eyes met, her eyes glaring, his entreating, and after a few tense seconds she stilled.

She dropped her hand. "You heard them. They have my sister. I'm going in with or without you."

"Not now. You don't know how many others are inside. They don't appear to be in any hurry. We'll come back later with reinforcements."

"No."

"Yes. I'll call the constable and set up men to watch. These men will still be here in the morning."

She read the look on his face. "Fine." Her brows lifted, and she smoothed her hair. It would be better for her to return alone under cover of darkness anyway. She could even walk the distance.

His eyebrows rose.

She answered his look. "You make a good point, and I'd rather have my sister in one piece."

He didn't look convinced—she'd have to do a better job at dinner, or he'd never let her out of his sight.

"We are working together." She shrugged. "So, that means I have to wait for you."

"Sometimes I wonder if our definitions of certain words in the English language might have different connotations." He quirked an eyebrow, but held out a hand to her.

They led their horses back to the south and exited the woods into the valley. They ended up farther away from the manor, but with the tracks leading the wrong way. They mounted and trotted back to the house.

A movement to her right alerted her. She turned toward the woods, but no one was there. Her senses went on alert. It was not an animal, she was sure of it. It might be a villager or even a poacher, but there was someone in the wood. She edged closer to Stephen. If it were one of Flanagan's men, she would need to protect Stephen.

Stephen made no comment, but he kept trying to guide her to the side. It was damn hard work protecting him when he kept putting himself in harm's way.

But they reached the manor without incident.

After she retrieved Faye she'd find out who was watching them. And which one of them they were watching.

Stephen spoke with the butler, and Audrey meandered into the library, tension still thrumming though her. Volumes towered from floor to ceiling. She loved books. They were at the same time an escape, safe haven, and hope for the future. She had books of her own, tattered and well used, but nothing like what Stephen and the previous dukes possessed.

She put her hand on the back of a Rousseau and started to pull it out. Someone coughed and she snatched her hand back.

Stephen stood in the doorway, lounging as usual.

"I wasn't going to take it."

"I never said you were. Did you want to borrow something to read?"

"Maybe later." She absently walked to the window. Darkness had descended upon the country.

"Why do you assume that I think you are stealing?"

"That's what I do, right?"

"And you automatically assumed I would find you guilty this morning with no facts to back any of the allegations."

"I'm a criminal. You hate us."

Although he appeared outwardly at ease, she felt him tense. "I don't hate you."

She shrugged.

"You don't trust me," he said.

"Why should I trust you?"

"Have I given you reason not to?"

She jerked a bit. "You don't trust anyone, Chalmers. I know you. So why would you ask it of me?"

"I trusted in you this morning."

"No, you used logic and reason to sort through the lies."

He shook his head and leaned back against the door, that same inner stillness at odds with his posture. "No, I knew you weren't guilty before applying logic and reason."

She remained silent, unsure how to respond.

His eyes were penetrating. "Dinner will be served soon. I'll see you there." He pivoted on his heel and left.

An uncomfortable feeling spread through her, and she walked away from the window. He was being nothing but kind and helpful. Unfortunately, this wasn't a simple lark. She had tried pretending it was, but it hadn't been a game for a long time now. She needed to harden her heart if she was going to make it to the end and save Faye. The plan had never included saving Audrey.

Audrey moved listlessly upstairs to change her clothing, then dragged herself to the immense dining room. Chandeliers gleamed across the expanse, creating an intimate mood at odds with her feelings.

Dinner was excellent, but she barely did it justice. Stephen was consumed with his own thoughts as well, and there was little conversation. She didn't know how to break the silence and wasn't even sure she wanted to. As long as he was preoccupied she could develop her own strategy, however depressing the thought of their lost intimacy.

After dessert and an uncomfortable silence, she stood. Stephen rose as well.

"The constable will take care of everything tomorrow."

She shrugged, not feeling what the motion indicated. The constable would just as well come to arrest her on the morrow. "Fine. Good evening."

She felt him watching her as she walked slowly from the dining room. She shut the door to her room, then locked it for good measure. She couldn't forget her mission.

She stripped to her shift and tucked herself under the covers. They were warm, bless the maid. A nap would restore her energy before she returned to the cabin. Time for Stephen to go to bed, time for the servants to go to bed, and time for the bastards who had her sister to become drunk and lazy.

Revenge would be sweet. Right now the men in the woods were the perfect scapegoat for her pent-up feelings—the confused ones for Stephen, the terrified ones for her sister, and the vengeance that she craved against Travers.

Audrey napped lightly and woke when she heard the footfall approach her door. There was an infinitesimal pause before they continued down the hall to the master suite. She stared at the ceiling. An hour later she was still staring at the same spot. By now he should be asleep. She tossed the covers and stepped on the plush oriental rug.

It took a few minutes to find her coat and trousers. As soon as her weapons were in place, she cracked open the door and peered into the hall. The corridor was clear.

She made her way down the steps, slipped into the kitchen and through the back door. A half-moon provided enough light to illuminate her way. She trotted to the east. Once inside the woods she stepped onto a trail and increased her pace. Years of running from the law gave her speed. She spotted the large oak tree she had mentally marked earlier and turned from the path. Slowing, she picked her way through the forest, trying to avoid stepping on anything that crinkled or rustled. She wasn't accustomed to the terrain and found it much more difficult to traverse than it had been in the daylight.

Finally, the thatched cottage came into view. Three men sat around the fire. She skirted to the back and sent up a prayer when she saw the partially open door. She snuck inside and stayed low to the ground. The idiots had left lamps glowing throughout the place. She poked her head into the first bedroom. Empty. Second one. Empty. A sound from outside caused her to crouch lower on the floor, knife in hand. Silence.

She moved to the final, room. Empty. She twitched her hand and straightened. Walking into the living area she noticed that no one had been held here, now or in the recent past. Anger and frustration whipped through her, and she sidled up to a curtained window, peeking through.

The three men were still drinking and smoking around the fire. The stranger she had seen earlier was smoking, a man with his back to her was staring toward the trees, and the older man was leaning against a log drinking from a huge jug.

She opened the door. "What the hell are you three rats doing here?"

The older man dropped the jug, spilling ale on himself. "By the devil, Hermes, what are you thinking of, sneaking up on us like that?"

She walked over and tapped her foot on the log. "Why are you here?"

The man who had been staring at the trees whipped around and stepped forward. She grimaced in recognition. "Flanagan told us to keep an eye on you so you'd not weasel out on paying up."

Audrey frowned and continued tapping. "Flanagan said you two had split from the ranks."

The older man grunted. "He needed help. Too many spoons in the kettle, so you might say."

They occasionally hired men from other rings or independents to do simple tasks when they had many irons in the fire, but why would Flanagan send anyone after her?

"I told him I'd ante up. And why would he send you, Beefy? Trying to get you out of his hair?"

The man who had been studying the trees glared. "Someday I'm going to tear off a chunk of yours. We'll see how fine you look then."

"Awww, Beefy, it sounds like you missed me."

"Call me that one more time, and I'm going to—"

"Leonard, cut it out," the older man said, picking up his jug.

Leonard's hands curled into fists.

Audrey turned to the jug man. "Chalmers knows Beefy." She smiled falsely at the large man

272

who was tightly gripping his hands, "Oh, excuse me, I mean, Chalmers knows Leonard."

She returned her attention to the jug man. "If you are going to be here, you should have at least left him behind. Was one of you in the forest today watching us?"

Leonard smirked. "Chalmers ain't going to recognize me. We're just keeping an eye on the two of you. Chalmers can't see two feet in front of his face."

She pulled her foot down from the log and rolled her eyes. "Right, and that's why he escaped from you on the bridge last year against the odds of twenty to one."

Leonard smirked, but it didn't touch his eyes. "Looking pretty cozy with the bloke, Hermes. Always knew you were after the fancy pieces." He spat. "Too good for the likes of us, weren't you?"

"Too good for you, most definitely."

The third man, the stranger, snickered. Leonard moved forward menacingly, but the jug man put a hand on his leg. "Leave her alone."

Jug man resumed drinking and leaned back against the log. "This is just a friendly follow along. As long as you're straight with us, we won't bother you or interfere in your plans, Hermes."

Audrey frowned but nodded. It was not an uncommon practice, but she had never been taxed with followers before. "Fine. See that you don't."

She checked Leonard's position before turning her back to the trio. He was too far away to reach her without warning, but she kept her eyes strained as far back as possible as she walked with her head forward. What a mess. Her least favorite thug and two extra dimwits to boot. She'd be lucky to get out of this without Stephen finding them.

While keeping an eye on Leonard was a very wise move, it also precluded her from seeing the person who stood directly in her path. She nearly collided with him, but a slight movement jerked her attention forward at the last minute.

"Plotting with the enemy, my dear?"

Chapter 16

Ｔhe jug crashed for a second time, and Stephen watched the three men scramble. The man smoking showed the quickest reflexes and dove behind the log. The man with the ale fell forward before following the man behind the log.

And the dumb lug who had been threatening Audrey didn't disappoint him as he lumbered forward, his fists clenched. Oh, this was going to feel good. Audrey put herself between them. Stephen pushed her aside and ducked as Leonard swung. Stephen used Leonard's forward momentum to pull him into a flip. The thug hit the ground hard.

"I'm sorry to say that I do not have a bat, Leonard. I've been looking for you." Stephen waited for him to rise. Better to have kicked him while down, but he had some pent-up aggression to spend. "Now I see why they bring you in for the jobs where the person is already bruised and beaten. Not much of a fighter, are you?"

Leonard rushed him again, and Stephen flipped him into a cluster of plants. He prayed they were poison ivy.

The other two men came out of their hiding places, guns trained.

Audrey stepped in front of Stephen. "We are going back to the house. You three are welcome to stay here."

The man who had been drinking stopped moving, but the smoker continued forward. Stephen was prepared to push Audrey out of the way. But the drinker stopped the smoker and nodded to them.

Audrey turned and pushed Stephen into the woods. Leonard was trying to rise and was begging for a few more lumps. Audrey must have divined Stephen's intent because she pushed him harder.

He allowed it only because now that Leonard was out of hiding he'd be easy to find. But he had threatened Audrey. Stephen's lips tightened, and he turned around, the smoker nervously raised his gun again and glanced to the drinker.

Audrey sighed and grabbed Stephen's hand. The gesture was so unexpected that he allowed her to pull him the rest of the way to the house. It was a silent journey. He had overheard the men say they would stick around to shadow Audrey. Leonard could wait.

She went in through the kitchen door, and he followed behind, not releasing her hand. She led him to the library.

"You followed me. Did you know I was going all along?"

She poured a glass of brandy, handed it to him, and sat on the sofa. He swirled the liquid, feeling no desire to dull his senses.

"Yes."

"Why didn't you stop me?"

"I had to know if I could trust you."

She leaned back against the sofa. "And do you?" The question was light, but he saw the tense line of her jaw.

"I might." He continued to swirl his brandy. "Or I might not."

He had to know if the suspicions that had formed tonight were correct. There were so many questions vying in his brain that he didn't know which to ask first.

He issued a statement instead. "You were with

the ruffians that trapped me on the bridge a year ago."

She folded her hands and looked him straight in the eye. "No."

"I overheard you talking. You witnessed my jump."

"Yes, but I was not with the ruffians, as you call them."

Stephen put the glass on the rosewood table and leaned against the hearth across from the sofa. "Then what were you doing there?"

"I followed Leonard and a few of the others."

"Asking you questions is like catching fish with bare hands. Why did you follow them?"

"I heard they were going after you. I wanted to see it for myself."

"Curiosity was all?"

She didn't blink. "Yes. I had observed you before, but not closely. Of course, you hadn't pegged me as Hermes yet, so as long as you chased me in the shadows I was safe."

Stephen's blood warmed. She was so confident in her abilities. So sure that she would have continued undetected. So strong. "Where were you standing?"

"I beg your pardon?"

"Where were you standing when they attacked me?"

One foot shifted, but the rest of her stayed still. She continued to look him straight in the eye. "I don't see why that is of any importance."

"You weren't on the bridge, I would have seen you."

"Then I wasn't on the bridge."

"You were on the bank, admit it."

A spark of defiance lit her eyes, breaking her calm expression. It only succeeded in heating him further. "Why bother asking me the question at all then?"

"I want to know."

She tapped her left heel against the floor twice. "Yes, I was on the bank. I could see most of what was going on and still remain undetected."

"So you saw what happened after I jumped in the water."

"You fell quite ungracefully into the sour pits of the river."

"And then?"

"Well, that pretty well frustrated the men who were trying to beat the information out of you on the bridge."

"Who pulled me out of the water?"

She didn't move, but he could almost feel her body tense. "The show was over, I left. I don't know how you managed to pull yourself from the river."

Stephen moved until he was standing over her, staring at the top of her head. She tilted her head back. Her brows drew together, and she rose and put her hands on her hips. "You aren't going to intimidate *me*, Chalmers."

He wanted her to call him Stephen. He wasn't trying to intimidate her; he was just having an unsure moment of how to proceed. She was so strong, and yet there was a fragile quality about her as if one small push would be the one to send her over the edge.

"Audrey, you pulled me out. And you nursed me. That's why you seemed so familiar. I remember you. It's like something out of a dream, but it was you. It finally makes sense."

She crossed her arms. "You've taken leave of your senses. Why would I have saved you? You were nothing but a pain in my arse."

She was gazing at him with wide eyes just as she had the other day when he had taken the documents from her trousers. Another light went on. "And that explains why you came through my window the other day. The footmen who saw you drop me off at my town house were in the front hall talking with Grimmond. You couldn't take the chance that they would recognize you."

"That's absurd."

He gave her a soft smile. "No, no it's not absurd in the least."

She sat back down and looked at her hands. "You are such a tenacious man. I was afraid you would remember. That's why I took you back to the town house inhabited by Lady Angelford. I couldn't risk keeping you with me any longer. I knew you were going to regain consciousness at any moment."

"Why did you save me? Your cohorts obviously didn't want me alive."

She waved a hand. "They were hired by outside men to do an extra job. It wasn't on Flanagan's orders."

"I know. The men who organized it were instructed to gather information concerning the death of Calliope's father. They have been taken care of. But that doesn't answer the question of why you saved me."

She shrugged. "I admire a good move as well as the next person. It didn't seem fair that after escaping from them, you'd drown from your injuries."

His thoughts were jumbled. "I've been searching for my rescuer. You."

"Why?"

Why? He didn't know why, he just had had to find her. His throat was dry, so he cleared it. "I was curious, that's all."

"Well, you found me." Audrey frowned. "I've been trying to discover who ratted me out. Care to enlighten me?"

Stephen shook his head. "No one ratted you out. The footmen knew you were a girl. I sent men all over the city trying to dig up information. Imagine my surprise when clues concerning you and your sister kept popping up. I merely connected them and started following you as the thief Hermes, rather than my savior."

Audrey looked disgruntled. "So my saving you led to you knowing my identity?"

"Yes." He paused. "Thank you."

"Ah, well, if I had known at the time that your investigation would bring you down on my head I might not have been so accommodating."

"You obviously did not learn from your mistake. You saved me again at the theater." He smiled. "Besides, if you hadn't saved me, I wouldn't have had the pleasure of knowing you."

There was a naked moment of emotion on her face as if that would have caused her pain, and lightning shot down his spine. The urge to grab her and never let her go was strong, but he sat next to her instead and leaned back. Every rational part of his mind said he shouldn't give in to this crazy obsession with her. Yet every other part urged him on. There was something very important about the moment.

"Where should we go from here, Audrey?"

She looked over at him and leaned the side of her head on the back of the sofa so that she faced his side. "Where can we go, Stephen?"

"I honestly don't know. All I do know is that I've never wanted anything so badly as to take you upstairs with me."

He looked both determined and resigned. Panic and excitement warred within her. She put up a last front.

"Out of gratitude?"

Stephen grimaced but didn't move. "Definitely not."

He was so honest. All of the men in her life had been anything but. Her normal defenses were failing under his steady stare and open air. Trusting him would only open her to further pain. She knew it. And something about the steady acknowledgment of spending the night together instead of falling into it in a fit of passion made the decision harder than it had been the night before.

Yet, there was tonight. One night to be free, not to think about the past, not to worry about the future. He wasn't promising anything, and neither was she.

"I want you to take me upstairs."

His eyes were gentle as he held out his hand. She took it and the warmth caressed her. He rose from the sofa and lifted her to her feet. They walked hand in hand down the hall and up the stairs. Each step brought her closer to his room, and each step caused the flurries in her stomach to increase and the weight of her burden to lift.

He opened the door and stood aside, allowing her the choice. She walked in and breathed in the pine scent. Sometime during the evening he had taken time to transport a few plants into the room. They were sitting in pots around the floor. He reached down and pushed one to the side. Nothing to bar the way to the bed. The covers were already pulled back but not rumpled. He had probably not even undressed for bed that evening.

She walked forward and sat on the edge, watching him as he lit candles on both sides of the bed.

She shivered, and he turned to her. "Would you like me to light a fire in the grate?"

Suddenly shy, she shook her head. "No, I am fine, thank you."

He knelt before her. Taking one calf in his hand, he began rubbing it. Up, down, circle, up, down, circle. The heat slowly started to spread as he worked his way up to her thigh. A tightened feeling in her chest caused her breath to catch as he switched his attention to the other leg, massaging it as well. By the time his hands reached her thigh her breathing was coming in short gasps. He lifted her onto the bed, carefully laying her down. He removed her boots pausing at the sight of her ankles.

Laughing softly, he removed the straps that kept two knives in place and tossed them to the floor. She looked over the edge of the bed as the steel disappeared into the shadows.

He pushed her back onto the pillows and ran a finger up her stockinged right calf and placed her feet under the covers. Both hands moved up her legs to her waistband. He slid her trousers down slowly. She barely felt the cool air this time as his hands lingered on her skin and he tucked his finger under her garter straps, where two reserve knives were strapped. The garters were for dresses, but they were her insurance in case she was captured. His fingers caressed the garters, then undid them and slipped them off as well. Two more pieces of steel hit the floor.

He tucked her legs underneath the covers. She reached for him, unsure whether to undress him as well or allow his exploration to continue.

She reached for him, but he simply caught her hand and tucked it beneath the pillow as he drew his fingers up and over her thighs, her hips to her stomach, pushing her shirt up and leaving a trail of heat in their wake. Her shirt was undone, and he lifted her back from the bed and removed it.

Two solid thunks resounded from the shirt hitting the floor. He looked at the trousers, which were still on the bed. Little knives were tucked into various sheaths. He placed the pants on the floor instead of dropping them. He chuckled and whispered into her hair, something about carrying a small arsenal. His breath caught in her left ear, and her head fell back. He kissed the side of her neck, and his lips trailed down and to her chest.

His right hand started at her ankle and trailed slowly upward on the inside of her leg. His lips continued their descent and his hand its ascent. Heat collided from both directions as he pulled a nipple into his mouth. Her hips lifted involuntarily as his fingers reached their target and wrapped around her. Dear Lord, she didn't think she could stand it. A faint warning caused her to tighten her thighs.

This man would not be a part of her future. He could not be. Stephen seemed to sense her indecision, and his hand stopped its motion, resting on top as his head lifted and rested against her neck.

Tragedy and romance; Shakespeare would be proud. One night. Just one night to keep the darkness at bay.

Audrey reached up and unbuttoned his shirt. She heard him catch his breath. She looked at his face, thrown into shadow and flame by the surrounding candlelight. Touching his face, she brought her mouth to his and kissed him with everything inside of her. He returned the kiss, and she felt him giving her a piece of himself. She grasped it, and her fingers moved to his shirt, pushing it off, then running her hands over the muscles underneath.

His warm hands roamed, making promises. Even his lips on hers made whispered promises that she knew could not keep for tomorrow. But they were hers for the night, and she gripped him as he moved his promising lips down her body and replaced his hands with them as she arched against the bed. Waves of pleasure washed over her, and she bit her lip as her head moved back of its own will.

Those whispering lips moved up her body, and she grabbed them to hers as he slid inside. She shuddered as he pushed, and her body accepted him completely. It was so right, so complete a feeling.

The light flickered over his features as he began moving above and inside her. She leaned her head back and stared into his eyes, mesmerized by the look there, the promise in their depths. The longer she stared into his eyes, the more the sensations intensified until wave after wave of pleasure crashed through her, and she buried her face against his shoulder, crying out in tandem with him.

Stephen drew the covers around her. Audrey hadn't shivered since her clothes had come off, but she seemed to be perpetually cold, and he didn't want her to be uncomfortable.

She had long since fallen asleep, but Stephen didn't think it would take much to wake her. In her line of work it wasn't a good idea to sleep heavily.

He frowned. He had chosen his line of work. He had lain many a night waiting for the enemy to sneak up and snuff him.

But she hadn't chosen her life. It had been forced

upon her, and she had succeeded in leaving it once, before being dragged back. She curled into a ball, not even trusting him in her sleep. What was he going to do with her?

One night with her had done nothing to satisfy his obsession. If anything, it had increased it, just as he had known it would. So many facets, so many fascinating angles—she was a puzzle waiting to be solved.

More than that, she was challenging—demanding and forthright. He thought about the pile of clothes on the floor. A woman with a damn arsenal of weapons strapped about her at all times. Not a blushing debutante. Not a schemer hiding in the shadows. Not quite honest, not quite noble, but with a set of guiding principles that she abided by. And although he knew the important ones, he wanted to know all of them.

If he were logical, he should walk away now and never look back. He was walking on the edge of a precipice. He knew it, Roth knew it, and James knew it. Hell, even James's bodyguard had mumbled it within his hearing. But Stephen couldn't turn his back on the most intriguing woman he had ever encountered.

"Nooooo!"

Audrey thrashed wildly at the covers holding

her under. Stephen reached out and brushed her hair. "Shhhh, it's just a nightmare."

She pushed his hand away and struck out. Stephen ducked to the side; her fist missed his chin by inches. He continued murmuring, trying to soothe her back into dreamless sleep. He stroked a finger down her back, and she curled toward him.

Newgate. Travers had put her there, and Stephen intended to make the man pay for that and much more before this was over.

The game would continue, only now there was a lot more at stake.

Travers approached the two men around the fire. Both men jumped, and one even grabbed his gun.

"Dammit, Hermes, I'm going to let Leonard at you if you do that one more—" The man stopped as he recognized the visitor. The man twitched nervously. "Begging your pardon, sir, I didn't know that was you."

Travers fisted both hands. "Had a late-night visitor, did you?"

"Well, er, yeah, she stopped by for a chat."

"Where's Leonard?"

The man twitched again and took a drink. "Followed them back."

"Them?"

"Yeah, the duke fella followed her here. They left together."

"Really?" Travers relaxed his fists.

The man said nothing.

Leonard crashed into the clearing. "Damn girl, I always knew she had it in for the high fly—" He stopped midsentence, just as the other man had done. Travers would have smirked if he hadn't been so angry.

"You were saying, Leonard?"

Leonard spat. He didn't quite have the brains of the other man. "Saw them going upstairs together."

"And you think that means what?"

He smirked and walked toward the fire. "If you had seen them, you'd know what I meant."

Unfortunately for Leonard, he walked right past him. Travers landed a punch. It didn't relieve his rage. He started to lean down to throw another, but the third man shifted his gun nervously and looked twitchier than the first. Travers straightened. *Funnel the rage, funnel the pain*. So Chalmers planned to continue taking everything that was his?

A fifth man entered the clearing, his dark clothing mirroring his expression. "Plans have changed. Tomorrow you will follow them. Somewhere along the pike before they get to London I want you to attack."

Leonard glared at the stranger and rubbed his jaw. "Just who are you?"

Travers felt the jolt of fear that always accompanied him in the man's presence.

The man scoffed at Leonard as if he were a small spider scuttling from his path. "You will do as you are told."

Something about his voice or demeanor alerted Leonard to scoot back a step. Leonard looked at Travers, who said nothing. There was nothing he could say to gainsay the man who had reached his side.

Leonard seemed to feel this was a good course of action as well, for he simply asked, "Where?"

"I don't care where. Pick a spot, just don't let them reach London." The man tapped a finger on the back of his knuckles. "Kill the duke, but spare the girl. Bring her to me."

Fear pulsed through Travers, but there was nothing he could do.

Leonard smiled.

Chapter 17

A clinking sound jarred her awake. She opened her eyes to see Stephen grimacing as he closed a large trunk.

"Sorry about that, I was trying to close the damn thing without waking you."

She raised her brows. "Trying to pack, then ditch me, Stephen?"

He chuckled. "And then spend all my time dodging you? I don't think so."

His gaze focused on her leg, thrown out from under the covers. "Of course, it depends on the manner of the dodging."

She lazily drew her leg up so that the sheet gapped and exposed a smooth, bare hip. "And what manner of dodging would you be interested in?"

A seductive smile spread over his face as he sauntered toward her. Her body tingled and responded as he trailed a finger along her toes and up her leg, creating tremors of desire before disappearing beneath the sheet to find the mysteries underneath.

Much later he kissed her with such burning sweetness that she thought she would burst from it. Even after a wild night in his arms, his gentleness touched her soul, creating within her a deep sense of peace. She sat up and admired his broad back, his long, tapered torso, and his tight bottom as he walked from the bed, unembarrassed by his nudity.

"I found a copy of the estate accounts dating back a few months. Logan must not have known about them." He sat back on his heels. "The estate is perfectly healthy. Just as we both suspected, there's nothing wrong with it. Makes it all the more curious why Logan would say I was penniless and use this property as proof, then end up murdered."

She propped herself on one elbow. "It does give one cause to wonder."

He looked at her. "We need to return to town and clear your name. Then we will find your sister."

Her fingers knotted in the sheet. He really would help her find Faye. He really would be her knight in shining armor.

"Audrey?" Stephen returned to the edge of the bed and gazed at her in concern.

She forced a smile and waved a hand. "Oh, I just have something in my eye. Let me get dressed so we can be off."

He looked doubtful, but moved from the bed to let her up.

She struggled into her trousers and shirt. Damn, he made her wish for so much more. She had to stop herself from running as she exited the room.

Again the maid said nothing about her sleeping elsewhere and helped her change into a traveling dress dotted with tiny rows of pearls. The feel of the smooth cool pearls was reassuring. Audrey couldn't help but run her fingers down the iridescent seeds.

They were packed and loaded in the carriage a few hours later. As long as they weren't waylaid by highwaymen they would be fine. She smirked. Bandits would be most surprised if they attempted to rob this carriage. In an earlier inspection, she discovered a cache of weapons. The man came prepared.

Stephen spread out estate papers on the seat and was making notes. Even though the ducal coach was top-notch, the macadamized road left something to be desired, and an occasional swear word punctuated the air from his side. He finally gave up and put the papers away.

"Are you enjoying this extra responsibility?" she asked.

He grimaced but then regained his carefree air. "If you had asked me that a week ago, I would have sneered at you. But one must adapt as one must. Now that I'm not going to have to hie off to some foreign shore to escape the creditors, this may be just the thing I need."

Envy swept through her. She had never met such a charmed individual. So together, so everything that she desired. A person able to put everything into perspective, sooner rather than later.

"Good for you, Chalmers."

He smiled. "You're calling me Chalmers again."

"I told you, Chalmers is your irritating side."

"Well, Audrey is both your irritating and your luminous side. Unfortunately for you, since you won't have access to the same type of key emotional information.

She grinned. Whatever else could be said for Stephen Chalmers, she truly *liked* him.

More than liked. That thought brought dark unbidden thoughts that she shoved aside. She was determined to make their last day together fun. Today it would be just the two of them—no baggage and no betrayals. Tomorrow would come soon enough.

She nudged him with her foot. "Tell me more about this luminous side."

A devilish glint caught his eye.

The air was fresh and warm. Billowing clouds formed interesting shapes through the windows.

"There's a hare being chased by a bear."

"And over there"—he reached across her, pointing—"a hound after a fox."

They talked about everything from the weather to their childhoods. Childhoods untarnished by death and disillusionment. Audrey came to life under his questions, talking about amusing antics that she and her sister had pulled. Pranks on the servants and contests with the local lads.

"I'd never seen my mother angrier than we she found I'd challenged one of the local boys to a race across the pond." There was a smile on her face. "Good thing she never found out that we actually went through with it later."

"Who won?"

She feigned affront. "Well, I did, of course."

It was the perfect ride. The perfect conversation with the perfect partner. Stephen was willing to overlook the sad expression that appeared in her eyes before she had started the banter. But he was determined to erase it permanently.

He watched the way she moved her hands as she talked. Elegant and refined. She tried so hard to be jaded and flippant, but the lacy garters he had stripped from her were more feminine than necessary. Practical? Yes, they were still able to sheathe her knives, but the embroidery was delicate, the lacing fine. She was unsuccessful in trying to hide her femininity underneath all of those layers.

How hard it must be for her always to present a tough façade and be in control. Never being able to laugh or weep. Stephen recalled how drained he felt after his parents died, but good friends and good fortune had helped him endure. Who did Audrey and her sister have to lean on? No, Audrey's life had been cutthroat since she was ten. She had been playing a much different game since then. And being female hadn't been an asset, which was probably why she usually eschewed the trappings of one.

But he had seen her touch the tiny pearls on her dress and the delicate baubles in her hair. She liked them. And God how he wanted her to be able to like them without guilt.

They dined on an enjoyable lunch with pleasant conversation at the Wayfarers Inn. It was still early as they decided to push on toward London.

Within a mile of London the first shot rang out.

Chapter 18

⌒◝◟⌒

The horses raced down the road out of control.

"If we're lucky, we'll make it in one piece," Stephen yelled over the noise. "Hold on."

No more were the words expressed than the coach hit a huge rut and a wheel cracked.

Stephen pulled Audrey into his arms as the carriage tipped, and they went tumbling into the side of the vehicle, now the floor. The horses had broken free. She could hear their retreating hooves as they scampered into the distance. Or was it their pursuers' hooves? She couldn't be sure.

Another shot punctuated the air, and something splintered against the side of the coach. She gasped as her lungs finally inflated. She had hit the ground hard.

She pushed off Stephen and grabbed one of the rifles in the sideboard. Stephen was already moving as well, and he had a gun in hand and was firing through the window at the top of their space.

"We have to leave the coach."

She nodded and tucked a pistol into a hidden pocket in her dress.

A rifle barrel caught her eye, and she grabbed it. Loaded. A shot was fired, and she lifted her hand and blindly returned fire.

Stephen peeked through the trap. "I'm going to fire through the top and draw their attention. You climb through the trap and run for those trees." He pointed to several large clusters a few yards away.

He barely gave her a chance to get situated before he started firing. He had lined pistols up on the floor and was reaching for a new one as she pushed through the trap. She fell ungracefully to the dirt and scrambled on all fours to the boulders, carrying the rifle in hand. Shots rang out behind her, but they were focused on the carriage and Stephen.

He pushed through the trap and she saw a movement in the dark. She tracked it, took aim and fired. A cry met her ears, and she pulled the pistol from her pocket.

Stephen dove behind a neighboring rock.

"I think there are three remaining. They can't have many shots left," he said.

"No, but they could have reinforcements."

"We can shoot, run, or meet them. You decide. What will it be, my lady?"

A fierce look flashed in his eyes, and Audrey felt a pitter deep inside her chest. A warm glow spread through her. And then a stream of pebbles hit her as a shot fired into the rock above.

They returned fire until the night was silent. She looked at her last pistol. One more shot and nowhere to run.

"Well, well, well, looks like we need to flush the hare, boys," a voice said from around the boulders.

Audrey looked at Stephen in confusion. Leonard?

"Flanagan will have your head, Leonard," she shouted.

"Not for following orders, he won't. Now be a good girl and come out."

"Flanagan wouldn't do that. Who are you working for, you little worm?"

"Don't like being betrayed, eh, Audrey? Too bad for you. Come on out. Oh, and bring your lover with you."

Flanagan wouldn't do this to her. She bit her lip. "You're dreaming, Leonard."

"Aw now, Audrey. All my dreams are of you, you know that."

She watched Stephen edge around the other side of his rock. "Don't make me vomit, Beefy."

"No, we don't want that." He sounded angry. Good. "We're all going to have a nice little taste of you. See if you taste as sweet as your sister." Rage and anguish whipped through Audrey. Travers had her sister. More importantly, Travers's men had her sister.

"What are you doing? This is not the plan," hissed the voice of one of the assailants.

Leonard continued, "Brewster over here says you will taste just like her. My guess is you'll be much more tart. I always liked a good bite."

Stephen quickly reappeared, his eyes wide as he worked his way toward her. "Audrey?" he said urgently. "Don't listen to him, he's trying to force a reaction to get you out in the open."

Stephen tried to reach for her across the distance.

"Sweet little Faye. Don't you worry though, Audrey, she was only an appetizer, I consider you the main course."

Stephen guessed her intent and dove toward her, but she was already running around the boulder and firing. The first man ducked and she threw the gun to the side, sparing no thought to him as she whipped a knife at the man on the right and launched into a dive. A gunshot sounded, and the man taking aim at her collapsed. Her dive brought her face to barrel with Leonard's gun. He smirked as he cocked it against her forehead.

His eyes lifted from her for a moment, and Audrey heard footsteps behind. Stephen. But he had already used his last bullet to save her. Leonard lifted the gun to take aim. She stabbed him in the leg and knocked the gun from his hand. He fell to the ground. She hit him. Then she hit him again. And again. From a distance she heard someone screaming in rage and pain, unaware that the sounds came from her own throat.

Strong arms pulled her upright. Darkness was all around her. Warm arms pulled her close and she stepped away from Leonard's prone body and buried her face against Stephen's chest, hysterical sobs escaping.

Stephen made soothing noises and stroked her hair. The three unconscious men on the ground were lucky to be alive. Their wounds, although not fatal, were bad enough to put them out of commission. Leonard was unconscious, the other two men were scooting away from him, one holding his side and the other holding his leg.

Stephen repositioned Audrey in his arms and slid back against a boulder. Voices from the woods were audible. Townsfolk and servants were quickly approaching. The gunfire must have surely alerted everyone in the London outskirts. Stephen looked at the faces of Leonard's companions. They were the two men from the previous night.

Audrey knew they were working for Travers. He had seen it in her eyes. It was the only way she could have possibly known that Leonard wasn't bluffing. Now was not the time to press for details.

He picked her up and headed to one of the horses left by Leonard's men. He set Audrey on top of one horse and took the reins of another. His coach driver was nursing a shoulder wound and what appeared to be a broken leg. Stephen rummaged through the carriage and gave him a pistol and a bottle of spirits. He would send his men back for him.

The villains would have to be left behind. Stephen tightened his lips. He would find them. He knew their faces.

He mounted the horse and took Audrey's reins. She showed no movement to ride herself, simply staring straight ahead.

He rubbed a hand over his forehead. Could he overcome the darkness in Audrey? Should he even try? He looked over at her, and a fierce protectiveness overtook him. The answer was yes.

He rode toward the city, pulling her horse behind. He took out-of-the-way paths to Mayfair and used a back path to his town house. Two servant boys were sitting on the rear wall. They jumped to attention when they saw him and grabbed the reins as he dismounted.

Stephen touched Audrey's hand. "You know he was lying. He wanted you to come out, and you did."

Her eyes focused on him for a minute before she gave him her hand.

Stephen's eyes were calming, but Audrey's pain was evident. She needed her sister. Needed to see that she was safe. Stephen lifted her from her horse. He was giving orders to the boys.

"Unsaddle and stable the horses. Tell the grooms that Murphy is injured on the London Road. Do so quietly and quickly, then find yourselves an extra dessert."

The boys scrambled off, eager to please their master. Audrey leaned back resting her head against his shoulder and allowed him to carry her to the door.

The shrubbery lining the house bounced in her view as he continued to carry her.

Stephen rounded the corner and as quick as lightning stepped back and deposited her in the bushes. An outraged cry lodged in her throat as she saw him make a silencing motion with his hand and then stride forward.

"Good evening, Your Grace. I am Barney Tyler, Bow Street runner."

Audrey recoiled into the prickly bush and barely noticed the pain.

"Good evening, Mr. Tyler. Please forgive my sad state of dress, it's been quite a trying evening."

"Indeed. We received word that a murderess was apprehended and in your custody."

Audrey's breath lodged in her chest.

"Yes, Mr. Tyler, that was the case."

"Was?"

"The hellion escaped. I've been chasing her the past few hours. Damn woman almost shot me."

The runner's voice was grim. "As soon as we find her, we will make sure she pays for that."

"That is an encouraging thought, Mr. Tyler. She had several men helping her."

"Gary, go have a look 'round back. We'll search the property, Your Grace."

A darted glance around the area showed nowhere for her to run except the way they had come.

"Excellent. I chased her just outside of the northern outskirts of London, and disabled a few of the men. They may still be nursing their wounds there. I was unable to linger."

He wasn't going to turn her in. Footsteps rounded the corner, and Audrey pulled her hair around her face, blessing her dark locks. The faint outline of a man passed her hiding place and continued into the darkness toward the stables.

"Quite understandable. Sounds like you did a fine job, Your Grace. Shall we talk inside?"

"Yes, the night is getting chilly. I feel sorry for anyone having to stay outside, but we do as we must."

Damn him for telling her to stay outside. She started to feel the branches poking into her ribs, back and bottom, but she dared not move. Two more men walked past, speaking in hushed tones.

She was stuck here, probably for a long duration. She scooted against the house, wincing as the thorns tore through her garments and into her skin. She pulled her knees up close, crossed her arms on top, and laid her head down. She would be able to hear anyone approaching. She palmed a knife just in case.

Leonard. Just one more name to add to her list for when this was over. She shuddered. What he had said about Faye ... wasn't it what she had been dreading? One of the many things that had kept her up at night, unable to sleep? Leonard had put voice to the fear, making it more urgent than ever to finish this quickly and free Faye.

She remembered the looks of the prison guards. The guards had been receptive to taking in two pretty female prisoners, especially after they had a look at Faye, with her wild red hair and sherry-colored eyes. They had been most receptive. No court, no jury, just straight to that dark little cell in that horrible-smelling prison.

All because of Travers. Leonard was working for Travers.

I know you will taste as sweet. Audrey flinched. Dear Lord, she hoped they were only trying to rile her. But she couldn't risk it. She had to get her sister now. And there was only one option left. Stephen might continue to help her, but he would want to do it in his fashion, and right now everything seemed to be moving too slowly. She could no longer afford the time.

Her last task was waiting inside. Within the house was her final bargaining chip with Travers, the one that would bring her one step closer to Faye. By the end of this, Faye would be safe. And what about Audrey?

Audrey peeked up from her crossed arms and watched the men scout the area. Somewhere out there Stephen was running interference for her, helping her. But tomorrow might be a different story.

As for Audrey? Well, Audrey would survive.

Chapter 19

❧❧

"**A**udrey?"

Stephen looked into the murky shadows along the stone wall. She had been left alone in the dark for over an hour. No alarm had been sounded, so either she had run or she was still ensconced in the thorny bushes. Hopefully her fear of dark, close places did not extend to foliage.

"They are gone, Audrey. Let me help you inside now."

Fear that she had truly left trickled through him. She wanted to hurt Leonard for what he had said. She could have gone back to try. One girl alone with three large men.

Even knowing she could take care of herself did

not stop the fear. Things had a nasty way of changing on you if you locked into the emotion.

A slight movement caught his eye, and he saw a faint gleam of skin. Walking closer, he could see her leaning up against the house, watching him.

"I'm truly sorry about tossing you in there."

"No problem, Chalmers. Rather here than being tossed into prison."

He extended a hand, and she grasped it. The chill of her hands seeped into his.

"There's a fire blazing in the study."

She nodded but said nothing. She walked stiffly into the house, and he could see the pale gleam to her skin and the weary look in her eyes. Still thinking about her sister. Stephen gritted his teeth. Hopefully Roth would find Faye soon.

He nodded at Grimmond as they entered the study. Cook had heated tea and warmed some biscuits, and they were arranged on a tray in front of the fireplace. Audrey collapsed onto the settee. Stephen poured the tea and handed her a cup. She took it and absently blew on the top.

"Audrey?"

She continued to blow on her tea and stare into the grate. "Why didn't you turn me over to the runner?"

"Should I have?"

She gave him an enigmatic look. "No. What did you tell him?"

"I only repeated what I said outside, expounding on how wily and clever you were."

She briefly smiled and sipped the tea. "Thank you for not turning me in."

"You're welcome."

She peered at him over the rim of her cup. "I don't really understand why, though. I know you view me as something of an oddity to examine, but I nearly killed Beef—, Leonard, tonight."

"I know."

"Your parents were murdered."

"Yes."

"Everyone else thinks I killed your solicitor. Why didn't you turn me in?"

The stirring of something akin to panic reared itself. He didn't want to answer that yet. "I haven't finished examining you yet?"

"I need to speak with Maddox to see if he knows anything."

Stephen switched paths readily. "What are you going to do?"

"Just talk. The man has a tendency to reveal more than he should. Sometimes he is not very bright."

"That showed when he sold you to Flanagan."

She shook her head. "It could have been worse. I saw Maddox speaking to Madame Devieve, not knowing at the time what business the woman conducted. Better Flanagan with his skewed morality than working for a woman like that."

Stephen went cold. Madame Devieve's establishment was well-known for the young faces employed there. They had been unsuccessful in closing the house down. Too many government insiders with a stake in the business had always foiled the attempts. Stephen tabled the dark thought. "Why did he have to sell you at all?"

She shrugged. "Gaming debts. The man has worse luck than I do when it comes to the roll of the dice or the turn of a card." The corners of her lips lifted slightly.

"What about your mother? Did he have gaming debts while he was married to her?"

Audrey looked into her cup. "She passed away before she found out what kind of a man she had married. Both of my parents were soft-spoken and scholarly." She gulped the hot tea. "They'd be ashamed if they could see me now."

He rubbed the back of her neck, and even more surprisingly, she let him. "What was life like after you joined Flanagan?"

"Hard, but Flanagan's not that bad." Her mouth

tightened as she followed his train of thought. "No, Flanagan is not part of this. He's tough, yes. Demanding, definitely. But he has rules. His struggle is external, not from a decaying soul. He isn't rotten like Maddox, not evil like Travers."

"Ah, so what should we do about the illustrious Mr. Travers?"

Her neck muscles tightened beneath his hand. "I will deal with him."

She put the cup down and stood.

He put a hand on her wrist. "If you trusted me enough to help you find your sister, why won't you trust me with the other burden you have been carrying around for the past few hours?"

She looked into his eyes. "But I don't trust you, Chalmers. Our deal was Newgate and finding my sister. I offered you information and money and in your reduced circumstances you accepted the offer."

"I don't want your money and never did."

"But you would then have to marry a useless young lady of quality."

There was something in her eyes that made his heart beat more quickly. "But I'd eventually have to marry a young lady of quality, useless or not, wouldn't I?"

314

She tensed, and he felt the reaction to his toes. She cared.

"I don't care whom you marry, Chalmers. Better a useless lady who will ignore your plants and other strange hobbies."

He gripped her shoulders. "What if I don't want to marry a useless lady?"

She took a deep breath and stared at him. "Would you sail across the ocean to be free?"

He rubbed a section of her hair between two fingers. "That sounds divine, but alas, no. The title is a burden, but it is my burden, and bear it I will."

She leaned into him. "Why?"

"Because others count on me now."

There was something naked in her gaze, but she pulled away. He wanted to pull her back, but his senses told him to proceed with caution.

She was going to leave England. Sail across the ocean and out of his life.

She was in profile, looking at her dirty fingernails. Dirt smudged her face. Her dress was tattered; some of the pearls had been ripped off in the confusion. He touched the small pearl necklace at her neck. It had somehow survived.

He wondered if it was hers and if she owned any jewels. He ran a finger down the beads. She was staring at him strangely, and it made his blood warm. He reached up and slipped a hand into the hair at the nape of her smooth neck. Her skin beckoned his hands to linger.

"Still intact?" Her voice was slightly breathless.

"Beautiful." But he wasn't looking at the necklace.

She stared at him for a moment, then touched his face. "You make me want things I can't have."

He touched his forehead to hers. "What about a hot bath?"

She nibbled her lower lip. "Yes, that would be divine."

He walked to the door and as usual Grimmond was hovering just within sight. He ordered two hot baths, both to be brought to his room.

Audrey stepped into Stephen's room as the footmen carried the last empty bucket out, closing the door behind. Stephen grasped her hand and slowly pulled her toward him and into his arms. She rested her head on his chest as he ran his fingers down her spine. It gave her chills and warmed her at the same time.

He tipped her chin up and kissed her. Warmth raced to her toes. She was safe here. For any night with him, she was safe.

Pulling her closer, his warm lips moved over

hers again and again. Warmth, then heat, then a blazing fire whipped through her. She kissed him back with all the passion he had incited. Fingers grazed through her hair and down to the buttons on the back of her dress. He simmered the heat in their kiss and tugged her lips gently between his.

It was like being wrapped in a moonlit forest.

Stepping away, he hooked a finger in the top of her undone gown and pulled. She shivered, not from cold, as his finger and the edges of the gown inched downward, exposing her upper body to his gaze.

He pushed the gown the rest of the way, and it pooled at her feet in a whisper of silk and promised passion.

He removed the rest of her clothes until she stood, clad in only her garters and stockings. And then those too were gone. He stepped back to admire his handiwork.

"Beautiful."

And under his hot gaze, she felt it. Emboldened, she stepped forward and undid the buttons on his shirt, pushing it back and over his arms. Her breasts rubbed against his chest as she tugged the shirt down and threw it behind him.

Threading her fingers through the hair sprinkled over his chest, she gave him a leisurely kiss before sliding down his chest and hooking her fingers into the top of his trousers. She undid them and pulled them down, allowing her body to slither down his. She heard his breath catch, and smiled as she slithered back up.

She took his hand and led him to his tub. There was a dutiful sparkle in his eyes, as if to say, *do with me what you will.*

And so she did. She pushed him into the tub and leaned over to grab the fresh, cedar-scented soap. Rubbing it across his chest and back, she let her breasts dip into the water, then touch him as she reached over and around him. Working her hands into a massaging motion, she covered his chest as she rained kisses along the side and back of his neck. She felt the shiver go through him and smiled into his hair.

She motioned for him to rise, and he cocked an eyebrow but did so. She dragged the soap down the hard planes of his stomach, down his thigh, and around his left leg. He really was magnificent. And for now, he was hers.

Running the soap back up and around his back, she leaned toward him and heard his breath catch. She ran her hands across the bar of soap, put it down, and touched him with her hands. He gave a low groan as she moved her slippery hands up, down, and around his length. He shuddered and sank into the water. Feeling victorious, she smiled, then lost it as he rose and swept her up.

"Stephen!"

He ignored her cry and plopped her into her own tub. Laughing, she watched as he lifted the soap, a wicked look in his eye.

Her laughter died as soon as he touched her. He lathered his hands and rubbed them over her chest in long, slow swirls, starting at her neck and working down to her breasts. His hand caressed her right breast, and he lightly ran fingers up and around the tip. Her head dropped to the cool edge of the tub, and she watched him through lids gone heavy as he washed both breasts, then replaced his hands with his mouth.

The cool edge of the tub provided some relief as her body automatically arched in response to his tongue. Delicious heat spread through her body, and she gripped the edge of the tub with both hands to seek some relief. Her body was on fire, and his swirling tongue enflamed her more.

He pulled back and lifted her so that she was standing. Reaching for the soap, he again lathered his hands. He drew his hands along her stomach, pausing for the briefest moment at her scar, then moved around her hips and down her thighs in continuous circular motions. Her body called out for him to stop circling and go straight to the area that needed him most, but he kept circling and grazing.

He washed her off and lathered his hands one last time. Her heart quickened, and she stepped toward him. She saw his smile as he reached for her. And then his hands were on and around her. Clever fingers pretending to clean and massage instead of inflame. He stood and nuzzled the side of her neck as one of those clever fingers slipped inside her. Her legs started to give out, and he pulled her back down into the water, then lifted her out and onto the bed.

Wet limbs tangled together, and she nearly came undone from the intensity of his gaze. He ran a hand over her as if she were made of the finest porcelain, and she pulled him to her, unable to bear the emotion pounding between them. Entering in one swift stroke, he whispered something unintelligible into her ear. She grasped him to her and took him over the edge with her as she caught the moonlight in her hand.

They stayed locked together for a long time, Stephen stroking her hair, Audrey stroking his back.

"How did you get the scar on your side?" Stephen asked mildly.

Audrey's heart quickened from its languid beat. "Would you believe I tumbled down some stairs and hit a fireplace poker?"

He rolled them on their sides, and continued to stroke her hair, not answering.

"You had a nightmare the other night."

She shook her head and picked at the corner of her pillow. "Sometimes that happens." She thought of Stephen's blond hair matted with blood and shuddered.

"How did you get the scar, Audrey?"

She sighed and shook her head. "I had a partner once. He ran with Flanagan a long time ago." It seemed centuries ago. Another world.

"What happened to him?

"He was very dashing. Women were always trying to lure him into dark corners. One finally succeeded." Her mouth tightened. "I arrived just in time to receive a knife in the side before she shot him. Reprisal for a job he had done in St. Giles against a rival. The rival was another pretty face that hated him and sent his doxy to get rid of the competition.

"I told Johnny never to trust a pretty face. But it's hard to say that to someone as pretty as Johnny was."

"Did you love him?"

She cocked her head, considering the question. "He was like the big brother I never had. He was bigger than life. He had a real talent for acting and pulled off a lot of the larger jobs that involved higher society. Therefore, we worked together a lot. But he started to believe he was invincible." She gave him a pointed stare. "Not unlike you."

"You think that I believe I'm invincible?"

"Aren't you?"

"No, Audrey. I can be hurt as easily as the next man."

"Ah, but I don't believe you, Your Grace. You are one of those people to whom everything comes easily. Charmed and charming." She looked into his eyes. "I hate you for it, you know."

"Yes, Audrey, I know." His voice was soft and he continued to stroke her back, not breaking eye contact.

Right before they fell asleep in each other's arms, she had the distinct impression he had just peered into her soul.

Chapter 20

❧

Audrey woke to the sweet smell of lilies. She opened her eyes and saw vases of flowers winking at her. Stephen sat on the edge of the bed.

"I need to go out. Feel free to use the library or anything else you might find. But don't go outside. Stay out of the gardens even. They are still looking for you."

He kissed her and left.

An hour later she was meandering through the conservatory, poking plants and smelling the flowers, when a servant knocked on the doorframe.

"Miss, a note arrived for you."

She opened the paper. It was from Travers telling her to meet him immediately at the Green Man. The writing was nearly illegible, and it alarmed her. Travers's usual handwriting was overly neat. She tapped a finger against the edge. Stephen had told her not to leave, but she hadn't actually agreed to his dictate.

Twenty minutes later she was dressed as a servant and tiptoeing through the back, carrying a bag of money from her case. She had left her case, hoping to make it back before Stephen and thus avoid any unpleasantness. A twinge of guilt assailed her, but she pushed it aside. Her sister was still in danger. Freeing her was still the number one priority.

Travers wasn't sitting in his usual spot. Instead he was up near the front, nervously watching the door. The relief on his face was evident when he spotted her.

"Do you have it?"

He latched on to her wrist. She tried to free herself, but some sort of terror had given him added strength. "No. I don't."

His grip tightened. "You *must* get it."

"I don't know if I can do—"

"I'll kill her! I'll do it! Bring me that pocket watch, or I'll do it!" Travers was shaking violently. No one seemed to be paying attention to his raving. The tavern was mostly empty; only a few lone figures were scattered throughout.

Travers ran a hand through his hair and she took advantage of his inattention and freed her wrist, scooting a few feet away from him. He seemed to be hanging on by a thread. "What is going on?"

"He'll kill us all. But I'll make sure he kills her first, with you watching." He pointed at her, hysteria driving his actions. He was breathing heavily and gave a mad laugh. "It's no use."

This Travers truly frightened her. "What do you mean? What happened?"

"He isn't pleased. Marston has been sniffing around, asking questions, confiding in friends. Too many people know. You didn't see his eyes." He nearly whispered. "They were mad. He wanted Marston killed, and Leonard blew the job."

Audrey didn't think Travers had any right to talk about wild eyes and madness at the moment.

"Who? One of the Hendrix brothers?"

He reached out and grabbed her wrist again. "No, you fool. The Hendrix brothers are nothing."

Fear pulsed through her, leaving her dizzy. Who had he gotten mixed up with? The Hendrix brothers were nothing?

"Oh, God, Travers. What have you done?"

He pushed her arm away. "Nothing. Just go get the watch."

"Let me ask Marston. He can help you."

Travers's eyes were dead. "No. If you tell him, your sister dies. *He* knows where she is. He'll do it if Marston finds out. He'll kill us all if Marston finds out."

"Let me get Faye. We'll help you. We'll leave Marston out of this."

"No. He found out about the watch. Nearly killed me when he found out I was using you to get it. Now he wants the watch as insurance. You have to get it for me."

Audrey wanted to again ask who *he* was, but Travers had shut down. She left him slumped in the corner, staring at the table. Shaking, she hailed a hack and headed back to Mayfair.

Too upset to follow her normal procedures, she never saw the man in the corner who slipped from the tavern.

She made her way to Flanagan's. It was a long walk, and she needed to stay alert. Her fragile relationship with Stephen was about to crack. She was going to renege on their agreement and betray him just as she had feared from the start.

She could tell him . . . but Travers's warnings sounded in her head. He hadn't been faking it—Travers was frightened, and that terrified her. No, she was going to have to do this one last thing and

326

hope that she could somehow make it up to Stephen. Maybe by rotting in prison.

By the end of the walk she was sweaty, tired, and miserable. She entered Flanagan's lair without problem, dumped the money bag on his desk, and plopped into a chair.

Flanagan's brow rose, but he merely spilled the contents of the bag onto his desk. "Leonard's fled the country again, but talk is that you killed him."

Audrey slouched in the opposite seat. "To be honest, I almost did. He followed me from the city. Said he was under orders to collect your money."

Flanagan tested a coin between his teeth and picked up another. "I wouldn't send minions after you, Hermes. You might be a right pain in the arse, but you've always honored a deal." He pawed through the rest of the coins and notes, then pushed them aside. "Just like I don't need to test the rest of these or ask for an accounting."

"Leonard and three others attacked us last night. I knew then he wasn't working for you."

"Nope. And I don't believe you killed that solicitor fella neither."

Audrey grimaced. "Thank you for that vote of confidence. Am I to take it from your comment that others believe I did?"

He nodded. "Many believe it."

"Well, the Duke of Marston doesn't. And he can vouch for my whereabouts that night."

Flanagan looked speculative. "But will he? You're going to be on the wrong side of him this time tomorrow, ain't ya?"

She stiffened. "It's no matter."

"Wouldn't say that. You're in deep, girl. But there might be some good news for ye."

Audrey's skin tingled. "You located Faye?"

"Not yet, but the boys are closing in. By the end of the week, I should think."

Her shoulders drooped. The end of the week was too late.

"Go home and get some rest, you look terrible." He paused. "Or would you rather stay here?" His too-perceptive eyes searched hers.

"No, I need to take care of some loose ends. But . . . thanks." This was new territory for her. Flanagan was a good man, but he had never been overly demonstrative.

He sat back and studied her. "I'll be glad to see you sail away, Hermes."

"What?" How had he known?

"Of course, it won't be the same here in London without you. But you were slipping away. I could see it in your eyes. Why do you think I let you leave Olympus?"

"I left because I wanted to."

"Aye, but I didn't have to release you. From the outside it wouldn't look to be in my best interests even."

She knew where the conversation was going, where she didn't want to tread, but it was as if Mesmer sat before her. "Then why did you do it?"

"You know why. A few more jobs, and you were going to end up like the bird that shot Johnny. Cold inside."

"What's to say I wouldn't still turn that way?"

He ran a coin through his fingers. "Only you, Audrey, only you."

The last time he had called her Audrey had been when he told her it was no longer her name—that Audrey was dead, and only Hermes remained.

Audrey had been born again, but a yawning chasm was still before her. The bridge that had been tentatively constructed in the last few days with Stephen was about to be broken.

She put a hand on his shoulder. "Thank you, Flanagan. I'll see you again soon."

"Expect so, expect so. Happy hunting." He looked back to his coins with a jerking motion.

Emotion clogged her throat. Oh, yes, those long years ago when she had been deposited in the back alley—things could have been so much worse. Maddox had done her a favor, though she'd never tell him so. Audrey turned and walked through the door. No gesture would be welcome. No gesture was needed.

She looked at the sky, the sun was sinking—it was growing late. Stephen would return to his town house soon, and she needed to get there before he did.

Retracing her steps through the back of the yard, she breathed a sigh of relief to see the conservatory in darkness. She had made it.

She stepped toward the door and an arm reached out and grabbed her.

Chapter 21

❦❦

"**D**ammit, Audrey," Stephen was still saying twenty minutes later as she was toweling off from her bath. He had been tight-lipped after seizing her at the door, but he had ordered her a hot bath after fully seeing her.

If she weren't still feeling so miserable, she would have kissed him for it.

"I asked you to remain here, and you left. You know you're a marked woman with the runners after you."

"Stephen, it's you someone is trying to kill. How dare you accuse me of taking risks when you always put yourself in jeopardy."

He seemed oddly intent. "One can't live a life in fear."

331

"Exactly! That is my point."

Something flared in his eyes, and it made her nervous. He got that look when he was about to declare checkmate. "Audrey, what do you want?"

"What do you mean?"

"What do you want from life? What will you do after you find your sister?"

"I don't know." She felt tired. "I suppose I'll wake up again the next day and go to sleep at night."

"And?"

"And that's it. I try not to think too far ahead. My motto is to live each day fully because you may not have another to experience."

"Sounds like you are afraid to live."

Irritation surged within her. "I can read your face and know what you are thinking. But it's not easy on the streets. People die all the time, Chalmers. It doesn't pay to stare at the stars and ignore the horse droppings in your path."

"If you don't have dreams, you're an empty shell."

She gripped her towel so hard that her hands hurt. "An empty shell is still a live shell."

"It depends on your definition of alive."

"Life is betrayal."

"Or maybe you betray life."

She launched herself at him. He caught her, wrapping his arms around her chest. She made a few primal sounds and struggled to pull free. He spun her around and stroked her hair.

Agonizing sobs poured forth. He picked her up and carried her to the large armchair against the wall. Sitting down, he cradled her in his lap. She gripped the back of his hair as if grabbing a lifeline.

As if sensing in herself that soothing noises weren't what she needed, she grabbed his face and kissed him hard. The next few minutes were a flurry of towels, hands, and lips.

Not bothering to move from the chair or waste energy doing anything that required time away from touching and kissing, they made love like there would be no tomorrow. It was wild, passionate, and slightly desperate. The actions of two people holding on until the end, desperately hoping for more and trying to extend the present.

It was sad, joyful, exhilarating, and heartbreaking.

They finally dragged themselves into bed and lay entwined, clinging to each other, not willing to relinquish the night.

She rested her head in the crook of his shoulder. He stroked her back until her breathing became even. She had told him that she detested him for his charmed life. But the only thing she hated him for was making her fall in love with him.

Stephen smoothed Audrey's hair and gazed at her sleeping features. The recurrent question was ever-present. What was he going to do with her? He closed his eyes, and soon his breathing was as even as Audrey's.

Audrey waited for Stephen to fall asleep. She had feigned sleeping so many times she considered herself a pro. This time she had truly earned the title.

She looked at his handsome profile, relaxed in sleep. Lord, he was good-looking. And thoughtful. And caring. And stable. He was the most wonderfully grounded man, but with a verve for life that would always keep him from being stuffy. Dear God, why had she fallen in love with this man?

Audrey slipped from his embrace, regretting more than ever her chosen path. There was no room for a man in her life. And if there ever were room, a woman like her didn't deserve a perfect man like Stephen.

She slipped into the closet and gazed at the bureau. Inside was the secret compartment she had never found. The compartment he had opened while she had been undressing for her bath. She bit her lip. That he had trusted her enough to open the compartment while she was even in the same house, no less in the next room over . . .

She swallowed and buffered her resolve. Kneeling, she turned a series of knobs, exposing the bounty beneath. It was an ingenious system. The lever was completely invisible until triggered. And the innocuous-looking bureau already contained a very easy-to-find hidden compartment, making the one underneath that much more devilish.

She opened the box and was startled to see the keepsakes within. Her white satin ribbon from the costume ball was on top. The last time she had seen it, he'd been caressing it with his fingers, a sad, pensive expression on his face. A miniature of a smiling blond woman was next to the ribbon. Her features proclaimed her a close relation. His mother no doubt. A heavy signet ring was alongside. His father's?

Audrey could scarcely breathe. He had placed her ribbon inside the box with his most private and treasured possessions.

Remorse clogged her throat as she moved the things aside. She had to think clearly, rationally—like Hermes, master thief. Some documents and items occupied the next layer, and she shifted them as well.

A dull glint caught her eye. A pocket watch.

She picked it up and examined the watch that Travers so desperately desired. Opening it she traced a set of initials and what appeared to be a family motto. It had to be a gift from Travers's father or brother. It looked like a family heirloom, which would explain Travers's bitterness.

This was the one item that she knew would buy her sister's freedom.

The item that would lead to Audrey's damnation.

Audrey reassembled the contents on top, pausing over the ribbon, miniature, and ring. She added a letter she had written earlier and locked everything in place.

Stephen would know it was she who had taken the watch, but perhaps he wouldn't check for a day or two. Just enough time for her to save Faye and, she hoped, make amends.

She dressed in her shirt and trousers, pocketed the watch, and stepped back to the bed. Stephen was sound asleep, breathing deeply.

The last few days with him had been beautiful and warm, like the summer. Their frenzied passion and the soft, whispered words in the dark had been a glorious autumn. And now the inevitable winter. Barren trees, frost, and cold nights. She had been walking down winter's path for so long. The reprieve with Stephen would forever be locked in her heart, a memory.

The clogged feeling threatened to overcome her, and she turned away. She abandoned her traveling case and slipped through the door, silent tears streaming down her face. Despair and regret mingled. She'd be fine. Faye would be saved and could make a new life in America, while Audrey accepted the responsibility for her actions. It was time for her to pay the price.

She stepped back onto the streets.

Stephen waited until he knew she had left the house. She moved noiselessly, but something inside him signaled that she had slipped out the front door.

He wiped a hand across his face and sat upright. She had taken the watch. He had known she would after one of his men had relayed the overheard conversation with Travers in the tavern. Stephen had deliberately shown her where the hiding place was.

And he had hoped she wouldn't steal it. Had known she would, but had desperately wanted to be proven wrong. The game was once more afoot.

Unless he accompanied her, she would be followed as soon as she left the house.

He activated the secret compartments and opened the box. He slid the ribbon through his fingers. The ribbon would remain in the box. A piece of parchment with her handwriting caught his eye and he moved into the light to read it.

He felt a stab of pain, then of resolve. The chase was back on.

Chapter 22

It took nearly an hour to walk to her house. She considered it an early penance. One last breath of free air and space to move her legs before it was snatched away.

She was in a miserable state by the time she reached the brick house. All she wanted to do was clean up and sleep. But as she approached the house she noticed something was peculiar. She checked the street. She had made sure no one was following, but there could easily be men watching for her return.

The shades were drawn in all of the downstairs windows. She walked past the house and around the corner. It took extra time to dart through the small backyards and around the gardens and fences, but caution was time well spent.

Scooting around the back of her house, she peered into the drawing room window. The shade was partially cracked. She could vaguely make out a shape in a chair. Maddox. A fist connected with his jaw, forcing his head to jerk back. Audrey pulled to the side.

Maddox's troubles had finally caught up with him. She chewed her lip, trying to decide what to do. He was the bane of her existence—always creeping in at the wrong moment, always ruining whatever she had going. How much easier life would be without him. It didn't take long to make her choice.

Audrey crept through the back door and down the hallway. The servants had probably bolted at the first sign of trouble. She pulled out the small pistol that Stephen had given her the night before. It was unloaded, but only she knew that. Peeking around the corner she saw one man pummeling Maddox. Blood dripped down his face. Lucky for him the attack had only just begun. Lucky for her they had put down their pistols while tying Maddox to the chair.

One man was the talker, the other the muscle. "You don't got the money, do you, Maddox? Marty here don't like it when there's no money to pay the vouchers. Don't you know who you're messing with?"

If the muscle was Marty Hendrix, that made the lippy one Stan. Taking aim at Stan she stepped around the corner, far enough to be out of reach of Marty the muscle.

"I assume you are the Hendrix brothers?"

Stan squinted at her and eyed his gun on the table. "Who the hell is this, Maddox? Honey, put that little gun down before you get hurt."

She kept the gun steady. "How much does he owe you?"

He took her measure. "A thousand pounds and another five hundred for our troubles."

"That's some pretty steep trouble."

The man opened his hands in appeal but was regarding her with interest, smelling opportunity. "The streets are hard, love."

Audrey grimaced, thinking about how she had used that same logic with Stephen. "Not fifteen hundred pounds hard."

Marty inched toward her. She pulled out a knife with her free hand. She had never liked guns much. Unreliable weapons, heavy and more deadly if the shot went well. Knives were much more efficient. You could immobilize a person without doing any lasting damage.

She took the handle between her thumb and index finger and pointed the blade to the ground. Her voice lowered. "I don't miss with these."

Marty stopped, while Stan sized her up.

"Always the women that cause the most trouble. What do you want, love?"

"I want you to leave the slimy piece of filth in the chair alone."

"Fifteen hundred and he's yours."

"I'll give you twelve, and that's final. I'm not in a negotiating mood."

Stan opened his arms. "And I'm feeling generous today. Where's the money?"

"Upstairs, and that puts us into a bit of a negotiations dilemma."

Stan smirked. "Tell you what, love. Me and Marty will take the slimy welsher out on the stoop. You can lock the door and run upstairs. You have the upper hand here, but don't do us false, 'cause he won't be escaping. We'll do the exchange in the doorway and be off. If you don't come to the door with the money, we'll just take our mutual friend with us. Deal?"

"Deal." Marty untied Maddox and heaved him toward the door. As soon as the three were out on the stoop, she locked the door and ran upstairs. Throwing open her secret compartment, she counted out the appropriate notes and hurried downstairs.

She opened the door. Stan was singing a vulgar drinking ditty. She shoved the money into his hands and grabbed Maddox's collar, dragging him inside. Dangerous situations always gave her an extra boost of strength.

Stan counted the notes and tipped his hat. "Pleasure doing business with you, love. Look forward to the next time."

"There won't be a next time."

She shut the door and turned to her stepfather, who was bleeding and defiant. He would never change. She wondered if that would be true for her as well. She seemed to be going in that direction.

Maddox wiped the blood dribbling down his jaw. They stood staring at one another.

She sighed and spoke first. "Travers's scheme is about to crash down on our heads. I will give you sufficient funds if you agree to leave England permanently."

He regarded her for a moment and wiped his face roughly. "I ain't gonna change, and I ain't gonna apologize. But I'll take your deal."

"Good. Pack your things now."

He didn't move, but continued to wipe a hand across his face while regarding her.

"I look like hell, so do you," she said in defense.

"I know where your sister is."

Audrey looked at him, stunned.

"She's in a farm warehouse just outside of town. Heard Travers describe her as a pig in a poke. Damn fool forgot that he had mentioned the farm before."

"Why are you telling me now?"

He shrugged. "I did love your mother. Best I could anyway. Didn't know what to do with you two. Didn't marry for you. I should have probably taken you two with me." He nodded. "Yes, you would have been useful."

He gave her the direction and turned to mount the stairs.

It wasn't the apology of her dreams, and if in fact he had taken them, it would have probably been even more of a hell, but something inside her lightened. She gave him the money and watched him leave, his things already packed and readied for flight.

Audrey sat on her bedroom floor and sorted through the items within her secret compartment. Her fingers caressed the butterfly pin. Travers had laughed at her when she had tried to give it to him. Claimed it had been a test to see if she could pull it off and, more importantly, if she *would* do it. She had, and how she had hated him even more after he had told her to keep it as a memory of a job gone well.

Her fingers closed around the exquisite pin. She looked at her small, cheap clock. She had time. No matter how badly she wanted to charge to Faye's rescue, she couldn't risk approaching the warehouse in the day.

If Maddox were correct, she knew Faye's location. The thought brought exhilaration and pain. Stealing Stephen's piece had been unnecessary. Who would have thought Maddox would help? When this was all over, she hoped Stephen would understand.

Tears choked her, and she tilted her head to staunch their flow. Hope was all she had. Stephen had nurtured that during the past few days. Redemption still hovered within her reach. She would make amends. Even if he rejected her explanation, it was the right thing. No, she amended. It was the only thing to do.

She changed into a day dress but kept her knives in place. She was going to offer herself to Calliope's justice. If the lady sought to punish her, she would have to put justice on hold in order to save Faye. And then she would return for her sentencing.

Audrey packed her necessary belongings in a

bag. The other things were replaceable. She couldn't risk returning to the house in case Travers or Stephen stopped by. Hailing a hack, she gave the driver the swanky Mayfair address.

Hopefully she could meet the marchioness alone, a cowardly thought, but if the marquess were in residence, she would still continue. She gave the haughty butler her card and waited in the foyer. The magnificent ceiling depicting the heavens caused her to stare.

"Please follow me." The butler led her into a room down the hall. A pleasant space filled with light and color. The marchioness was arranging flowers in a large vase.

"Good afternoon, Audrey. I'm delighted you've called. Tea please, Templeton."

The butler bowed and exited the room.

"There is no need for tea, Lady Angelford, I am simply here to return something that belongs to you."

"Please call me Calliope. Now then, what is it you want to return?"

Audrey withdrew the beautiful blue pin and held it out to her on her palm. "I stole this from you the night we met."

Calliope took the pin and looked at her thoughtfully. "I expected as much when I noticed it missing later. Why do you now return it?"

"Because it was taken under the wrong circumstances."

The edges of Calliope's mouth lifted. "Thank you for returning it. I like your honesty."

"No offense, Calliope, but did you hear me say that I stole that from you?"

"Yes, yes you did." She tapped a finger on top. "Will you continue to steal?"

"No. I am happy to leave it behind. To leave it behind as a career, that is—I would do almost anything for someone I loved."

"Yes," Calliope said simply. "I sense that passion in you."

Calliope picked up two stems from a stack on the table and handed her one. "Would you care to help me with the display? Tea will be here soon."

Audrey looked at the stem in bewilderment. She didn't know the first thing about floral design. Or any useful household skills for that matter.

"Did you know how to create floral arrangements before marrying the marquess?"

Calliope looked at her. "Yes, although it was not a passion of mine."

"I don't know the first thing to do." She surprised herself with the admission. She hated not knowing how to do something, and hated even more admitting her weaknesses to someone else.

"Well, I don't know how to pick a lock. Perhaps we can help each other. It has always been a skill I've wished to learn."

She twirled the stem and looked at Calliope. "You are the oddest courtesan I've ever met."

Calliope laughed. "I'm a caricaturist. Acting as a courtesan was just a ploy to cover the fact. I thought Stephen would have told you."

"He would never divulge a secret if he cared deeply for that person."

Calliope stopped and looked at her. "No, he wouldn't," she said quietly.

Uncomfortable under her regard, Audrey followed Audrey's example and placed the stem into the arrangement. "A caricaturist. You spoof the ton?" She paused. "But however did you do it?"

"Do what?"

"Marry a peer knowing society's expectations and standards."

Calliope chose a long, bluish-purple flower and caressed its blossoms before placing it in the arrangement. "I won't lie and say it's easy. A marquess marrying a commoner, even a commoner with a partially noble lineage, is not acceptable to many in society."

Calliope shrugged. "People say things. I can hear them whisper at parties, then smile to my face. Being observant does have its disadvantage." She smiled. "But, it really doesn't matter. If you love someone, and want to share your lives, you find a way to make it work. You ignore the naysayers. You ignore the gossips. You live life as you please. And if you truly love someone, it's enough. The other things become immaterial."

Longing rushed through Audrey. A deep yearning to have that type of relationship with Stephen. "But I'm a thief. I have no claims to the nobility. Even had my parents lived, I most likely would not have had a season."

"Stephen doesn't seem to care. Why do you?"

"Stephen should care. He's a duke. He has a responsibility to his title. Besides, it's a moot point. Stephen wouldn't have me now even if he wasn't a duke." She bowed her head, aching inside.

Calliope covered her hand. "I feel your pain, Audrey. But, you have to make your own choices. And so does Stephen."

A noise in the hall caused Calliope to look up. "That would be James. He is home earlier than I thought." She looked at Audrey. "Would you want to stay for tea with James here? I will understand if you prefer not to. Perhaps you would be more comfortable in a few days after things get worked out?"

"If they get worked out," Audrey muttered, and looked for an escape. The marchioness was giving her an out. She would deal with her reparations to the lady later.

Calliope put a hand on her arm and guided her to a rear door. "Oh, don't underestimate Stephen's resolve. Things will work out, have no fear."

Audrey scooted through the kitchens, surprising the kitchen staff on her way. Calliope had given her new hope. If she got through this right and tight, maybe, just maybe, she would have found a new friend. And if she were really lucky, maybe the man of her dreams.

He was tired of playing games. All he wanted now was to find Audrey's sister, bundle Audrey up, and take her back to the country, where they could sort things out.

With that in mind, Stephen walked into Bessington's study, pushing past the sputtering butler. The earl looked stunned, but he hid it quickly. "Marston, to what do I owe the honor?"

Bessington motioned for the outraged butler to leave, and Stephen walked to the desk, tapping his walking stick as he did.

"I've come to let you know what I've decided."

"Good. I can have all of the papers drawn up within the day."

"Excellent."

Bessington looked relieved.

"Perhaps you can include the part about being blackmailed. Simply for the sake of thoroughness."

Bessington's jaw dropped. "Pardon me?"

"When you write up the papers about the fake marker from Vernon and collaborating in illegal shipping activities."

"Now see here, Marston—"

Stephen leaned across the desk. "No, Bessington. The game is over."

The earl went white. "I don't know what you are talking about."

"Did you know we engaged the same solicitor, Bessington?" Stephen asked it as if it were a question of no importance.

Bessington fingered his cravat. "Yes, I did, actually."

"And?"

"He had been with me for years."

Stephen tapped him on the chest with the end of

his cane. "Perhaps if you tell me where he is, I will choose to drop the investigation into your affairs."

Bessington sputtered, and his forehead dampened. "He was murdered."

"Then dig him up, I want to see the body. What did our dear solicitor Logan tell you about Vernon?"

"Nothing."

"Come now, Bessington. He had to tell you something. Perhaps if Clarissa married Vernon and produced an heir, an unfortunate accident might befall Vernon, allowing you control of both estates?"

Bessington flinched. "Never. He introduced the idea of a match between Clarissa and Vernon. But that was it. I was surprised when he introduced the notion of a match between you and Clarissa."

"Why? Because he hadn't allowed a match between Clarissa and the eighth duke, Thomas?"

Surprise flashed across Bessington's face. "Yes. Exactly." The top of Bessington's forehead was beaded with moisture. He dabbed at it with his kerchief.

"He pushed strenuously for the match with Vernon. I was shocked when he refused with Thomas."

"Such a forthright solicitor! Why didn't you replace him?"

The earl's face turned ashen. "I couldn't."

"Why is that? You are an earl, he is merely a man of affairs. Doesn't sound like the balance of power that most have with their solicitors."

"I couldn't."

Stephen tapped his fingers on his walking stick. "He found out about that nasty little affair at the brothel, didn't he?" Bessington fell back in his chair. His white face registered the truth of Stephen's accusation. "Resorted to a bit of blackmail?"

Stephen leaned forward. "You have five minutes to tell me everything. I won't resort to blackmail, so tedious really. I have a much more effective solution in mind if you're not forthcoming."

Bessington didn't need to be asked twice. He had already been broken. He tripped over himself to explain. Logan had been blackmailing Bessington and had set him up in the shipping scheme to secure his cooperation. For his part, Bessington had thought the match between Vernon and Clarissa, then Stephen and Clarissa, would be perfect. Either would have been the match of the season, and his darling Clarissa would be happy. He adamantly denied knowledge of or any role in planning any murders. His eyes didn't quite meet Stephen's though when he said it.

Bessington was colorless and shaking by the

time he was finished. Stephen decided to leave one of his men with the earl so that he didn't try anything silly like committing suicide.

Stephen returned to his house to find Roth waiting for him. "Excellent timing as usual. What did you find?"

"Faye Kendrick is being held in a building about an hour outside of town. There were other men watching the place. I'd guess they were Flanagan's men. I decided not to delay my return. The girl is doing fine. They have her drugged and trussed, but from what I could see, no harm has been done. The number of men guarding her tripled, so I decided to come back for reinforcements."

Stephen raised a brow. "Getting soft, Roth?"

"Yes, and cautious. If I don't watch out, I might fall all the way to your level."

Stephen smiled, but his mind was already planning a rescue. "Audrey will be there. My guess is that she is supposed to exchange something for her sister."

Roth raised a brow. "Do you know the nature of what she is trying to exchange?"

"A pocket watch."

Roth stilled, and Stephen nodded in answer to the unspoken question. "Yes, it is what you think it is. I let her steal the pocket watch that Brandon's father gave me."

Roth gave him a cryptic look, but simply said, "Have you contacted James?"

"Yes, he should be here anytime now."

"What are you going to do with the Kendrick sisters when this is through?"

"I don't know. It depends on Audrey's answers." He shook his head. "She doesn't trust me."

"But you trust her." It was a statement.

"It's hard to maintain trust when it's one-sided. But I do trust her in some weird manner. I knew she was going to take the piece. I've known it since I realized Travers was involved in this business. The watch has both monetary and sentimental value."

"Why didn't you arrest him before?"

"Not enough hard evidence. In addition, he made threats against Audrey and her sister. Retribution if anything happened to him. I thought it easier to let him muddle his way around and bury himself."

"And you didn't want to scare off the bigger fish."

"No." Stephen's voice was soft. "I didn't want to do that, but maybe I should have."

"Well, I took care of Travers's men, so there will be no worry from that quarter. Not unless we put her in Newgate ourselves." Roth raised a brow.

"That is still up in the air," Stephen bluffed.

James walked through the door. "We ready?"

Stephen pushed up from the desk. "Yes, let's go."

But James didn't move, almost as if he were fighting an internal battle.

"What is it?"

James exhaled, and he and Roth exchanged a glance. "I don't know that I want to clutter your perspective, but fair is fair. Miss Kendrick returned the pin that she stole from Calliope the night of the Taylors' ball."

Stephen tensed. "When?"

"Today, not more than an hour ago. Calliope didn't tell me about the visit until the girl was safely out of the neighborhood."

Stephen absently played with a pen on his desk. "Well, I'll be damned."

"Join the crowd," Roth muttered.

"What are you going to do about her?" James asked.

Stephen didn't answer.

Chapter 23

⟨⟨◦⟩⟩⟩

Audrey dismounted and led the horse she had borrowed from Flanagan into a copse of trees. She tied the mare to a small tree and set out on foot for the last mile trek through the woods. She was dressed in trousers, and this time carried two loaded pistols. One was strapped under her trousers on the inside of her left ankle and the other in her right pocket.

A decrepit farmhouse sat at the edge of the property, a barn nearby. The house was unlit, but light peeked through the poorly placed boards in the barn walls. Audrey crept to the side and peered through one of the holes. Faye was trussed against one corner. Two guards hovered nearby, and two others were playing cards. The sight of her sister lifted her spirits. She appeared to be knocked out or sleeping.

Audrey crept around the structure. There were doors on both sides. Two escape routes.

She walked to the horses and made shooing motions with her free hand. They nickered. She did it again, and one of the horses whinnied.

She ran behind a nearby tree. A guard exited the barn with a gun in his hand. He approached the makeshift paddock, and as he walked by, she whacked him with a heavy stick. He slumped to the ground. She tucked his gun in her waistband and dashed behind a tree closer to the barn. She wasn't strong enough to lift the fallen man.

A second guard called from the open door. "Fred?"

Fred's friend wasn't too smart as he too walked down the same path and helpfully turned his back. He joined the unconscious Fred in the dirt.

Audrey ran to the barn door. There would be no third opportunity. She dove into the building and fired at the guard nearest her. She caught him in the leg, and he dropped his gun as he screamed. The fourth guard turned to fire. Before Audrey could react a streak knocked the guard into the wall and began pounding the daylights out of the man.

"Faye!"

Faye looked up from the damage she was inflicting, even with her hands tied, and leaned unsteadily against the wall. "What took you so bloody long?"

"Excuse me?"

"Dear Lord, sis, I would have been out of here myself tonight if you hadn't finally decided to show."

Audrey freed Faye from her bonds and they hugged fiercely. Faye limped over to the other side of the bed in the corner and Audrey was surprised to see a man on the floor, his hands tied. He had been completely obscured from view. "Lucky for me they brought this one in. They only gave me half a dosage by accident."

Faye was fumbling with the man's knots, and Audrey rushed to help. She put her gun down and untied the ropes. The man's head lolled to the side.

"What are we supposed to do with him? And who is he?"

"Edward Logan, the Duke of Marston's solicitor."

Audrey sat back on her heels. "Well, well. They can't pin it on me after all."

"Well, well, pin what? No, on second thought tell me later. We can't linger."

A new voice responded. "I agree. Lingering is unwise."

359

Audrey whipped around to see Travers standing in the doorway. She grabbed for the gun.

"Please don't do that, my dear. It will only make things messy." Travers looked nervous. He kept switching his gaze between them.

Audrey removed her hand from the gun. "Fine. I have what you want. The watch for Faye, then we'll be on our way."

He walked to a spot where he could see Logan's body and seemed satisfied by what he saw. He was gaining confidence. "I must commend you on the masterful job of stealing the watch."

"Let's go, Faye."

"Yes, Faye will be able to leave. You however are going to stay. I have a new job, but this time it's for your sister. A little gambling hell to infiltrate. I hear she has uncommon luck at the tables."

Audrey didn't look at Faye, but she could feel her tensing. Audrey placed a restraining hand on her arm. "Fine. Faye, you go."

Travers narrowed his eyes. "First, where is the watch?"

"Faye goes free before I give it to you."

"Show me you have it first."

Audrey reached into her pocket. A cold steel blade and the heavy weight of gold pressed into her hand. The blade knicked her skin as she palmed it sloppily. She used her thumb to secure the piece on top.

"Put it on the table, then step back." His greedy eyes devoured the watch as if it were his salvation.

"Faye, leave."

"No, I'm not leaving you h—"

Audrey pierced her with a look. "Now."

A defiant expression came over her face, but she walked toward the door. Two steps from it Travers grabbed her and put the gun barrel to her throat.

"I'm not going to ask again. Put the piece on the table, then move away." Audrey gripped the piece tightly but put it on the table. Having been caught unprepared, all of her bargaining chips had become useless.

He motioned to one of the battered guards to retrieve it. Audrey moved the knife into a throwing position and bided her time.

Travers crowed when he examined the treasure. "Get the ropes from my saddle," he said to the guard.

Faye had an opportunity to escape from Travers's hold, but she was watching the doorway to her left as the guard disappeared. One of the guards Audrey had felled must have awakened for her sister to be so distracted. Audrey inwardly cursed. There were two guns trained on her already, she didn't need four.

Travers chuckled again. "Well done, well done. I can't wait to see if your sister manages half as well as you did. How I wish I could see the look on Chalmers's face when he discovers the watch my father gave him is missing and realizes it was you who betrayed him. That watch is a family heirloom—and my father never went anywhere without it. Should have been mine. My blasted father didn't even give it to my brother. No, he gave it to Chalmers to replace the heirloom that was stolen from Chalmers's father when he was robbed and murdered."

Audrey's heart dropped. It had been in his personal compartment, so she shouldn't be surprised at its sentimental value, but she knew Stephen would never forgive her now.

Travers continued to crow. "Oh yes, I wish I could see the look on his face."

"You can see it now if you'd like."

Audrey jerked her attention to the door to see Stephen casually leaning against the jamb, pistol in hand. Roth slipped inside and was removing the pistol from the remaining guard's hand, while his own was shoved against the man's neck.

Travers stiffened, and his pistol dug deeply into Faye's chin as he positioned her in front of him. Audrey nearly stopped breathing.

"Surprise. Surprise. Your contacts really are superb, Chalmers. Not that someone like you would do with less than the *best*, eh?" He sneered at Stephen. "Come to steal my watch again, Chalmers? Disappointed in our little Audrey?"

Travers turned so that Faye remained a shield in front of him. His back was to an empty wall.

Audrey coiled herself to move. Travers was keeping them all in view, but he knew he had lost, and that made him extremely dangerous. Travers wasn't going down without a fight, and Audrey knew that he was going to take Faye or Stephen with him.

Stephen caught her eye. "It would have made things so much easier if Audrey had fully trusted me, no matter what you threatened her with. But she's done nothing that can't be rectified."

He was asking her to trust him now. She looked at the barrel lodged in Faye's chin, then back to Stephen. He was asking her to trust him with Faye's life.

Audrey nodded and saw some of the tension around his eyes relax. He regained a negligent air and waved his pistol around in a deceptively carefree manner. "How about we make a deal, Travers? You give me the watch and all of the papers and information that Audrey went to such trouble to gather, and I will leave you with the ladies?"

"I know you, you bloody saint. You won't let me take the girls or get away. Damn sense of justice." Travers inclined his head in Audrey's direction. "You should join forces with me and take out your lover, Audrey dear. He'll just throw you to the hangman. Ask him."

Stephen waved his pistol. "Quite possible."

Roth had the guard in front of him and was inching forward toward Travers. Travers saw the motion and yanked Faye backward. Audrey saw the glint in her eye. *Oh, dear*.

Stephen must have seen it too because he was moving forward and shouting. "Get down."

She followed his command without question.

Four things happened in quick succession. Faye knocked Travers's hand away and elbowed him in the throat. Roth pulled the guard back so as not to interfere. Stephen reached Travers and wrestled the gun from his hand, and the Marquess of Angelford appeared and made quick work of tying his hands.

Audrey ran to Faye, who was staring wide-eyed at the three dangerous-looking men. Faye whispered from the side of her mouth, "To tell you the truth, I'm not sure we aren't in worse trouble now."

Before Audrey could explain the situation, Faye fell forward. "Oh thank you, gentlemen. My poor sister and I were kidnapped by these awful monsters. You saved us." Audrey tried to stop her, but Faye was already dabbing at fake tears and grasping Lord Roth's sleeve.

Faye gave Roth a watery smile and thanked him as she backed toward the door. "Thank you again. Come sis, we must be off while these wonderful saviors take care of these villains. Mum is probably beside herself." Faye sent a tearful glance her way, but kept backing through the door. Roth's eyebrows lost none of their height, and he looked almost amused.

Faye sent her a meaningful glance meant to hurry her along, but Audrey was rooted in place. Stephen was squatting with his arms resting on his knees. He was staring at her.

Faye had reached the door. She peered out, sent another smile Roth's way, and walked determinedly to Audrey, clasping her arm and dragging her forward. "My sister seems to be having a spell. No worries, she will be fine."

They hadn't gone but a few steps when Stephen cleared his throat. "Roth, take Icarus outside."

Faye stumbled at the name, and Audrey automatically reached to steady her. "I'll explain later. Go with Lord Roth."

Faye looked stunned, and Roth seemed to find it funny that now Faye was on the other end of being dragged through the door.

Moments later Audrey and Stephen were alone. "How did you find us?"

"All along Roth was searching for Faye."

She nodded mechanically. Of course he had been. She shouldn't have expected anything less.

Audrey extended her hands in front of her. "I suppose you mean to arrest me, Your Grace."

"For which crime would I arrest you?"

"I stole from you and betrayed you in so doing."

Stephen didn't move. "I would have given the pocket watch to you had you but asked," he said softly.

Yes, he would have given it to her. He was the one man she really could trust. She had given him all of herself last night, the surest sign she trusted him. But she hadn't trusted herself. And now surely neither would he.

"I know." Her voice broke.

He shoved his hands in his pockets. "I could have said something. I wanted you to turn to me

366

on your own, but it was too early. I rushed your fences in every way."

"No, I just wasn't willing to let you have that much power over me."

"I know, but I lusted for it."

"Travers told me that his partner would kill Faye if I confided in you. He was terrified of his partner, and that frightened me."

He shook his head in a distracted manner. "I should have told you what I knew. We could have taken down Travers and Logan days ago."

Audrey's heart stopped. She felt the terrified sensation wash through her. "Oh Lord, Stephen, what did you say?"

"He said you could have taken me down days ago, dear girl. Surely you aren't deaf?"

Stephen's head whipped up to stare at the man holding Audrey's discarded pistol. "What rock did you crawl out from under?"

Logan laughed unpleasantly. "I've been here the entire time, enjoying the show. Travers showed an uncommon amount of nerve, kidnapping me this afternoon."

He sent a sardonic look in Audrey's direction. "I think he actually might feel something for you. I told him you all had to die. In a gloriously tragic

manner, of course," he said flippantly. "But Travers
got cold feet. Oh, he was ready to use you for his
own ends, yes, but kill you? No, he refused to do
so. I misjudged him."

Logan shrugged and moved forward.

Audrey was in such shock she had forgotten she
was still holding her knife. She worked it forward
in her palm. "Did Travers throw us in prison on
your orders?"

He sniffed. "No, Travers was already setting up
his petty shipping schemes when I approached him.
Of course, he latched right on to my plans. I had all
the contacts he needed, and the foresight to carry
the plans through. He would have gotten nowhere
without me. The shipping scheme was amusing, but
I just did it to further my own ends. And if Travers
really did end up in a powerful position like Exchequer or Prime Minister, all the better for me in the
future. Travers was willing to go along with everything for a bit of power. And he quite hates
Chalmers," he said cheerfully, turning to Stephen.
"So I used my connections at the docks to hire some
thugs who wanted a bit of revenge on you anyway.
You have no trouble making enemies. I picked a few
men that already had a past with Audrey here, just
in case I needed to use her as a scapegoat."

He shrugged. "I just used everyone who might

want revenge on you. Made the whole thing much easier. Alas, no one could do the job properly. So it falls back on me."

Stephen looked bored. "All of this for a few extra pounds, Logan?"

"No, you fool. I did it all for the dukedom."

"The dukedom was doing fine by itself."

"Vernon was ruining the dukedom," he shrieked. "It would have really been in the ruinous state I showed you had he stayed in control. He was a stupid man, but I underestimated him. He caught on to me; he started hiding the books, hiring other men. Somehow he guessed that I was skimming from the top."

The quality of his voice changed. "Mind you. It was just enough to be comfortable. I deserved it after all those years kowtowing to the idiots who were always in power."

"You murdered Vernon."

"Of course I did. He deserved it."

Audrey's mouth dropped open, but Stephen didn't seem surprised. He must have already known.

"And Thomas?"

Logan spat. "No, Thomas was a gem. Idiot boy, pliable. Thomas was perfect. I could rule through him. He made the perfect duke, keeping everything in order and letting me make all the decisions. But he had to go and get killed in that riding accident. I should have crippled him, so he'd be bedridden."

"You're horrible," Audrey breathed.

He shot her a nasty look. "All good leaders seem horrible to those that don't understand them or stand against them."

If only they could stall him, surely Roth or Angelford would appear around the corner at any moment? Stephen continued to look bored, but she could feel the tension wafting from him. No, his friends were on their way back to London. They had left Audrey and Stephen alone to talk. No one was returning.

Stephen stepped away from her, drawing Logan's attention.

Logan turned to him. "And then you came along. The worst sort. A free-flying, carefree gallivant who could care less about the title."

Audrey gripped her knife. "That's not true, and you know it."

"Perhaps, but he would actively manage the estate and be overly generous with the tenants, thus cutting into my profits. I gave him a chance to stay his execution," Logan said.

"By marrying Clarissa?" Stephen asked as he

inched forward, trying to keep Logan's attention away from Audrey.

"Yes. I control Bessington. It would have been genius."

"And then after producing an heir, I would have had a small accident?"

"Oh, most definitely," Logan said with relish.

Audrey pulled her knife into position. "It surprises me how poorly you underestimate your foes. Did you really think Stephen wouldn't discover what you were doing?"

Logan snarled at her. "Look at you defending him. You're just a two-bit thief and probably a whore as well."

Stephen launched himself at Logan. Everything seemed to be happening in a speed so slow that Audrey could hear the scrape of Logan's finger pad over the trigger as he pulled it back. But Audrey was already in motion, throwing her knife in a practiced line.

"Argh!"

Stephen grabbed Logan and slammed his arm against the wall, causing the gun to fall to the floor. But Logan wasn't paying any attention to Stephen or the gun. All of his attention was focused on the knife blade embedded in his hand. Blood spurted from the wound, and he screamed again.

Faye came tearing back inside, Roth and Angelford hot on her heels. Conversation erupted from everyone at once.

There were ten minutes of explanations and disgruntled looks before the others left with Logan. Stephen peered under the bed and announced that he and Audrey were finally alone.

He put his hands on her shoulders, and she leaned into him.

"So what happens now?"

"Logan goes to prison. They won't be kind with his sentence since he murdered a peer of the realm."

"Travers?"

Stephen sighed. "I don't know what to do about Travers. Maybe we should foist him on the Americans or Australians."

He said it jokingly, but she flinched. She had been planning to foist herself on the Americans, but it was going to hurt to hear him say it.

"What about me?"

"I suppose that depends on you, Audrey."

"You talk in riddles again, Stephen."

"What would you like to do?"

Her insides coiled. "I suppose the best thing would be for you to send Faye and me to the Americas as well. You would have no further worry of the two of us pillaging the countryside."

He pulled back from her and ran a hand through his hair in an agitated manner. "Is that what you desire? To leave for a distant shore? Is there nothing for you here?"

A strange clenching began in her stomach. "You know there isn't. That there never can be. I will never be able to escape my past here."

"No, Audrey, I don't know that at all."

"You would tire of me quickly. You would want me to change."

"Not change, bend, adapt to new circumstances and challenges. Be willing to take a partner." He sighed. "Audrey, I know life hasn't been easy for you. But we can work through that."

Hope bloomed, and she tried to tamp it down. "We can?"

He smiled his rogue's smile. "Life is unfailingly kind to me; so as long as you stick by me, we'll do all right."

"You deserve someone better."

"I deserve someone I love, and that's you."

The bonds around her heart cracked, and she quickly tried to reconstruct them. "You mistake infatuation, Stephen."

"Do you love me?"

Her brain was scattered. "It doesn't matter. You are a duke. I'm a soon-to-be-re-retired thief. You need to marry for money and prestige and all of those things. Oh, I suppose you weren't offering marriage." She bit her lip in embarrassment.

"Do you remember what you wrote on the parchment you left for me last night?"

"I said I would not run."

"But aren't you running now?" He lifted her chin and leaned his forehead against hers. "Didn't I once tell you that the prickly plants were my favorites? Or how much I love ferns, with their ability to survive no matter the condition?"

She nodded, and he kissed her.

"Will you marry me, Audrey Kendrick? I swear our life will not be dull."

"I'm scared, Stephen."

"I know. As I said, we'll work through it." He rested his chin on top of her head.

She cleared her mind and took a deep breath. "I do love you." She peeked up at him. "I had even admired your very fine assets last year while tending you."

Stephen laughed and kissed her forehead. "Let's go back to town. I have a fancy to admire your very fine assets as well."

She stopped him and placed a hand on his chest. "I will marry you, Stephen Chalmers. And in so doing place both myself and my sister into your care."

He smiled at her gently. "And I will take every care of the trust you place in me."

He slipped his hand into her trousers and she gasped. He withdrew it just as quickly. A heavy weight remained, and she realized he had just given her the pocket watch.

He lightly touched her cheek, and tears sprang into her eyes. And when he took her in his arms the darkness vanished completely.

Don't forget to stock up on these "school supplies"
coming this September from Avon Romance...

Taming the Barbarian by Lois Greiman

An Avon Romantic Treasure

Fleurette Eddings, Lady Glendowne, craves adventure and passion. But she never dreamed she'd find it in the arms of a warrior from centuries past. Fleurette finds it hard to resist this sexy flesh and blood man, but she's been keeping a dark secret. Is Sir Hiltsglen there to seduce her—or to betray her?

Wanted: One Sexy Night by Judi McCoy

An Avon Contemporary Romance

Lucas Diamond is supposed to keep his eyes on the stars . . . not on the sensuous, impossibly perfect woman next door. Little does he know that Mira has an important mission to accomplish, one that will throw Lucas's whole universe out of whack. Because Mira is definitely out of this world—and Lucas is about to learn just how far out!

Still in My Heart by Kathryn Smith

An Avon Romance

Brahm Ryland, the most scandalous of the Ryland brothers, lost the one woman he truly loved, Lady Eleanor Durbane, to an idiotic mistake years ago. But when he receives an invitation to a shooting party at her home, he knows his opportunity to make amends has come at last. If only Eleanor will give him that second chance he's always dreamed of . . .

A Match Made in Scandal by Melody Thomas

An Avon Romance

Wealthy and successful Ryan Donally thought he'd gotten over his boyhood love for beautiful Rachel Bailey. But then one moment of unrestrained passion forces them into a marriage neither can afford—nor bear to give up . . .